THE YANKEE PRIVATEER

THE
YANKEE
PRIVATEER

By

DEREK YETMAN

Breakwater Books
P.O. Box 2188, St. John's, NL, Canada, A1C 6E6
www.breakwaterbooks.com

A CIP catalogue record for this book is available from Library and Archives Canada.

ISBN 9781550819236 (softcover)

We acknowledge the support of the Canada Council for the Arts.

We acknowledge the financial support of the Government of Canada through the
Department of Heritage and the Government of Newfoundland and Labrador through
the Department of Tourism, Culture, Arts and Recreation for our publishing activities.

Printed and bound in Canada.

Breakwater Books is committed to choosing papers and materials for our books
that help to protect our environment. To this end, this book is printed on a recycled
paper and other sources that are certified by the Forest Stewardship Council®.

 Canada Council Conseil des Arts
for the Arts du Canada
 Newfoundland
Labrador
 Canadä

For Gregory,
from Grandad

ONE

INDEPENDENCE

St. John's, May 29th, 1780

T he bright peal of the noonday bell is no more than a muffled clang in the narrow, fog-bound channel. A shroud of mist dampens all, including the courage of some on board the swiftly moving schooner. On she blindly sails, every scrap of canvas sheeted home as taut as human strength will allow, and her skipper indifferent to the peril. He paces the sharply tilted deck and stifles a yawn as the hourglass turns.

The crew waits, lines in hand and nerves stretched thin, listening to the muted roar of a breaking swell. A moment more and the raging surf appears through the grey veil, sooner and nearer than expected. The powerful surge climbs far, far up the sheer sandstone cliff and falls away in cataracts of foam. Few care to look at it or at anything else, other than the man whose attention is taken by something high in the rigging. The dismal roar grows louder and every mind now wills the man to speak.

"Off sheets and haul," he says at last. Unlike those who bellow, heave, and cleat for all they are worth, he has a voice as calm as his demeanour. The schooner comes smartly about and none are more relieved than the two barefoot boys who sit astride the jib-boom. The elder, feigning indifference, is heard to say: "Told ye. Skipper likes to take a bit o' seaweed when 'e tacks."

The younger boy is flushed with excitement. Neither he nor his companion has ever been on so large a vessel and never on one that is armed for war. The thrill and the wonder of it all are too much for words. The schooner heels to her new course and the breathless boy looks back, over the line of 6-pounder guns and through the web of rigging. The skipper's cocked hat and boat cloak glisten and his weathered face shows the faintest hint of approval.

The bark of the schooner's long-barrelled musket pierces the fog to announce her approach. The echo clatters and bounds away between hidden walls of rock as the puff of smoke sweeps astern. They enter the harbour, where the subsiding wind carries them past the grim, watchful batteries and through the many brigs and sloops that swing at anchor. A large shape looms in the mist and a moment later the schooner rounds up to the cry of "Douse all!" Her sails disappear and she comes alongside a frigate, as gently as a bird to its nest.

———o———

The captain of HMS *Maidstone*, 28 guns, was standing on his quarterdeck with hands clasped behind his back. "Well done, sir," he called down to the schooner. "She might have been built with you in mind."

Jonah Squibb looked up at the approving face of Captain William Parker, who had been kindness itself since Squibb and his crew had arrived in St. John's the day before. The big gaff topsail schooner with the unsavoury name of *Independence* was the frigate's prize, captured a week before on the Grand Banks with no more damage than a neat round hole in her fore topsail. At one hundred tons and more than a hundred feet in length, she was a valuable catch, even without her Holland-bound cargo of Virginia tobacco. Earlier that morning Parker had insisted that Squibb take her out "to see how she answers," as he put it.

"A fine vessel, captain," Squibb called up to the quarterdeck. "She points higher than anything I've known. Eager in any breeze and a joy to handle."

Parker smiled and nodded. "Yes, that she is. And there is no limit to what she can do, with the right man at her helm." Squibb said nothing, uncertain as to the meaning of the compliment, or indeed if it was a compliment at all. It was not the first time he'd felt some discomfort, for twice on the previous evening Parker had alluded to the "right man" being needed for the prize.

"Do not forget the governor," Parker added as he walked away, still smiling to himself.

Squibb had not forgotten his meeting with Governor Richard Edwards, whose letter he carried in the pocket of his coat. It was by no means heavy but it pressed against his ribs like a round shot, full as it was with the weight of his unanswered questions. It had arrived in Trinity a few days earlier and Squibb had left his home immediately for St. John's. Now, as then, he was eager to know the reason for the summons. But first he intended to return to his own schooner, which was anchored further up the harbour. He called for his crew to man their small boat and they did so quickly, being already late for their midday meal. Squibb raised his hat to the frigate as he took his seat in the stern of the gig. The officer of the watch returned the compliment and the oarsmen lowered their sweeps.

It was a short pull to the waiting *Amelia*. She was a smaller schooner than *Independence*, with no naval ensign at her stern and no heavy guns poking from her bulwarks. She was a modest trading vessel, in fact, but beloved by her owner all the same. Squibb had purchased her off the stocks in Trinity ten years earlier, just as master builder Charles Newhook had caulked the last of her seams. Since then, she had taken him many times from Cape John to Fortune Bay to collect fish, and on annual trading voyages to Lisbon and Cadiz with a stop in the West Indies. But these last few years had put an end to all of that. The war with the rebel colonies to the south had changed everything that was familiar.

The loss of trade was not the only disruption in Jonah Squibb's life. Nor was it of much importance compared to the death of his beloved wife, more than two years earlier. An epidemic of typhus had come ashore that spring, brought by the crew of a Salem privateer that had sailed into Trinity harbour and landed on Hog's Nose in the dead of night. The raid was not a success. Two of the villains had been killed outright and a half-dozen more captured before the boat made off. But the prisoners had infected their captors and the illness spread rapidly through the harbour. His Amy would not rest while any neighbour was in need of care. She saved the lives of many before being taken herself, a cruel reward for her labour and kindness.

Since then, Squibb's own life had slowly fragmented. His livelihood was all but destroyed, owing as much to his grief as to the Yankee depredations. His stepson, Ethan, had gone away as soon as he turned sixteen, no longer able to rely on his father for either love or comfort. Nearly a year had gone by without word of him and every day Squibb fought the pain of the boy's absence. The rum he'd shipped so often from the Indies, once a pillar of his prosperity, became for a time the enemy to that same good fortune. He'd abandoned his beloved books in his misery, leaving the neatly shelved and well-thumbed volumes to moulder in the darkness and damp. For weeks on end he'd been unable to move from his house or stir himself and think of the future, such was the depth of his despair.

Amy had been his childhood sweetheart, and their separation during his years in Britain's navy had done nothing to lessen their love for each other. Near the end of the Seven Years' War she'd believed him dead, so long did she go without news of him. She reluctantly married another man and, when next Squibb saw her, she was the widow Toope with a fine young boy named Ethan. Their affection was rekindled and, within a year, Squibb was released from the navy. He returned to Trinity and a new life as husband, father, and merchant captain. He had loved that new life, but now the memory of it was little more than a painful reminder of what he had lost.

The letter from Rear Admiral Edwards, Newfoundland's naval governor, was vague but there was no mistaking its urgent tone. He wished Squibb to come to St. John's as quickly as possible. The message was unexpected, but so was Squibb's reaction to it, for the words had stirred some old, almost forgotten sense of allegiance. He'd quickly rounded up the remnants of *Amelia*'s crew and any others who were idle, orphaned, or likely to starve over the winter months. They were facing him now as they sat to their oars, some with hope in their eyes, some with relief at the prospect of even a week's wages, and others—the younger ones—near bursting with excitement. They were all known to him and all were more or less honest and dependable. He could rely on them, but in return he bore the responsibility of their welfare in these uncertain times.

A navy longboat was waiting in the lee of *Amelia*, and Squibb had only to step across from his gig. The coxswain spoke and the sailors gave way as one, their long oars lifting and dipping with precision. The fog was thinning as the boat moved off and Squibb peered at the ridge that lay north of the harbour. At one end, the faint outline of newly built Fort Townshend was just visible. At the other, old Fort William crouched in the gloom above Maggoty Cove. Between the two, the town straggled down to the shoreline, many of the wooden buildings covered by spindly flakes of drying fish. Here and there a stone chimney protruded from the platforms like a smoking finger, the acrid smell mingling with the other odours of the town and harbour. Nearly two thousand people lived here now, perhaps half of them soldiers and sailors. The other half, it was said, were tavern keepers.

The boat was headed for the King's Beach, where an old and less than complete frigate was moored bow and stern. She was HMS *Proteus* and Squibb had marked her out when he entered the harbour the day before. Her useful sea days were clearly at an end and she'd become a store ship with boats coming and going, laden with men and supplies. Most of her spars, cordage, and other useful parts had been cannibalized by the needy ships of the naval squadron. Her powerful guns had been thinly distributed among the outlying settlements, where resident fishermen and planters were expected to defend themselves. The longboat came alongside the hulk and Squibb quickly climbed the ladder. A young lieutenant, likely an aide to the governor, he thought, offered him his hand.

"Welcome aboard, sir."

Once again Squibb felt that he was being treated rather better than his former rank and experience deserved. He'd resigned the navy as a lieutenant after eleven years and although his record was good, it was hardly enough to merit his cordial reception by either Captain Parker or the governor's aide. He followed the young man aft, removing his sodden boat cloak and hiding his surprise when a servant appeared and took it firmly from his hand.

"We are rather in a muddle at the moment," his escort confided as they walked along the gundeck. The young man was plainly dressed in blue uniform coat, buff waistcoat and breeches, but there was no mistaking the quality of the tailoring. "The governor's office at Fort Townshend is finally ready and we are moving house."

The spacious cabin was guarded by a stony-faced marine who saluted as the lieutenant stooped through the low doorway. Squibb ducked his head and followed. Watery grey light from the broad array of stern windows filled the sparsely furnished space. To his right, a couple of seamen were passing boxes through an open gun port. On the left sat the governor himself, wearing a faded yellow dressing gown over his uniform and signing papers with a long quill. He wrote furiously, as rapidly as two funereal-looking clerks could place the documents before him. The lieutenant ushered the sailors from the cabin and, with a nod to Squibb, left by the low door.

He stood before the desk, his hat under his arm and his coarse woollen coat steaming in the warm dampness. He had never seen the man in the old-fashioned wig before, though he knew something of him. Richard Edwards had been made Rear Admiral of the Blue only the year before, after a creditable action with his 90-gun *Sandwich* at the Battle of

Ushant. He had also been appointed governor of Newfoundland immediately thereafter. The surprising thing was that Edwards was very old for
the post, at least sixty-five. And equally odd was the fact that this was his
second term as governor. The first had been more than thirty years ago.
Still, Squibb reasoned, who better to be in charge in time of war than a
man who knew the place so well? What he hadn't known, until Parker
remarked upon it, was that the governor had married a Carbonear girl
during that first term in Newfoundland—the former Julia Pike, daughter of a prominent Conception Bay merchant and shipping agent.

Squibb concentrated his wandering thoughts as the man at the desk
threw aside his quill with a growl of exasperation. The black-garbed
clerks hurriedly withdrew to a corner of the cabin to sort and pack their
sheaves of paper. The governor reached for his snuff box and seemed
to notice his visitor for the first time. He was very stout, perhaps even
portly, with the scarlet jowls of a man who enjoys his food and drink.
Despite the man's evident irritation, Squibb noted something else in the
penetrating gaze. The face before him showed an intelligence that he
had rarely encountered in senior officers. The lines around the eyes also
revealed a penchant for good humour, and as if to confirm the observation, the governor sat back, smiled broadly, and gestured to the only
other chair in the cabin.

"Well, damn it all, sir," he boomed in a seagoing voice. "I am pleased
to see you here so soon." In another life Squibb would not have dared
to sit in an admiral's presence, but as a mere civilian he allowed himself
the liberty.

"Thank you, sir. It was a swift passage. That is, I came in my own schooner, sir." He perched on the edge of the chair, feeling like a midshipman
about to be examined on trigonometry. The governor's gaze did not
waver, nor did Squibb's sense that the man was studying him closely.

"Yes. The *Amelia*, is she not? I believe I saw you come into the harbour." Thick fingers toyed with the silver snuff box as he spoke. A servant
quietly entered the cabin and placed a tray with a finely cut decanter

and two glasses on the desk. The governor poured the wine himself. "Parker's been taking care of you, eh? Damned fine Madeira, this. Taken from a Marblehead smuggler a week ago."

Squibb accepted the glass of wine and said nothing.

————o————

Richard Edwards regarded the man before him with interest, noting the steady hand that took the offered wine. A most unfortunate name for a sailor, he thought, but this young Jonah seemed to bear it well enough. The governor had the advantage of knowing quite a bit more about Squibb than Squibb could possibly have guessed. He had a very clear knowledge of his naval service under two previous governors—Graves and Palliser—and of their high regard for him. He also knew that he'd studied navigation under Cook, that he was a native Newfoundlander, and that he was strangely attached to this remote rock in the sea. All this, and the fact that he likely knew the local coast as well as any man alive, made this former lieutenant a subject of great interest to the man charged with the defence of Newfoundland.

"Yes," the governor mused. "It seems that everything we consume comes from our captures these days. We no longer trade with the New England rebels, of course, and bloody little comes to us from England or Nova Scotia. The wretched merchants and their insurers are too frightened of losing a ship or two. As a result, it is a choice of either freezing or starving to death this winter. Do you know that we require over twelve thousand bushels of coal to heat our ships and quarters in the winter months?"

"Ah no, sir. I did not."

The governor did not pause, for the question had been rhetorical. "But this year coal is not to be had, not at any price nor from any place. I have just signed orders to have nearly a thousand cords of wood provided instead. And do you know that what provisions we have will not last us through the winter months?" This time, Squibb refrained from comment.

"It is a fact. A damned vexing fact. I have been encouraging the garrison and townspeople to plant more vegetables if they wish to see next spring. But will they listen? No, sir, they will not. Everything we need is in short supply and the rats are already eating the candles." He shook his head. "Not a good sign, Mr. Squibb."

As he spoke, the governor studied the man who was listening so attentively. The records showed Jonah Squibb to be thirty-six years of age, with seagoing experience far beyond his years. The clear grey eyes were steady and confident, the left one faintly encircled by a web of fine scars. Quiberon Bay, the governor had read. Squibb had been a mere youth in that famous naval battle with the French. He'd been on the old *Royal George*, which had been in the thick of it. It was an obscure piece of information, but Richard Edwards preferred to know the sailors with whom he dealt.

"Which brings me to the point, Mr. Squibb. This unholy war with the colonies is threatening to bring Newfoundland to her knees." The governor did not miss the look of immediate interest.

"As I'm sure you know, France and Spain have joined the rebels and together they have made the destruction of the Newfoundland fishery one of their primary objectives, knowing as they do that it is one of Britain's most important assets. As for the Americans, as they are calling themselves, they have only a handful of ships in their Continental Navy. These are of little significance. But they also have over two hundred privateers in commission and a fair parcel of them are in our waters at this very moment."

The governor pushed his chair away from the desk and grunted to his feet. "Which means, sir, that our sole industry is in rapid decline. The backbone of it, the migratory fishery, is down to fifty ships this year, compared to five times that before the war."

"But surely, sir, the resident fishery can fill the void." The governor's eyes were still on him as Squibb added, "I have always believed that the local population can do much more for themselves, sir. And for England, with the proper support and encouragement."

The governor walked stiffly to the stern windows. "You may be right, young man. But the resident fishery is diminished as well, between the reluctance of our merchants to back it and the number of men who either have returned to the British Isles or are serving in our ships and regiments. Four years ago, both fisheries produced six hundred and fifty thousand quintals of dried cod. Last year the total was not a third of that. Our convoys are being attacked and fishing premises are being looted and destroyed. Soon there will be little point in any of us being here."

"Is there a solution, sir? A practical one?"

The governor turned from the windows and looked hard at his guest. He smiled and scratched his ample belly. "Yes, I believe there may be. These damned raiders are, for the most part, merchant mariners and fishing masters with no stomach for a fight. I have the ships to engage them, thanks to some handsome prizes that we have captured. What I do not have are capable and experienced officers to command them." He drained the last of his wine and sighed wistfully at the empty glass.

"As you say, Mr. Squibb, there must be more that the local people can do in this time of great need."

———— ◊ ————

William Parker laughed and shook his head as he passed a bowl of last year's potatoes, newly boiled. "Did you not see it coming, Jonah? Not even a suspicion?"

The newest officer in the Newfoundland squadron took the bowl and laid it beside his plate. It was early afternoon of the same day and the two were dining informally in *Maidstone*'s cabin, attended by a steward and a severely scrubbed ship's boy. Jonah Squibb was wearing a slightly worn uniform coat, a gift of congratulation from the captain. Its single gold epaulette on the left shoulder had taken up a permanent place in the periphery of Squibb's vision.

"The truth, sir, is that I did suspect something of the sort. But more along the line of serving as a pilot for coastal patrols." Squibb speared a piece of salted fish with his fork.

"Hah! Then what a shock to be offered a commission again. And a promotion to master and commander!" Parker raised his glass. His thinning blond hair framed a round, cheerful face, while the wide smile showed his large, uneven teeth to good effect. Parker was a few years older than Squibb, but their brief acquaintance had established the two men as being of much the same mind. "And now you have a ship of your own. Here's to your future success."

Squibb raised his glass. "Thank you." They drank the toast and the steward refilled their glasses with Madeira. "And may I add, sir, that I am very pleased to serve under you. Your success at sea is no secret."

"Success is a relative word, Commander." Parker laid his glass aside. "But cruising with you and *Independence* will double our chances of stopping these marauders. And to be perfectly frank, it should make us both a little richer. Having the governor buy the schooner into the service has made me and my crew very happy, you know, and keen for more of the same." He nodded to the boy, who brought a pitcher of water. The fish was very salty.

"Now then, I have to ask, have you given any thought to changing the name of the schooner?"

Squibb paused in his choice of potatoes. "Why would I do that, sir? With all respect."

"Well, the name *Independence*. Does it not smack of . . . of rebel sentiment?"

Squibb tried not to smile. "Yes, sir. It certainly does."

Parker stared for a moment, then laughed aloud and threw his napkin on the table. "By God, sir, I like your way of thinking. Those damned Yankees will never suspect a thing! Here's to a fruitful partnership."

They drank the toast and after eating heartily, the captain sat back to light his pipe, falling to his own thoughts as they awaited the fig pudding.

After a brief silence he roused himself and said, "Forgive me. I sometimes find myself brooding over this endless war."

"Yes, it is almost as long as the last one."

"Nearly six years and no end in sight. We've had our successes and rewards, but there have been so many losses. In ships and countrymen. Dear friends, some of them, killed or out of the service because of their wounds."

Squibb swirled the wine in his glass, thinking of dear friends of his own. Sam Skiffington, for one, killed in the second year of the war. His old friend Friday Froggat, whose body was never found after the bloody battle at Flamborough Head. And Silas Blackhouse, his ship lost with all hands in '78.

"I was also thinking of the last schooner we had in our squadron," Parker said. "She was very like *Independence* and was with us until a year ago."

"Reassigned, was she?"

The captain smiled sadly. "She was not. *Egmont* was on patrol in Trinity Bay and one blustery day she met with an armed Yankee brig by the name of *Wild Cat*. The schooner gave chase, the brig fired first and a few of our own were killed. And, sadly, *Egmont* could not reply. The fact is, her powder was wet. She was boarded and taken, and a prize crew sailed her away." He nodded to the steward, who placed another bottle of the captured Madeira within reach.

"A few days later the two vessels crossed the path of our frigate *Surprise* under Captain Reeve. There was another fight. This time *Wild Cat* was captured but *Egmont* got away, though most of our people were released. *Wild Cat*, by the way, is sitting just off our bow. She is now HMS *Trepassey*. Another fine prize taken into the service."

Squibb shook his head. "The fortune of war. We have all seen its fickle nature."

"Aye, we have indeed." Parker reached for his glass. "Today is Friday, is it not? The toast of the day then. May we meet a willing foe."

Squibb raised his wine. "And may we have the sea room to fight him."

A short time later the two men emerged onto the deck of the frigate, their pudding with its doubtful figs settling uneasily. The late afternoon sun was shining dimly through the cloud cover. As Parker walked his guest to the entry port, a midshipman came up and saluted.

"Message from the governor, sir."

Parker opened the sealed note and chuckled as he read it. "We are to have a second dinner, Commander. Governor Edwards is entertaining the prominent townsfolk this evening to celebrate the completion of Fort Townshend. We are expected to attend and will fail to do so at our peril. It will hardly be the social event of the season, but the food may be better."

That evening, shortly before the appointed hour, Squibb passed uneasily through the main gate of the imposing fort. Tall, bearded sentries stamped to attention and saluted. They were Fraser's Highlanders, the 71st Regiment, which had seen long service in Newfoundland. Squibb had arrived early to familiarize himself with his surroundings. Social gatherings had never been his natural element and he had not attended one in years. And he also wanted time to explore the high stone ramparts of the new star-shaped citadel.

Squibb strolled across the square and climbed to the Grand Battery. The sturdy gun platform offered sweeping vistas of Signal Hill, the harbour and south side, all the way up the river valley to the west. Its massive 24-pounders were capable of accurately hitting a target at a distance of a mile and a half. Squibb could also see the new Military Road, which linked Fort Townshend with Fort William to the east. It seemed a formidable defensive position, but he was no soldier and knew better than to form opinions. Still, there was no mistaking what an eminent bastion it was, or what herculean efforts had been needed to complete it in five short summers.

Other guests had arrived while he was sightseeing and were crossing the wide central parade square to the governor's residence. Squibb descended the stone steps and joined the flow, stepping into the house as the evening gun echoed around the harbour. Servants were taking cloaks and capes, and Squibb helped himself to a glass of wine from a tray, realizing too late that it was the ubiquitous Madeira. In the large reception room, Governor Edwards and Lieutenant Colonel Hay, the garrison commander, greeted the guests as they filed in. An imposing woman with iron-grey hair stood at the governor's side, her benign smile a counterpoint to a sharp and intelligent gaze. Squibb bowed to them both and was introduced to Mrs. Edwards. She gave him a welcoming nod while her eyes raked him from stem to stern. He passed on to the colonel, who glanced at his second-hand jacket, grunted and turned to the next arrival.

There were many coats of army red in the room, along with a scattering of naval blue. Here and there a black or brown civilian suit mingled with the varied colours of the local ladies' dresses. There were no officers' wives other than Mrs. Edwards, the custom being for them to remain in England for the six months or so that their husbands were stationed on the island.

Squibb spotted his friend Parker with a small knot of navy men and wandered over to its fringe. An animated conversation was in progress and a red-faced senior captain, his shoulders adorned with two faded epaulettes, was saying loudly, "It came in the Portsmouth packet, I tell you, direct from Whitehall. I watched the admiral break the seal myself."

"*How* many sail of the line did you say, Keppel?" This from a small, wiry commander with a glass in each hand.

"Seven! With three frigates and a cutter. What a Frenchman like de Ternay could do with that number of ships, I shudder to think. Not to mention the troops in a dozen or more transports! Good Lord, there must be a couple of regiments!"

"You say they sailed from Brest on the fifth of May?" This time it was Parker who spoke. "Why, they could be here even now!"

"Exactly!" said Keppel.

"But their destination isn't known," a tall scowling lieutenant offered. "And so large a force must be bound for New England."

Squibb was listening to the exchange with a keen interest and had edged into the circle. "Admiral de Ternay is no stranger to St. John's," he put in. All heads turned to stare. "It was he who took the town in '62."

"Commander Squibb!" Parker smiled. "Allow me to introduce you. This is Keppel, who has *Vestal*, Baskerville of *Cygnet*, and Lieutenant Gardiner, *Bonavista*. Gentlemen, may I present the newly appointed commander of *Independence*." The officers, with the exception of Gardiner, nodded and mumbled a greeting.

"What's this you say?" Baskerville asked. "De Ternay was here in the last war?"

"He was, sir. He took the town after landing troops at the Bay o' Bulls. They marched overland and our small garrison had little choice but to surrender. His ships then entered the harbour and the town was his."

"How do you know so much about it?" Gardiner demanded.

"I was on Lord Colville's flagship when he sailed from Halifax to retake the town."

"Well, well," the red-faced Captain Keppel said. "Perhaps you know more of his thinking than we do. What do *you* believe de Ternay is up to, Commander?"

Squibb shook his head. "I cannot say, sir, except that when last here he put the town to the torch and sailed away in the dead of night. He abandoned his troops, and after a short bombardment they surrendered to us the next day."

"Typical!" Baskerville snorted.

"But such a force!" Parker exclaimed. "Can it be intended for Newfoundland?"

"If it is," Keppel declared, "it will be the end of the war for us. What have we? A handful of frigates and a dozen smaller craft. And no more than five or six hundred infantry and artillerymen. No, gentlemen. Make no mistake, de Ternay will be on his way to Rhode Island or some such place, where his force can influence the course of the war."

Just then a bell sounded and dinner was announced. The little party broke up and Squibb was conscious of Lieutenant Gardiner's stare as he took his leave. The guests entered the dining hall and the servants directed them to their places.

Squibb was pleasantly surprised to find himself next to a young woman, already seated to his left. Her face was turned to her neighbour, but he noted her distinctive maroon dress that he assumed to be fashionable. She glanced at him when he pulled in his chair and he gallantly bowed his head. On looking up, he found himself before a pair of penetrating blue-green eyes. His first impression was of the ocean, of its colour as well as its depth. Her eyes seemed to take him in entirely, appraising not only his outward manner and appearance but also his entire character and disposition. He had the startling sensation of having his inner thoughts examined. And all the while, her composed features betrayed nothing. She did not speak or smile, and before Squibb could bid her good evening, she had turned away again.

Released from her captivating attention, he looked around the table. The man on his right was deep in conversation with his neighbour, as were the people seated across from him. Squibb sat unbothered for some time, stealing occasional sidelong glances at the young woman. Her braided auburn hair was complemented by the colour of her fashionable dress and was pinned in loops. Her earrings were the same colour as her eyes, a type of turquoise perhaps. His impression was of a person of poise and refinement, quite unlike the merchant wives and daughters, who were making the most of the governor's food and drink.

The soup course came and went. Squibb rearranged his cutlery while he awaited an opportunity to speak. None came until he resorted to clearing his throat—perhaps a little too loudly, he realized. The noise caused her head to turn a degree, perhaps out of concern that he might be choking on a bone, but enough to give him an opening that he was quick to seize.

"Allow me to introduce myself, ma'am. I do not believe we've met." Her head turned a little more and he added, "Commander Squibb. Your servant."

Her eyes took him in again. "How do you do, sir?" Her features were arranged to be civil and nothing more.

"Very well, thank you." The lengthening silence that followed threatened to end the exchange. She had not introduced herself and he tried to think of a question that would draw her out. All he could manage was, "Do you live here, ma'am? Or are you visiting?" It was poor effort, he knew. Who would be visiting St. John's in the middle of a war?

Her smile, so unexpected, immediately set him at ease. "You may say that I am visiting, Commander. Boston is my home."

"Ah," said Squibb. It had been a very long time since he'd engaged in conversation with a young lady, and it showed. She looked away as a plate was handed between them.

"A terrible business," he said. "This war, I mean. I hope you have not been too greatly affected by it."

"I would say that I have been very much affected by it, sir."

"I am grieved to hear it, ma'am. Boston is a stronghold of these 'united states,' I believe. It cannot be easy to live among such—"

"I think, sir," she interrupted, "that the war is possibly more difficult, and certainly more complicated, for civilians than many naval gentlemen can imagine."

It was a polite rebuke, clearly indicating it was time to change the conversational tack. "Are you acquainted with Governor Edwards?" Squibb ventured.

"In a manner of speaking," she replied. The remarkable eyes lifted and probed his inner being once more. "I am the governor's prisoner."

———— o ————

At two o'clock on the following day, Squibb stood before the small crew of *Amelia*. The dozen men and boys waited expectantly, most of them with smiles on their faces. Their skipper's blue naval coat with its golden epaulette had drawn no comment or indication of surprise when they'd first seen it, as if the *Amelias* had known all along why the governor had sent for him.

Squibb was pleased that all twelve crew had volunteered to join him in his new command. The chance of filling their pockets with prize money was at the heart of it, he knew, but no matter. He was in desperate need of hands and any motivation would do. Even so, he could not take everyone. *Amelia* would have to remain in harbour and a few would stay on board while she was laid up. For this duty he chose the two eldest men and little Henry Spurrell.

Henry was the youngest of them, a wide-eyed orphan whose earlier excitement was still palpable until he was told the news. Squibb had brought him along because his prospects in Trinity were bleak. The boy's late parents, who were carried off by the typhus, had left him nothing and Henry had been living rough in Goose Cove, half-starved and running wild. Squibb was unmoved now by the child's expression of dashed hope. It stood to reason that young Henry would meet with greater disappointments in his less-than-promising life.

"When do we put to sea, sir?" It was Israel Miller, a dependable middle-aged man who stood his own watch on *Amelia* and would be a great asset to *Independence*.

"In a matter of days, I imagine. As soon as we receive our orders. Now then," he said, raising his voice, "I have something to tell you. Two of your shipmates have been favoured by the naval authorities and are now acting warrant officers." He removed two folded and sealed papers from his pocket.

"Robert Hogarth is to be the ship's carpenter and Mr. Miller our new master's mate. As naval ratings, the rest of you will answer to them and they will take charge of getting us settled aboard our new vessel. As you know, she is much the same as the old one, except a mite larger."

"And a mite faster, sir." The men laughed and looked at the rotund joker. Simeon Ballett reddened and tried to hide behind his mates.

"True enough," Squibb smiled. "And all the better to catch some of those fat Yankee prizes." The men nodded and grinned at one another. "And now that you are all navy men, let us begin with a naval tradition. Mr. Miller, your first duty is to issue these sailors their ration of rum. You will all know, I'm sure, that the King's birthday is just a few days from now. You may toast his royal health before dinner. Now carry on."

Squibb made his way to the cabin, high-spirited whoops and laughter following him below. In the small space he removed his coat and was about to sit down when Eli Bailey put his head around the door.

"Mr. Miller's compliments, sir." Eli was all of fourteen years old and clearly pleased with his appointment as steward. He had already made plans to lord it over his friend Henry. "Would you be free to see him directly?"

"My compliments to Mr. Miller and tell him to come at his convenience."

"Aye, aye, sir." The boy knuckled his forehead in naval fashion and retreated.

Squibb sat in the semi-darkness and waited, examining the small cabin that would be his new home and thinking of the sudden change in the course of his life. He would not have said it a week ago, but this was the best way forward. And Amy would have approved of it. He had mourned her for two years and only now was he beginning to feel that it was time to live again. Anything was better than being aimless, lonely, and miserable in the house on Mackerel Point. He picked up his letter of appointment from the desk, noticing for the first time that it was dated a day before his meeting with the governor. Richard Edwards had apparently been confident that his offer would be accepted. A sharp rap intruded on Squibb's thoughts.

"Enter!" Miller, short and square, opened the door. "Mr. Miller, please take a seat."

"My thanks for your recommendation, sir." The new master's mate still held his warrant in his hand. He lowered himself onto a locker, his short clay pipe clenched between his teeth. "Let me say that I look forward to serving with you, sir."

Miller was somewhat formal in his demeanour, but that hardly mattered when a cool head was needed in a crisis. They had seen more than a few of those in their years of sailing together. Squibb recognized something else in his shipmate's words. "Is there a 'but,' Mr. Miller?"

"Not exactly, sir. More of a question or two, if you don't mind me asking."

"Ask away. If we are to work together, we must be honest and direct with each other."

"Aye, sir. That is my way of thinking as well." He removed the pipe and examined it. "It's the crewing of this here schooner that I'm wondering about. We have a few prime hands, right enough, but none have ever served a naval gun, nor have any experience with such a large rig."

"I share your concerns, believe me. And I'm hoping that the governor will share them as well. We'll need a gunner and a boatswain at the very least. What else, do you suppose?"

Miller considered the question for a moment. "What about a surgeon, sir? Or a surgeon's mate? We're likely to be in harm's way from the sound of it. Then there's marines. Marksmen, like. Our lads can fire a musket at a rabbit well enough, but 'tis not the same as shooting at a man who's shooting at you, now is it, sir? Then there ought to be a third hand to stand a watch. If something happened to you or me, or both of us, what then?"

Squibb was making notes on the back of his commission. He'd been over these and a hundred other questions himself, but he wanted Miller to know that his ideas were being taken seriously.

"Then there's supplies. Who'll be in charge of them without a proper purser? And ship's boats. There's but one gig right now. That's six oars and no room for more than a dozen small men. Not much, now is it, sir? And a sailmaker would be blessing, wouldn't he? We don't even know what canvas is aboard of her, do we, sir?"

The mate paused long enough for Squibb to complete his rapid note-taking. "This is all good, Mr. Miller. I will have to take some of it up with the governor, I can see." From the deck above them came a burst of laughter and cheering. Both men looked at the overhead planks.

"I'd best be going up, sir. That John Cooper is the devil with a bit of rum inside him."

"Carry on, by all means. And thank you for this. I'll go to the governor and try asking first, then move on from there." He scanned the list in front of him. "After all, there's not much point in being master and commander if you can't make a few demands."

———o———

That same afternoon, in the governor's large new office at Fort Townshend, Squibb learned a valuable lesson about making demands.

"Hell and damnation, man!" Governor Edwards declared, rather more forcefully than Squibb thought necessary. "Did I not make myself clear when I said that the squadron is short of everything? That includes warrant officers as well as rope and tar!" He moved to his desk and picked up a handful of papers. "Pursers, boatswains, surgeons and gunners! Do you think I can conjure them, sir?" He threw the papers down and glared across the room. Squibb said nothing and hardly dared to breathe.

The governor shuffled his bulk, robed in the tattered yellow gown, to the chart table and back again. Squibb saw that seat of the gown was well worn. Governor Edwards reached for his wine glass, emptied it, and when he spoke again the irritation had receded and something of his natural good humour had returned.

"Pay me no heed, young man," he said. "It has been a trying day. My wife has always said that patience is like a Newfoundland pony—it carries a great deal and trots a great way, but it will damn well tire with overuse."

"Allow me to apologize, sir. You have many things to occupy you. I should not have presumed—"

"Nonsense, nonsense." The governor waved his hand. "It was I who got you into this, so I shall do all I can to help you. First of all, we will find you a gunner's mate and a boatswain's mate—a couple of experienced men who are ready for promotion. In fact, I will offer acting warrants to attract a few volunteers. As for a purser, you will perform the duty yourself. It is not unheard of, as you know. And you will not require a surgeon as you will be cruising in company with Parker, who has an excellent man aboard. Now, what else was there? Oh yes, a second master's mate. That is perhaps the most difficult. However, I shall have a look round and see if we have a qualified midshipman who can be parted with. How is that?"

"That is excellent news, sir. Thank you very much." Squibb hesitated, reluctant to push his good fortune, but necessity forced him to speak. "There is also the matter of my crew, sir. At present I have just the men who arrived with me. Not enough to work the schooner properly, let alone manage the guns. And no marines at all, sir." He stopped. The flinty look had returned to the other's eye and he feared that he had gone too far. But the governor merely pinched the bridge of his nose and sighed.

"Very well, Commander. I will have the captains send you what men they can spare. If more are required, they will have to come from Captain Parker. And as for marines, I will speak with Major Pringle, who commands the new Corps of Newfoundland Volunteers. He may have a few infantrymen who would serve the purpose. But"—the governor raised a thick finger—"I make no promises, young man. I am doing this because I want you to get to sea as quickly as possible. Do you understand?"

"Yes, sir. And thank you, sir. I am very much aware of your kindness."

"Kindness!" The governor glared at him and released a belch from somewhere deep within. "Can't say I know the word."

MISS ADAMS

St. John's, May 30th

Eli Bailey was waiting with a message in his none-too-clean fingers when Squibb returned from Fort Townshend. Distracted by competing priorities, he thrust it, unread, into his pocket, where it remained forgotten until late afternoon. He came across it while rummaging for a key and held the smudged and crumpled square of paper to the light. He saw that it was faintly pink and that the sealing wax was imprinted with the letter H, likely from a signet ring. He broke the seal, noting the graceful handwriting, and saw that it was from someone named Miss Harriett Adams. She expressed her pleasure at having met him the previous evening and was, to his great amazement, inviting him to dine.

Harriett Adams. He repeated the name aloud. He remembered everything about her and now he was in possession of her name. They had said very little to each other after her startling admission, but it was not for lack of willingness on his part. He'd been brought up short by the speeches, and when they'd ended, the ladies had withdrawn while the men drank their brandy. Escaping the room at last, he'd been waylaid by the governor's wife, who wished to know more about her husband's newest commander. Mrs. Edwards was a formidable woman and he'd had no chance of escape. She had extracted every detail of his life and career within five minutes. Satisfied for the moment, she'd let him go, but by then Miss Adams was nowhere to be seen. He read the invitation again, this time in delightful anticipation of another dinner, until he realized it was for that very evening. Pleasure was quickly overtaken by alarm. The state of his clothes and his person! And he was expected in little more than an hour!

The schooner's bell pealed the hour as Squibb emerged from his cabin. He was freshly washed and dressed in his second-hand naval coat, now scrubbed and brushed so vigorously that it was a lighter shade of blue. He wore his best cocked hat and a new neckcloth, clean shoes and breeches, and stockings that had hardly ever been mended. Eli Bailey took a final swipe with a brush as Squibb stepped into the boat.

Miss Adams lodged at The Rising Sun, a tavern and inn on the Upper Path, and he was at its door within minutes of landing. He paused outside long enough to catch his breath and scrape the mud from his shoes. The ground floor housed a taproom with a warren of snugs and small rooms that were popular with the merchants and gentlemen of the town. A narrow central stairway led to the upstairs chambers. This was guarded by a desk and an old woman of resolute appearance, whose scrutiny he came under the moment he walked through the door. Squibb touched his hat to her and enquired of a dinner hosted by Miss Harriett Adams. Without a word she inclined her head to a door on the right. He nodded his thanks just as the door opened. A maid, seeing him approach, stood aside and curtsied.

The first thing Squibb fixed upon as he walked in, not without some disappointment, was a table laid for six. He had somehow formed the notion that he'd been invited to a more intimate dinner. A glance at the room and its other guests showed that this had been wishful thinking. His disappointment was forgotten at the sight of Miss

Adams herself, standing beyond the table, auburn hair flowing over her shoulders. She was talking with two gentlemen and close by stood two others, one of whom—Lieutenant Gardiner—fixed him with a look of annoyed surprise.

Miss Adams turned her gaze upon him as he approached, favouring him with a smile as she held out her hand. Squibb took the delicate fingers in his and kissed them in what he hoped was a courtly manner. Those fingers had never seen a day of toil, unlike those of his late wife, he thought with a tinge of guilt.

"How very good of you to come, Commander," Miss Adams said.

He made a small bow and smiled. "How could I refuse, ma'am? There is so much that we have not had the opportunity to discuss."

His only wish was to talk with his charming hostess, but introductions were required. The first of these was to a clergyman, the Reverend Edward Langman, who was the Church of England missionary for St. John's. Squibb had seen him at the governor's affair and took him for a severe man. He had a thin, disapproving mouth and a look that seemed to find others deeply sinful. Next was a smiling, prosperous-looking young fellow named Thomas Slade, a merchant captain from Toulinguet, or "Twillingate," as the English called it. Slade was at pains to appear friendly and shook his hand a trifle too long. He was presented last to Mr. Gridley Thaxter, a ship's surgeon and, Miss Adams declared, a fellow American.

"A fellow prisoner, sir," Thaxter gently corrected as he bowed, "but one who has been given parole." He had the appearance of a well-bred man in his early thirties, his manner polite and relaxed. He smiled in spite of his capture and detention. His powder-blue coat was slightly frayed at the cuffs and hem. "I was aboard a continental privateer that ran out of luck last month," he said.

Squibb returned the bow. "I wish I could say how sorry I am, sir." Miss Adams laughed and everyone but Gardiner smiled at the pleasant sound.

"To my great embarrassment," Thaxter said, "this is my second time as a prisoner in St. John's. I was aboard a vessel that ran out of luck last year as well." He shook his head at the run of bad fortune and added, "I think I shall give up the privateering life after this."

Squibb found himself smiling at the man's good humour and asked him what he did to occupy his time. "I have been making myself useful among the American prisoners. Many have been wounded and are suffering from the scarcity of food." As are we all, Squibb was tempted to say. If Americans wished to avoid wounds and scarce food, they ought to stay away from Newfoundland.

The maid caught the attention of her mistress, saving him the need to say anything as the guests were asked to take their places. They did so, and a wine that looked suspiciously like Madeira began to circulate. He took very little and saw what might have been approval in the steely gaze of the clergyman. Langman was in fact the first to address him, stating that they were all most fortunate to be invited to one of Miss Adams' dinners. The occasions had become known throughout the town for their refined dining and conversation, he said.

Miss Adams playfully scolded him for a flatterer and turned to Thomas Slade, who was already refilling his glass. "I am eager to hear more about your latest exploits, Thomas," she said. To Squibb she added, "Have you heard of Mr. Slade and his *Exeter*, Commander?"

"I regret I have not, ma'am. You have a ship, sir?"

"An armed brig, Commander. Which in fact belongs to my uncle, John Slade." Squibb was familiar with the name. Slade's was a prominent merchant firm. "She is now the largest English privateer on the northeast coast."

Squibb glanced at Thaxter and the others. A very odd party, he thought. Not merely enemies in principle, but actively so. "Have you encountered any American vessels this year?" he asked.

"No, sir. It has been quiet thus far, but the summer has only just begun. I will begin patrolling the coast when I return there next week."

"You will certainly be a deterrent," Squibb politely offered. Privately he wondered whether a brig manned by fishermen and officered by a well-fed merchant captain might be more of an inducement to the enemy.

Gardiner had been listening and now broke into the exchange. "Yes," he said, "Slade and company decided to go into the privateering business last year, after their premises at Twillingate were looted by a Yankee raider. And to add to the offence, the rebels gave the entire stock of supplies to the people of Twillingate. Imagine that!" He chuckled and added, "I dare say that your chief duty, sir, is to keep Slade's goods from the poor, rather than taking enemy vessels."

An awkward silence followed as Thomas Slade's face took on a disturbing hue. The insult was plain and intended to provoke. Squibb could not imagine Gardiner's motive, aside from what seemed to be his habitually offensive manner. More interested in the *Exeter* than in calming the waters, he asked, "What is the tonnage of your brig, sir?"

"As if he might know," Gardiner said under his breath.

Slade swung his crimson face toward his tormentor just as the door flew open and the soup arrived in a bustle of tureens and servants. Miss Adams was visibly relieved, and Squibb smiled at the clergyman, remembering his remark on well-bred conversation.

It was to Reverend Langman that Squibb turned as the meal progressed, hoping to break the strained silence that had fallen over the dinner party.

"How long have you been in Newfoundland, sir?" he asked.

The clergyman laid his spoon aside and smoothed the napkin on his lap. "I took up the Lord's mission here in 1752, Commander."

"Twenty-eight years is a long time, sir. No doubt you have been busy."

The piercing eye flashed at Squibb, judging whether the comment was meant to be droll. "Yes. My work has been demanding, and not just here at St. John's. Twice each year I travel to the north and south, baptizing and marrying, and encouraging those in remote harbours where the word of God is rarely heard."

Squibb nodded. He had been raised in a home that worshipped daily, though his own attention to God had lapsed. "I admire your dedication, sir. May I ask if you will return to England in your retirement?"

"I will not," Langman answered without hesitation. "My wife and infant daughter lie buried in the churchyard here, and I intend to join them when my work is done."

Servants returned and cleared the table, and then began laying out the fish course. When they had left, Langman raised the subject of the war, asking the Americans what they saw as its principal causes. Thaxter lost no time in enumerating the grievances, beginning with Britain's taxation of the thirteen colonies to pay for the Seven Years' War.

"That disgraceful imposition," he stated, "was met by protest, with the dumping of tea in Boston harbour. Britain then chose to introduce what we call the Intolerable Acts. The port of Boston was closed, the government of Massachusetts was dissolved, and the colonies were forced to pay for the lodging of British troops who were sent to New England to keep the colonies in check. Intolerable, I may add, is the polite word for what your King has imposed upon his own people."

Squibb listened as the list of outrages went on, culminating in the declaration of independence in 1775 and the start of the war. Thaxter had barely paused for breath, and it was plain to Squibb that he was in the presence of an ardent revolutionary. Miss Adams, meanwhile, had said nothing but nodded politely from time to time. Gardiner, however, was showing signs of impatience by the time the surgeon had finished.

Squibb heard him mutter, "Liberty! What nonsense!"

Thaxter heard the comment as well and quietly asked, "You said something, sir?" For the second time that evening, Squibb feared that the lieutenant had gone too far, a suspicion confirmed by the acid tone of Gardiner's reply.

"Much of what I have heard, sir, comes from a man who has chosen to ignore essential truths. Yes, the colonies were taxed, but the tax was to pay for the cost of protecting them during the war. In fact, your people were taxed more lightly than the inhabitants of England. But I'm sure you know that already. And so you declare your independence rather than pay a tax. Do you honestly hold that a new nation can exist without taxation or even a higher authority to direct its affairs? It is a muddled notion of liberty, sir, invented by ignorance and adopted by folly."

The tension in the room was broken once more by servants bearing food, but this time Miss Adams did not look relieved. Squibb thought she looked distinctly uncomfortable.

"You must pay more attention to the dinner I have ordered, gentlemen," she said with an edge to her voice. "This dish contains the best quality *bacalhau*, and the dried chickpeas were a rare find."

They returned to the meal with compliments on her taste in Portuguese cuisine, but had eaten little when Gardiner resumed his harangue.

"And what of slavery, sir?" he demanded. "Where does this stand in your new liberty? Or is it liberty for some and not for others, based upon the colour of their skin? Slavery has been unsupported in English law since 1772 and now you fear the colonies will be forced to follow. Is this not the true basis of your so-called revolution? Is it not fear and greed that motivate many in New England, perhaps even yourself?"

Squibb looked around the table. The other guests might have been turned to stone. Slade sat motionless with a fork halfway to his mouth and Miss Adams' throat was deeply pink. Thaxter broke the silence, his face suffused with anger.

"Enough, sir!" he seethed. "If insult is your purpose, you have succeeded!"

This is the tipping point, Squibb thought. Gardiner was about to be called out, to defend his words with sword or pistol. The man merely picked up his glass and smiled into its contents.

"I will have an apology, sir," the surgeon loudly insisted. "Not for myself, but for the lady whose presence you have forgotten."

Gardiner ignored him and studied the glass. "My deepest regrets, madam," he said. "When one talks to a fool it is sometimes necessary to speak in a manner that he comprehends."

The legs of Thaxter's chair scraped the floor as he pushed himself back from the table and onto his feet. "You will give me satisfaction, sir!"

Gardiner stared back at him. "The only satisfaction you will have is knowing that I am prepared to overlook your rashness. You would challenge a man who has seen more bloody decks and dead traitors than you could ever imagine? The death of one more rebel means little to me, sir, so stop your foolish tongue while you have the chance."

Squibb sat back. The surgeon's mouth gaped and his face was pale. "Gentlemen! Gentlemen!" Reverend Langman implored.

Thaxter regained command of his voice. "Have you forgotten your own bloody decks, sir? What of *Egmont*, eh? It was my privilege to have been on *Wild Cat* when we took your vessel. And the only dead men that I recall were your own."

Gardiner sat stock-still and said nothing.

"So now, sir," the surgeon pursued, "will you satisfy me by naming a time and place? Or do you fear another defeat at the hands of a true American patriot?"

The two men locked eyes in undisguised loathing. Gardiner raised himself slowly to his feet, his body stiff with the effort of controlling himself. His voice was barely audible as he said, "You will hear from my second, sir." Still staring at the surgeon, he added, "Again, my apologies, madam. If you will excuse me, I must attend to urgent business."

And with that he was gone, leaving Thaxter on his feet, unable or unwilling to move.

Miss Adams looked around the table with an expression of resolve. "I believe we have had our fill of politics for one evening." Her tone left no doubt that she intended to recover her role as hostess.

"Sit down, Gridley. Thomas, please pass the wine at your elbow." The gentlemen did as they were told and she turned to Squibb. "I don't know what you think of our manners, Commander."

Squibb had been thinking more of Gardiner's outrageous conduct. "You bear no responsibility, ma'am," he replied. "A wise man once observed that when forms of civility are violated, there remains little hope of kindness."

She gave him a brief, tight smile. "Dr. Johnson did put things rather well, didn't he? I think we will have the coffee now, Sally."

———————— ◦ ————————

Squibb went aboard *Maidstone* at dawn the next morning. He and Parker had agreed to an early start on readying the schooner for sea, and the captain was waiting for him with breakfast just laid.

"Perfect timing, my friend," he said, rubbing his hands in anticipation before removing the cover from a dish of fried eggs and salt pork. "No doubt you worked up an appetite last evening, with such delightful company."

Squibb smiled at the probing comment. "It was less delightful than you imagine. Miss Adams is very charming, but the conversation was largely political. A couple of her dinner guests left much to be desired. Did you know that she and her cousin Winslow were taking passage to France on the *Pallas*, out of Boston, when one of our cruisers captured them on the Banks? They are now the 'guests' of the governor until transport can be arranged."

Parker poked the eggs with a fork. From across the table Squibb had caught a whiff and wondered about them as well.

"As for that," Parker said, "there is more to her story, you know. Did Miss Adams tell you about her cousin?"

"No, she did not."

"His name is Winslow Warren. The name meant nothing to me, either, until the governor told me. He is quite a catch, it seems. His father is none other than James Warren, paymaster general to Washington's Continental Army and president of the Massachusetts Provincial Congress. What's more, his mother is Mercy Otis Warren, propaganda writer for the rebel cause and, as the governor puts it, fomenter of unrest and harridan of revolution. Why he was bound for France is an unanswered question, but surely it involved nothing of benefit to England. I would say that son Winslow is quite a big fish, wouldn't you?"

Squibb thoughtfully buttered a piece of stale bread. "And where is this Winslow Warren? I haven't met him."

"It would be alarming if you had. Miss Adams is permitted the freedom of the town, but Warren is kept in close confinement. I understand that he is now housed in the admiral's former cabin on *Proteus*. The frigate has been turned into a prison ship with several hundred American sailors below decks. Warren enjoys some privileges and, of course, he is permitted visitors." Parker paused to sniff the pork.

"What will happen to him? And to Miss Adams?"

"Warren is to be sent to London. It would have been done by now, except for the alarm over de Ternay's fleet. No doubt he will be exchanged for one of ours, eventually. But it may take some time. It isn't every day that the rebels capture an Englishman of equal importance."

"And Miss Adams?"

"Oh, I daresay she will be sent home as soon as something can be arranged. One egg or two?"

Their dubious breakfast eaten, the remainder of the morning was spent in transferring supplies from *Maidstone* to *Independence*. Casks of beef and rum, small barrels of powder, spoons and square wooden plates, signal flags, coils of rope of every imaginable size, buckets of tar, boxes of cartridge, nails and hammocks, cutlasses and tin mugs, copper kettles and firewood for the galley, and on and on. Miller was tasked with supervising the work, allowing the two officers a chance to ponder the schooner's main armament. Her new commander was not entirely happy with the eight 6-pounder guns.

"Would you tell me, Captain, how you took her that day?"

"Why, we had a long chase of it," Parker said. "It took six hours or more, but we finally came within range and gave her a ball. You saw the hole in the fore topsail, I'm sure. They had no stomach for a fight with a 28-gun frigate and that was the end of it."

"Indeed. But why were you able to catch her? Normally this schooner would outrun anything in these waters, would she not?"

Parker pursed his lips. "Well, it seemed to me that she was poorly handled. What are you getting at?"

"I believe these guns may have overburdened her. A six-pounder is, what? Sixteen hundredweight?"

"Yes, I should say so."

"Eight guns for a total of some thirteen thousand pounds. And their six-pound shot, at fifty per gun, amounts to another twenty-four hundred. What if we replaced them with four-pounders and reduced the number of shot to twenty-five per gun? Guns and shot would come to less than ten thousand pounds."

"Yes, I see what you mean. Thousands of pounds lighter and she would fly, make no mistake. But are you forgetting that your weapons have to protect you, while convincing the enemy to strike his colours?"

"Ah, but that's exactly the point, sir. *Independence* doesn't need to do either of those. She has you and *Maidstone* for that."

Parker nodded as he considered Squibb's meaning. "Then we rely upon the schooner for the chase, with her improved speed, and upon the frigate to seal the deal." A grin crept across his round face. "Well then, we shall certainly change the guns. But there is one thing more to consider: I strongly advise you to keep a six-pounder as a bow chaser. A very effective argument it can be, in my opinion."

"Agreed. Swift of heel and with teeth to bite."

Their lively discussion was interrupted by the master's mate. "Beg pardon, sir, but there are some new hands arrived for the schooner." Two boats had come alongside while they were talking, one full of sailors and the other carrying a detachment of soldiers.

"I will leave you to it, Jonah."

"Thank you, sir." Squibb turned to Miller. "Bring the seamen aboard first and send for Captain Parker's clerk. He will enter them in the pay and muster books."

The sailors with their bags and chests came aboard and Squibb was pleased to count a dozen new hands. His satisfaction was dispelled, however, as the clerk set about recording their names and ratings. Fully half were landsmen with hardly any knowledge of ships or the sea and the few true seamen were sullen and surly. It was clear that the squadron's captains had taken the opportunity to rid themselves of unwanted company. The only welcome additions were the two acting warrant officers—a boatswain and a gunner. The latter, slump-shouldered and pallid, looked as if he were suffering from last night's rum. On the other hand, he had a sharp and knowing eye, and his lengthy pigtail was a mark of long service. The other man was a bearded and powerful-looking figure, who stood eyeing the rigging with a professional interest. As Squibb looked more closely, the man's face seemed vaguely familiar. It was not until he caught his eye that Squibb realized who he was. He crossed the deck and grasped the grinning boatswain's hand.

"Titus Greening! By heaven, what a surprise!"

"How d'ye do, Mr. Squibb?" the man replied. "I volunteered straight away when I heard it was you, sir."

"Well, my thanks for that, Mr. Greening, as I should more rightly call you. Congratulations on your acting warrant." Greening was clearly pleased and proud of his new position. Squibb had not seen the man in twelve years, not since they'd sailed together on the little *Dove* on the northeast coast. He was a promising seaman even then and was now worth his weight in gold to *Independence*.

"We will talk later. I have a few ideas regarding the rig. Get yourself squared away first." Greening knuckled his forehead and turned to one of the *Amelias*, who was idling near the hatchway.

"You there!" he called in a voice that would carry in a gale. "Shoulder this chest and take it below. Then report to me for some proper work." Squibb smiled and walked away. The new boatswain was wasting no time in establishing his authority.

With the sailors dismissed to their berth, Squibb remained on deck to watch as the red-coated infantrymen, a drummer among them, clambered over the rail. The men, from the Newfoundland Corps of

Volunteers, had been recruited from the town and surrounding bays to serve in defence of the island for the duration of the war. At first glance Squibb felt they inspired even less confidence than the boatload of so-called seamen. Their uniforms were far from uniform and one man seemed to have lost his tricorn hat. But at least they had their muskets. A solidly built sergeant with a cast to one eye came over the rail in an agile manner, making one experienced soldier among them. Behind him came a slim, long-legged ensign, whose hat hid his face as he pulled himself up from the boat. He wore the colourful officer's uniform of the Volunteers, a blue jacket with red cuffs and lapels and contrasting white buttons and waistcoat. Once on deck, the young man straightened his sword and looked up.

Squibb stood frozen, momentarily stunned by the sight before him. His eyes told him who it was, standing there so tall and straight, but his brain was slow to accept it. He had wished for so long and so hard to look upon that face that for an instant he could not separate what was real from what he had hoped for. Watching him with evident calm was his stepson, his sixteen-year-old stepson, whom he had not seen or heard from in nearly a year. The boy was fuller, his features a little more defined, and his hand whipped up as he saluted the schooner's commander.

"Ensign Toope and eleven other ranks," he announced in a firm, clear voice. "Reporting as ordered. Sir!"

There was a long, awkward pause as Squibb came to grips with himself. The emotions of confusion, relief, and happiness fought one another and became entangled with the many questions that overwhelmed him. He regained enough self-possession to acknowledge the salute, but words were another matter. Others were watching and he forced himself to speak.

"Take these men aft to the marines' berth, Mr. Miller." His voice sounded normal to his ear and he added, "The sergeant will mess with the gunroom. Mr. Toope will report to my cabin when you have shown him his quarters."

The stern cabin of *Independence* was not large enough for Squibb to pace. He stood behind the small desk and waited. It took but a moment for the knock to come. Young Bailey opened the door to admit Ensign Toope. Ethan had grown taller in the past year—Squibb was certain of it. He stood now with his hat beneath his arm, his fair-haired head bent forward under the beams.

"Please sit," Squibb said, and the young man sat, bolt upright and watching him with a steady eye. "Ethan…" Squibb began, then faltered. He had no idea what he wanted to say, and yet there were so many things that needed to be said. He tried again. "Ethan, I am so very, very pleased to see you."

Ensign Toope sat very still and replied, "Thank you, sir."

Squibb looked at the lad he had raised as his own since he'd married the boy's mother. There had been so much love among the three of them and yet, at some point after her death, it had become misplaced. He was grasping for it now, a precious thing that was just beyond his reach.

"Ethan." He repeated the name without meaning to. It had been a long time since he'd spoken it aloud. His stepson looked away and shifted in his chair, his composure less intact. Squibb gripped his hands tighter behind his back.

"Ethan, where have you been? Why did I not hear from you?" There were so many questions he wanted to ask, but he stopped as the young man looked at him evenly.

"If I may be frank, sir?"

"My boy, I am not the commander of this schooner right now. I am your father. Talk to me. Please."

The ensign swallowed and stared at the hat in his lap. "I was angry with you, sir. I think you know that. I took a boat to St. John's and found work on the docks. I would have joined the navy but there were no openings for midshipmen. I had a notion of sailing away. Anywhere would do.

When I heard that the Volunteers were being formed, I decided to enlist, so here I am. I didn't write to you for so long that, when I finally thought I would, it seemed too little, too late." He paused in his careful choice of words and glanced at his stepfather. It was all that Squibb could do to keep the tears from his eyes.

"To be truthful, sir, I am here because my company commander sent me. I cannot pretend that it is my choice or that all is forgiven. I am sure you will understand that. However, I am prepared to do my duty and more, if required." The boy's face was neutral, his features controlled. "Should you wish to have someone in my place, you must speak with Captain Graham of the Volunteers. I think he will do as you wish."

Squibb steeled himself to speak with as little emotion as he could muster. Still his voice cracked.

"Oh, Ethan. I am so very sorry. My grief at losing your mother clouded my judgment in a way that I would never have thought possible. You are as dear to me as ever your mother was. Then and now."

Squibb drew a deep breath and studied his son's face, seeking some evidence of understanding or forgiveness. The young man did not move and his face was unreadable.

"I am overjoyed to see you again, Ethan. And I will not be asking to have you replaced, unless you wish it."

Ensign Toope stood up, his head again bent awkwardly beneath the beams. He meant to leave and Squibb could think of nothing more to keep him, to get him to talk or to listen. There would be other opportunities, he told himself, and he must not rush the boy or impose his authority. The ensign managed a salute.

"Thank you, sir. I must see to my men." He turned and left, pulling the door shut behind him.

Squibb stood alone for some time, moving only to stare through the small window high up in the stern. Once or twice he shook his head and put his handkerchief to his eyes. Eli Bailey, his arms full of muster papers, opened the door, looked in, and quietly closed it again.

The officers commanding ships of the Newfoundland squadron received their orders late that day, delivered to each ship by one of the governor's black-clad clerks. Along with his sealed papers, each man received a summons. The governor was convening an immediate council of war, to be attended by all senior officers of the land and naval forces at St. John's. The threat of invasion by the French was considered imminent.

Independence was still moored alongside *Maidstone*, and Squibb was invited to share Parker's boat as they responded to the call. They discussed their orders while they were rowed across, both men in good spirits at the prospect of putting to sea the next morning. They smiled at the jeers and indecent offers of the harbour women and climbed the steep slope to the new fort with the other officers who had come ashore. It was an unusually warm day for early June and all were gasping and regretting their heavy broadcloth coats by the time they arrived at the fortress gate. The sentries of the 71st had been replaced by those of the 42nd, the Royal Highlanders. The duty, Squibb had heard, was rotated to appease the intense rivalry among the Scottish regiments.

The naval officers soon joined a half-dozen redcoats in the governor's office, where chairs had been placed in a semicircle before the imposing desk. Pipes, long and short, appeared from pockets, and the rich scent of captured Virginia tobacco soon filled the air. The governor himself entered the room a few minutes later and called the council to order. He had foregone the yellow dressing gown, perhaps as a mark of the meeting's gravity.

His secretary began with a roll call, and the exercise gave Squibb an opportunity to put names to faces. The first was Major Pringle, commanding both the Engineers and the Volunteer Corps. He seemed an active, capable man whom the governor evidently relied upon. There were also MacDonald of the 71st, Grant of the 42nd, and a couple of others, including Lieutenant Colonel Hay, Royal Artillery and garrison commander.

On the naval side, he heard the names of Keppel, Baskerville, and Gardiner, the last glaring at Squibb from across the room. Also Reeve of the frigate *Surprise*, Berkley from the *Fairy* sloop, Stanhope of the *Trepassey* brig, and Luttrell of the old 50-gun *Portland*. Parker and Squibb made just nine from the navy, not counting three or four others who were at sea. All awaited the governor's words with intense interest.

"Gentlemen," he began. "You are aware that a large French squadron left Brest some three weeks ago, sailing westward in company with what I can only describe as a small fleet of transports. There can be no doubt that this is an invasion force. The only question is where this force is bound. In the absence of further intelligence, we must assume the worst and prepare for the defence of St. John's." He paused, and immediately a half-dozen voices rose up.

"Order!" he cried, his colour rising. "Listen to me, damn it. I shall begin by outlining the priorities that have been decided upon by myself, Colonel Hay, and Major Pringle, and which are contained in your orders. You will have an opportunity to comment in due course.

"First of all, signals in the event of an attack, whether by day or night. Pay particular attention to these. They are of vital importance to our being prepared to meet the enemy. Number two, while in port the larger vessels will be moored to serve as floating batteries. These will cover the approaches from the Narrows and the low ground to the west of the harbour. Stanhope to be in charge. Thirdly, sailors belonging to the smaller vessels, when in port, are to man the guns of the three southside batteries. Hay will organize and command. And as for our final priority, it has already been taken in hand. This morning an anchor chain from *Portland* was secured across the harbour entrance."

The governor dropped the paper he'd been consulting and looked up. "These measures are in addition to those contained in your individual orders. On land we will be redeploying our troops and artillery to best advantage, including strong points at Kitty Vitty and Petty Harbour. Some of you naval officers will be employed in moving men and guns to the outlying batteries at Torbay and Bay o' Bulls. Others will begin patrolling the Banks and coastal waters to give us early warning of Admiral de Ternay's arrival. Now, to put this plainly, gentlemen, we have our backs to the wall. You know how many troops and ships we have. Damned few against so large a force. And if that were not enough to worry me, there is reason to believe that the French would be welcomed by many here in St. John's."

In spite of his interest in what the governor was saying, Squibb found his thoughts straying to Miss Adams' dinner at The Rising Sun. The governor would not be pleased to hear of Gardiner's intended duel. Such a thing was irresponsible, not to mention foolish, when there were enemies enough to fight.

And then there was Miss Adams herself. He'd been reliving the evening in his head and could easily repeat every word she'd spoken, complete with her manner of saying it. Everything about her was firmly imprinted on his mind. He wondered if she would still be in St. John's when he returned.

"...just as he did in '62, as Commander Squibb will confirm."

Squibb felt his face warming as everyone in the room looked his way. Caught out like a daydreaming cabin boy, he had only half-heard the governor's words.

"Therefore, we must not rule out an overland attack," the governor resumed. "I will end here by saying that there are some in this town who sympathize with the rebel cause and would see the arrival of the French as an opportunity to do great mischief. The Irish make up the majority of our population, and I need not tell you how many of them are in your ships' crews and regiments. We also have a large number of prisoners, many of them free to wander the town. Care must be taken, gentlemen, that we are not undermined from within!"

The governor sat back and a lieutenant, who'd been standing behind him, leaned forward to whisper in his ear. It was the same well-dressed young man whom Squibb had met the day before. "Oh yes, and we have reports that rebel privateers have stepped up their attacks on towns and shipping. A large vessel attempted to take the settlement of Mortier last week but was driven off with the loss of twenty of her men, thanks to the efforts of Sergeant Young of the 84th Regiment. The worthy sergeant, whom I have mentioned in my dispatch to Whitehall, was there recruiting and managed to organize the fishermen in defence of their property."

"Well done, the 84th!" cried Hay, much to the satisfaction of the regiment's commanding officer. The other soldiers sat stone-faced.

"Also to our credit, the privateer brig *Tyger* and her crew were taken on the second of this month. My congratulations to the officers and crew of *Cygnet*. That is all very good, of course, but alone these efforts will not turn the tide of this war. In recent weeks we have lost a half-dozen of our merchant and fishing ships to these raiders. It cannot continue, and I am relying on all of you to do one thing only—to carry out your written orders with energy and diligence. Should you fail to do so, I can damn well promise you a court martial to find the reason why!"

The governor glowered at the array of blue and red coats before him. The lieutenant stepped up to the desk and said, "Governor Edwards will now entertain any relevant observations you may have, gentlemen."

It seemed to Squibb that the ensuing talk was far from relevant. It consisted mainly of the Highland officers manoeuvring to gain some tactical advantage over one another. The naval men offered one or two comments on the need for stores and timber, to which the governor bluntly observed that their ships must resupply themselves from their captures. In the end, their host's patience, like the pony, tired with overuse, and the council of war was adjourned.

Parker and Squibb walked down to the harbour together, eager and impatient to get their vessels ready for the morning tide. Their assigned task was to patrol the entire eastern and southern coast of the Avalon Peninsula, from the northern Cape St. Francis to Cape St. Mary's in the south. They would likely be at sea for two weeks or more, and the prospect pleased them both. As they neared Parker's boat, Squibb raised the subject of Lieutenant Gardiner and his unsettling behaviour. Parker gave him an apologetic look.

"I should have told you sooner, Jonah. It has nothing to do with you personally, but John Gardiner is highly resentful that *Independence* was not given to him. That is all."

"But did he have reason to expect her?"

"Not that anyone can say, I assure you. You see, Gardiner was in command of *Egmont* when she was taken. A court martial was held, of course, and he was found to have acquitted himself honourably. But still, these things have a way of sticking to a man. He kept his crew and was given *Bonavista* shortly after, but she's the mule of the squadron—old, slow, and crank. And now he deplores the fact that you have command of *Independence*." Parker glanced at his friend before adding, "It doesn't help that you are newly returned to the service, either."

"Or that I am a mere colonial."

"Exactly," Parker conceded.

Squibb was not surprised. He had encountered that particular prejudice before. "Did you not say that *Egmont* was lost because her powder was wet?"

"That's right. I'm not sure how that came to be, but of course when the critical moment arrived, the situation was impossible. In any event, the court martial did not hold Gardiner responsible."

"And yet a hint of something remains," Squibb observed.

"Well, as to that, the responsibility ultimately lies with the officer commanding, does it not?"

"Yes. But it does seem unjust, all the same."

Parker smiled. "Perhaps. Gardiner seems to think so."

Squibb pondered the matter as they were rowed across the harbour. Did this explain the lieutenant's behaviour toward Thaxter, or Slade? Gardiner seemed for all the world like a man with something to prove. Or disprove. Could the loss of *Egmont* haunt him so strongly? Other men had certainly lost their ships but gone on to lasting and prosperous careers. Only the previous year Captain Charles Everitt had wrecked his 32-gun *Arethusa* after an engagement with the French *Aigrette*, and yet he was about to commission a new frigate, HMS *Solebay*.

The crew of Parker's boat was a hearty set of seamen who made the small craft fairly skim across the water. They were rapidly approaching the schooner when two things caught Squibb's attention. One was the sight of a fair-sized boat, upturned and secured on the deck of *Independence*. He had almost despaired of getting another before putting to sea and there it was, looking for all the world like an eight-oared pinnace. The other was a uniformed and unfamiliar figure who stood near the schooner's wheel. At the stern rail the marines under Ethan were standing in close order, evidently awaiting their commander's return. As Squibb climbed onto the deck they came to attention and the stranger saluted.

"Midshipman Salter, sir. Joining *Independence* as ordered." Squibb could have danced for joy. He had all but given up on having another mate to stand a watch but here, at the last minute, was a godsend. Not that Salter looked like much of a godsend. His uniform coat was badly tarred in places and his face had a wary, uncertain look. His mouth was rather small and his chin was nearly hidden in his collar. But he did meet Squibb's eye for a moment and he was standing quite erect for a midshipman.

"Are you fully qualified, Mr. Salter?" was Squibb's first question. The young man appeared to be only eighteen or nineteen years of age, but a midshipman's value, Squibb knew, could only be measured in knowledge and experience.

"Yes, sir. I am soon to sit my lieutenant's exam."

"Excellent!" Squibb replied. "And what ship do you come from?"

The midshipman blushed and replied: "*Bonavista*, sir."

TOAD'S COVE

St. John's, June 1st

T
wo bells in the morning watch, with the sky growing lighter behind Signal Hill and the wind fair for departure. At the last bell, the boatswain's mate in charge of *Maidstone's* forecastle signalled the waiting midshipman that the anchor had been hove short. The midshipman relayed this to the officer of the watch, who in turn announced the fact to the frigate's captain. With a barely perceptible nod, William Parker unleashed a chain of orders that saw the 593-ton ship bring her anchor home and swing her bow to the Narrows. Men aloft released the main topsail even as a party at the foremast heaved away to raise the outer jib. The frigate slowly paid off to the westerly breeze and made her stately way toward the open sea.

Similar events on board *Independence* did not go quite as smoothly. The crew had cast off from the frigate's side at the stroke of the bell, her foresail and staysail hoists manned and ready. But at the command, the foresail's throat halyard jammed and only the quick instincts of the quartermaster at the wheel prevented a collision. The schooner wallowed alongside her much larger consort until the problem was corrected, then took up station in her wake.

The commander of *Independence* stood near the aft rail and said nothing. His thoughts would be known in due course, but for now Squibb's mind was on the fact that two-thirds of his crew were green men and it showed. Salter, as officer of the watch, stood near the wheel and dared not look at him. The voices of Greening and Miller drowned all else as they attempted to bring some order to the mainsail hoist. Just then the frigate let drop her fore topsail. It filled with a crack, propelling her well ahead of the struggling *Independence*. In contrast, the schooner's mainsail now crept up the mast, the hoops rattling to Greening's shout of "*Heave, ye buggers, heave!*"

The massive sail was finally up, though it took some moments for the peak halyard to be tightened and the gaff raised. The commander's expression betrayed nothing throughout this performance. His mind was working on the many things to be addressed over the coming days.

The defensive chain across the Narrows had been lowered and once beyond it, *Maidstone* began to set all sail, including her topgallants. The midshipman turned to Squibb, but before he could ask his question the commander quietly said, "Carry on, Mr. Salter."

"All sail!" the young man bellowed. "Mr. Greening, all sail if you please!" In slow succession the remaining canvas appeared, including the main topmast staysail. This, too, took an inexcusably long time, but soon the schooner began to answer her helm in a lively manner. She capered up to the ponderous frigate, which brought, to Salter's apparent relief, an approving nod from the skipper.

Miller made his way aft and said by way of apology, "I'm sure things will improve, sir."

Squibb looked aloft. "There can be no doubt of that, Mr. Miller." He studied the sails, noting the round, neatly sewn patch on the fore topsail. "Now, Mr. Salter, the deck is yours. Mr. Miller, all warrant officers to my cabin straight away."

Squibb went below, passed the marine sentry slouching outside his door, and ducked into the small cabin. The others followed, finding seats where they could, until the space was jammed with half a dozen somewhat embarrassed-looking men. Squibb sat at his small desk and regarded the assembled company.

"First of all, we will not be discussing our present sorry state." There was evident relief all around. "We will focus instead on improving what we can over the coming days. I will begin with Mr. Salter. I have informed him that he is to be in charge of training. Mr. Greening and Mr. Tompkins"—Squibb glanced at the boatswain and the ill-looking gunner, to whom he had barely spoken since he came aboard—"you will advise and assist in this, the former with regard to sail handling and general deck duties, and the latter in everything related to the ship's guns. Particularly our long six, as it will be our bread and butter when it comes to a chase. Understood?"

"Aye, aye, sir," the two men answered.

"Now then, Mr. Toope." He caught his stepson's eye. "Your men will, of course, train under yourself and Sergeant Parrell, as far as their duties as acting marines are concerned. But I expect them to be familiar with the ship's guns and know how to pull on a rope as well. You will work with Mr. Salter in this regard."

"Yes, sir."

Squibb turned to Robert Hogarth, the former Trinity Bay boatbuilder who was now the ship's carpenter. "Mr. Hogarth, I believe you have had a chance to see what needs to be done, though precious little time in which to do it."

The carpenter nodded. "Right enough, Mr. Squibb."

"Then immediately following this, you and I will inspect the vessel, end to end, and I will hear what you have to say about her hull."

"Aye, aye, sir."

Squibb sat back in his chair and looked around the cabin. "You are no doubt wondering where we are headed and what my orders are.

The simple answer is that we are to patrol the near eastern and southern coasts in company with *Maidstone*. We will be looking for a French squadron, nearly the size of a fleet, with up to ten men o' war." Glances were exchanged around the room and Squibb watched for signs of alarm or trepidation. There were none and he carried on.

"One final item: the matter of command." Here again he had everyone's full attention. "Mr. Miller is an experienced navigator and one whom I trust in all matters of seamanship. He will therefore serve as first mate. And as this is a King's vessel and therefore a fighting ship, I am naming Mr. Salter as the second. He has the experience we require in gun drill, discipline, engagement tactics, and the like."

Squibb pushed his chair back and rose, prompting the others to do the same. "Mr. Hogarth, I will join you directly. Would you remain a moment, Ensign Toope?"

The warrant officers filed out and Squibb sat again before regarding his stepson. They had not spoken beyond the bounds of duty since their first discussion in this cabin. Ethan preferred, it seemed, to keep their interaction on a professional footing, and Squibb could only comply. What the crew made of their distant relationship he could not say. His stepson cut a dashing figure in his uniform, he had to admit, though how much he had learned about soldiering in so short a time was another matter. It was something he intended to find out in the coming days.

"Have you settled in?"

"Yes. Thank you, sir." Ethan's neutral look, perhaps a soldier's habit in the presence of a superior officer, was disconcerting.

He was a handsome lad, Squibb thought, even though he'd inherited George Toope's ears. He had his mother's nose and mouth and it was comforting to see her in his features. Squibb laid the thought aside for now and focused on the matter at hand. What he wanted for the present, more than anything, was to have his stepson succeed in his new role. It was the boy's first opportunity to show his worth, and Squibb intended to provide what guidance he could without being seen to favour him.

"I wish to say, Ethan, that I am pleased with your conduct and attention to duty thus far."

"Thank you, sir."

"It is early days, of course, but if you continue as you have begun, I have no doubt that Major Pringle and the Corps will be very pleased with you at the end of our voyage. You hold the most junior of commissioned ranks and you must have an eye to promotion if you wish to make this your career."

"Yes, sir," the young man nodded. "Captain Graham did say that he had faith in me when he signed my orders."

"Good. Now tell me about your men. Sergeant Parrell is an experienced man, I believe?"

"Oh yes, sir. Fourteen years under arms, including two with the Royal Irish in the New England war."

"And the rest of them?"

Here the ensign's face turned glum. "Captain Graham said he was giving me ten picked men, sir. I thought it was very good of him until I realized he'd picked ten of the worst. Half of them are awkward, at best, and the others are the hard nuts, sir. More used to the gaol than anything else."

Squibb ruminated on this a moment before saying, "Well then, the captain must have felt that you were up to the challenge. I think you are as well."

His stepson coloured a little. "Thank you, sir." He shifted in his chair and reddened more deeply. "I think it only right that I tell you, sir, that Captain Graham's daughter and I have . . . we have formed an attachment, sir."

Squibb was both surprised and pleased. He and Amy had been about the same age when they'd come to an understanding. "And what is her name?"

"Nancy, sir." The young ensign could not help but smile at the sound of it. "I would be happy to introduce you when we return to St. John's."

He nodded. Could this be an offer of reconciliation? Was the boy ready to forgive him for his neglect? The thought encouraged him.

"I am looking forward to it already. And congratulations." Squibb had thought of his stepson as a boy for so many years, it was hard to acknowledge that he was indeed a young man. But a man he was, sitting before him, and a King's officer to boot. It was time, he decided, to treat him as such.

"There is another matter that I must raise with you. And I am not certain how to put it. You see, like your 'picked men,' more than half our crew has come to us from other ships of the squadron and I fear their captains were happy to be rid of them."

"Yes, sir. I have heard Salter and Miller mention it."

Squibb had been thinking about Salter in particular, and why Gardiner had let him go from *Bonavista*. Did he simply wish to be rid of him, or was there some other reason? He felt the schooner heel slightly and judged that the helmsman had edged her onto a southerly course. Cape Spear would be abeam to starboard.

"Well then," he continued, "you are aware of how we sit. As the officer commanding this ship's marines, you have the responsibility of upholding my authority, by force if need be, in any crisis. Furthermore, anything that appears amiss must be reported to me immediately. Do you understand?"

"Of course, sir."

Squibb leaned forward and rested his elbows on the narrow desk. "I know that this smacks of spying on your shipmates, but that is not my intent. The other officers will have their eyes and ears open as well. I am reminding you because you are new to all of this. We are at war and we must not forget that, even for an instant."

"I understand, sir."

He was silent for a moment. "Can I ask you something, Ethan?"

"Yes, sir." The neutral gaze returned.

"Why did you choose to fight in this war?" The young man looked at him but said nothing. "Was it because of what happened to your mother?" There, he had said it. The question had been on his mind since Ethan had come aboard. As both father and commander, he needed to know his son's motivation.

"I felt it was the right thing to do," came the rely. "Our home and way of life are under threat. You always told me that we must be prepared to defend what we hold dear."

Squibb studied the closed face. "It has nothing to do with anger or notions of revenge?"

"No. That would be pointless, would it not?" The answer, phrased as a question, told him that his son was wondering about Squibb's own motivations.

"Yes, it would certainly be pointless. And apt to affect one's judgment, in general and at critical moments. I was angry for a very long time after your mother died, but now that has passed. The sadness remains and always will, I think. But there is no bringing her back, no matter what the outcome of this war or how we conduct it."

"Then we must be strong and resolute, yet merciful in victory."

Squibb smiled. He was being quoted. Had he known that his words would lodge so firmly in his child's mind, he might have considered them more carefully.

"Thank you. My question has been answered and the matter is closed. Now, let us carry on. We both have much to do."

The below-deck inspection with the carpenter buoyed Squibb's confidence in his vessel. He had taken Parker's word that she was seaworthy and now he wished to have the opinion confirmed by Hogarth and by his own observation. Beginning at the forepeak, where the hawsers and other cordage were stowed, they examined the solid timbers and fine workmanship of her Yankee builders. Her hanging knees were rather small and her side planks somewhat thin, but that was the price paid for her speed and agility. Moving aft, they inspected the forecastle, where the majority of the crew were berthed. The men slung their hammocks, ate, and otherwise lived in the dark cramped space when not on duty.

Returning on deck, they looked into the galley, which was little more than a cookshack. Here Simeon Ballett, the cook, worked and slept while they were at sea. He shared the small space with Eli Bailey, Squibb's steward. The unexpected visit flustered Ballett, who was elbow-deep in flour as he prepared a late meal for three dozen men. In his confusion he dropped the bowl. The visitors quickly retreated before a cloud of white dust.

Farther aft, Squibb and the carpenter descended the ladder of the stern companionway. At the bottom were the hatches giving access to the hold, the length of which Hogarth had previously crawled to ensure the integrity of the timbers that supported the ship. Stored there, below the waterline, were shingle ballast, round shot, and the water butts. There was also a large watertight and spark-proof magazine that held cartridge bags and kegs of powder for the guns. The only access to this area was by way of the lower deck hatches. Squibb instructed the carpenter to double the locks.

Forward of the companionway were the marines' berth and the gunroom, where most of the warrant officers would sleep. Aft of it were the two small cabins at the stern, one of which would serve as the wardroom for Miller, Salter, and Ethan. Tight alongside was the door to the commander's cabin with its marine sentry, who stood more nearly at attention since his officer had had a word. With their survey complete, Squibb thanked the carpenter for his diligence.

"Carry on then, Mr. Hogarth," he said. "You have your orders, and please tell Mr. Miller to relieve Mr. Salter and send him to my cabin."

Salter was soon sitting on the other side of the desk, and Squibb came straight to the point. "I would like to hear your plans for training the crew, Mr. Salter." He had little time for niceties now that they were at sea. The midshipman showed no sign of distress at the sudden demand, answering with a show of confidence.

"The starboard watch will begin exercising the guns with Mr. Tompkins at four bells, sir. Mr. Greening will take the marines in hand at the same time. Later in the morning we will switch them over and start in with the larboard watch as well." Miller's shouted commands to the sail trimmers came down to them from the deck above. "Do I have permission to use a little powder, sir?"

"You do indeed, and even an empty cask as a target if you can find one. Now tell me, Mr. Salter, where did you serve before landing on *Bonavista*?"

The question may have been anticipated and the young man replied with only the slightest hesitation. "I was with *Egmont*, sir. Lieutenant Gardiner commanding."

Squibb nodded. Parker had said that her crew had been transferred intact. "And you were captured with him last summer, only to be liberated by *Surprise* the next day?"

"Yes, sir."

He regarded the midshipman. "I see. Tell me, if you would, how *Egmont* was taken."

Salter licked his lips before answering. "The cartridges in her guns were wet, sir. Or damp at least. When she engaged *Wild Cat*, the guns would not fire."

"So the cartridges had been sitting in the guns for some time?"

Salter's look met his own. "Yes, sir."

"Do you know how this negligence came about?"

"Mr. Gardiner had ordered the guns loaded and run out as soon as we saw the enemy, sir. But we had a long wet beat of it before they engaged us."

"So that was how the powder became damp, do you think?"

"I believe it was the case, sir. Though Mr. Gardiner swore it had been tampered with. The Yankee delivered her broadside and *Egmont* could not defend herself." He looked at his hands and added, "They boarded and our losses were two dead and a dozen wounded."

Squibb studied the young man as he spoke, hoping to divine something more of his nature. He seemed forthright and honest enough, a competent officer in training who was about to take his next step up the ladder. "Are you on friendly terms with Mr. Gardiner?"

The midshipman swallowed, nervously perhaps, before replying. "I would not say so, sir."

"And why is that, do you suppose?"

"I cannot speak for Mr. Gardiner, sir. But it seems he cannot trust anyone who served on *Egmont*."

"I see. Well, enough of that, Mr. Salter. You are now third in command of this vessel. As such, please tell me what you think of her."

Salter's face betrayed his relief at the change of subject. "She is very light in construction, sir. She was never built as a warship or even a privateer. The Yanks added guns to prey on unarmed merchantmen and nothing more. We would be best to avoid a fight with anything heavily armed."

"Yes, of course. But she is ideal for speed and deception, is she not?"

"Aye, sir. May I ask what you have in mind?"

Squibb met the young man's watchful eyes.

"Nothing specific, but she was captured just a short time ago and word will not have spread among the enemy so quickly. With her name still plainly visible we will no doubt have certain advantages. And opportunities."

Salter nodded, still watching. Squibb wondered if his own full measure was being taken.

"I think I understand, sir," the midshipman replied. "You mean to engage the enemy, but on your own terms and in your own good time. Ruse and artifice are valuable weapons and you intend to make full use of them. All warfare, of course, is based upon deception."

Squibb regarded his new second officer. There was more to this young man than he had assumed.

———— o ————

The light was waning when Squibb came on deck to take his watch. They were two miles out from Bull Head with the frigate another five miles to seaward. Parker's plan was to use the schooner as an inshore scout while *Maidstone* remained offshore to detect any vessel sailing out of sight of land. From her main masthead a lookout would see anything that attempted to slip past them, even far out to sea.

The air was cool and the wind remained light from the west, moving the ships south at a steady three and a half knots. The watch on deck had little to do and Greening was taking the opportunity to teach the new hands a few basic knots. The landsmen were attentive, though slow to catch on. Squibb watched them for a few moments, noting with approval that the bosun had a great store of patience. He walked the length of the deck and returned to the man at the wheel. It was Sam Hiscock, an experienced *Amelia* whom he had rated quartermaster.

"How does she feel?" Squibb asked.

"Right enough, sir. Like a fine young horse what needs a firm hand."

"In that case, bring her up to windward and see how she likes it. I want to look into this harbour." Hiscock swung the wheel and *Independence* turned briskly to starboard, immediately picking up another knot of speed.

"Stand by sheets, Mr. Greening," Squibb called. The schooner skimmed past Columbine Point and Useless Bay on a southwesterly course into the Bay o' Bulls. In the failing light he saw the colours flying above the battery on Gun Ridge and had no doubt that the officer of the small garrison there was examining him as well.

"Mr. Greening, the private signal. Mr. Tompkins," he called to the wheezing gunner. "We will give them a salute, if you please."

A minute later a pennant rose snapping up the foremast and the voice of a single 4-pound gun rang out. It was answered immediately by a signal flag and a much louder boom from the battery. They neared Quail Point and Squibb briefly scanned the inner harbour with his glass before snapping it shut.

"Take her out, Sam. Mr. Greening, prepare to come about."

The schooner's bow swung to starboard as the boatswain herded his men into position. The tack was carried out in a competent manner and Squibb nodded his approval. They bore away with the wind astern and the sails quickly set on opposite beams like the wings of a goose. *Independence* left the harbour and resumed her station abreast of the far-off frigate.

The first half of the night passed uneventfully with a clear sky, brilliant stars, and the same steady westerly. A few hours before dawn the wind veered into the northeast. Squibb awoke as the motion of the boat changed and the sails were reset. He slept solidly again until sunrise, when Eli Bailey entered the cabin with a mug of steaming coffee. Sacks of beans had been captured by *Cygnet* a week earlier and generously shared among the ships.

"Mr. Salter's compliments, sir, and I'm to say the wind has gone nor'easterly and brought the fog." Bailey hesitated a moment. "Oh yes, and that we're coming up on Cape Ballard. I'll fetch your breakfast directly, sir." He laid the mug where it could be reached from the swinging cot and closed the door behind him. Squibb swung his feet to the deck.

Cape Ballard. He quickly calculated that they'd covered some thirty nautical miles during the night. Gulping down the coffee, he dressed and went on deck, where Miller was taking over from Salter. Tompkins was preparing the newly awakened watch for gun drill and Greening was explaining the ropes to the marines up forward. *Maidstone* was not visible through the fog, but he knew she was out there. Any variation in her sailing would have been signalled by a pre-arranged number of guns. He cocked his ear and listened for a moment, hearing little beyond a few low voices, the creak of hemp, and the swirl of water along their side.

"Send a reliable hand aloft, Mr. Miller."

"Aye, aye, sir." He watched as a sailor climbed the larboard shrouds to the masthead, a long glass slung from his shoulder. Squibb had no firm reason for sending a man aloft, and yet something was bothering him. He could not say what it was, but somehow or other he sensed that they were not alone in the fog that engulfed them.

The lookout had hardy reached his perch when his cry came down: "Deck there. Something to loo'ard. Can't rightly make it out."

"Where away?" Miller called.

"Gone, sir. No, there it be again. Half a mile or so off our wind'ard quarter." Squibb was scrambling up the windward shrouds before the man had finished speaking. He took the glass from him and followed his pointing finger. He saw nothing at first, until a dark shape became visible for an instant. Surely they were well past the Renews Rocks, he thought, and there were no other islands near their position.

"There it be again, sir," the lookout cried in his West Country burr. "Looks to be movin' north, away from us." Squibb had a brief glimpse of the shadowy form and it was definitely moving.

"Deck there," he bellowed, "full about." The schooner came about with much less warning than was usual. Fortunately, most of the experienced hands were on deck and the sails were trimmed handily. With the breeze now on the schooner's starboard bow, the helmsman pointed her straight at where the dark shape had been.

"Bring her up a touch, Mr. Miller." Squibb did not intend to chase the wraith, but rather to intercept it. "Just so," he called down as he estimated the point of convergence. He stayed where he was, one leg entwined in the ratlines as he scanned the distance.

Minutes passed and yet the spectre did not reappear. At length he passed the glass to the lookout.

"You've a good eye," Squibb said. "But I think we've lost whatever it was."

"I'd stake my pay 'twas a vessel, sir. And not a small 'un." The man's bearded chin was thrust out in respectful defiance.

Squibb clapped him on the shoulder and began his descent, shouting down as he went: "Resume course, Mr. Miller."

He returned to his cabin for breakfast but was too distracted to know what he ate. His mind was fully taken up with the object he'd seen. It was certainly a vessel, perhaps a fishing shallop, but it was moving at a speed equal to or greater than his own. And it had almost certainly altered course after *Independence* had come about. Otherwise he would have crossed its wake or seen it again, however briefly. The only explanation was that the vessel had seen *Independence* change her course and had done likewise to avoid her.

The fog was beginning to lift and for a brief moment he considered altering course again. But he shook his head, reminding himself that his orders were to seek out the enemy, not to chase a phantom boat to God knows where. A single vessel amounted to very little when the fate of the entire island rested on his diligence.

The morning wore on and brought with it an accident that, oddly enough, gave him the opportunity to speak with Captain Parker sooner than he'd expected. The gun drill had been progressing tolerably well, the hands going through the motions without actually firing the guns, until one of the new men put his foot where it should never have been. A carriage wheel with its thousand-pound burden rolled over his toes without as much as a tremor. The man's screams alone were enough to alert *Maidstone's* surgeon that a patient was on his way.

When the frigate was in sight the schooner ran down to her before putting a boat in the water. Squibb joined the moaning sailor for the pull across and was greeted by the captain as he climbed aboard. As it happened, Parker had the more important piece of news to deliver. The cutter *Coureur* had caught up with *Maidstone* that morning and delivered new orders: *Independence* was to return to St. John's while the frigate continued her patrol alone. It was unofficial, of course, but *Coureur's* skipper had hinted that there was civil unrest in Carbonear, apparently over the use of the town's church. A show of naval authority was required and only one of the smaller vessels could be spared.

It was not good news. Policing religious squabbles was a distasteful duty and Squibb felt his zeal for the naval life begin to evaporate. Less than twenty-four hours at sea and *Independence* was being recalled. For the first time he wondered whether he'd been too quick to accept the governor's commission. Parker consoled him by saying he should be back in a matter of days. Squibb was not so sure.

On his return to the schooner, he gave the necessary orders and paced the deck as *Independence* began to retrace her route. The man who'd been aloft was coiling down a line on the forecastle when Squibb paused to speak to him. "It seems," he said, "that our *Coureur* got the best of us this morning. It was she that we saw, returning to St. John's after delivering dispatches to *Maidstone*."

The man squinted up at him and scratched his whiskered chin. "Beggin' yer pardon, sir, but ain't *Coureur* a one-masted cutter?"

"Yes, she is."

"Well then, it weren't her we seen."

Squibb stared at the sailor. "What are you saying?"

"What I saw were too big for a cutter, sir. Two masts and no mistake. Maybe a hundred ton or even more."

The day was well advanced when the first distant, overlapping booming caused Eli Bailey to remark, as he cleared the dishes, that there was weather on the way. Ignoring the boy and grabbing his hat, Squibb rushed on deck. Two men were already climbing the shrouds and others were staring northward and listening intently.

There it came again—not thunder but multiple shots from weapons of various sizes, the sharp crack of swivels interspersed with the deeper note of 6-pound guns, or possibly nines. It was Salter's watch and Squibb had no cause to urge him on. He'd already called for the main topmast staysail and in little time at all the schooner had gained another half-knot of speed.

One final great crash in the distance and then silence.

The air was now hazy, with visibility of a mile or less, the wind still from the northeast and rising. The log board by the wheel showed their position as a mile or so southeast of the islands that lay off Toad's Cove. *Independence* was on the starboard tack. The fight, if that was what it had been, had taken place in or very near that cove, Squibb judged. There was no doubt that it had ended, however, and he instructed the quartermaster to bring them closer to the land.

Minutes later one of the lookouts hailed the deck. "Vessel lying to! Dead ahead."

Squibb scrambled aloft and immediately recognized *Coureur*. She was indeed lying to and there was a great deal of activity aboard her. Far more men were on her deck than made up her small crew. The situation seemed clear enough. She'd been taken in a sharp action and a prize crew was preparing to get her underway.

He watched her while *Independence* drew closer, until from the corner of his eye he caught movement in the direction of nearby Fox Island. The island lay to the north and east of the cutter and as Squibb adjusted his glass the outline of a slim topmast came into focus. It was all that was visible of a vessel moving steadily from left to the right and otherwise hidden by the grass-capped mound of rock.

"Put your helm down, Sam," he called in a calm, firm voice. "Stand by to tack." He continued to watch as the vessel emerged from her concealment and turned straight for *Independence*.

She was a square topsail schooner, at least as large as his own, and her sides were pierced for eight or ten guns of indeterminate size. There was no mistaking her intent as additional sails appeared in quick succession, her topsails catching the following wind to startling effect as she bore down on his ship.

The bow of *Independence* was swinging toward a new easterly course, but the approaching schooner was upwind and able to change direction at will. Squibb was fully aware of his desperate position. A square topsail schooner with the wind abaft the beam was as fast as anything afloat, which made the reflex to head downwind and run away from her exactly the wrong thing to do. His own vessel was a gaff topsail schooner and ideal for sailing upwind. On a close reach, as he was now, he could possibly outsail this interloper and avoid the intersection of their paths.

Independence responded to the change as he knew she would. With the breeze in her teeth he felt her tremble, eager to escape the clutch of the sea and take to the wind. Her angle of heel became more pronounced, every stay and shroud groaning with the strain of his close-hauled heading.

Salter was standing near the wheel, appearing uncertain, until Squibb told him to look lively. He seemed to rouse himself, quickly sending men to their stations and ordering small adjustments to the sail trim. The schooner gathered speed rapidly and her voice took on a different tone. Her lines hummed and thrummed like the strings of a finely tuned instrument, the pitch climbing ever higher.

Squibb knew that he was gambling everything. A single spar or rope, stretched beyond its endurance, would bring the day, and his naval career, to an inglorious end. He glanced at the enemy and saw her heading change slightly, to better bring her prey within reach. At that moment her colours ran up to the masthead. It was the rebel flag, a circle of thirteen white stars upon a field of blue, with red and white horizontal stripes.

Staying to fight was not an option. His crew was untrained and barely capable of running out the guns, whereas this Yankee privateer had the look of an experienced hunter. She was close enough now that he could see the men who crowded her deck, at least double the number of his own.

"Bring her up," he called as he descended the shrouds. Salter stood by the wheel, waiting expectantly, and he directed him to ease the foresail sheet. Was he imagining it, or did *Independence* immediately take on a hint of added speed?

"Now the main." Yes, there it was again. The sound of the water rushing past took on a more urgent note. He heard Greening's call for sail trimmers and then the boom of the first ranging shot from the privateer.. A 9-pound bow chaser, he judged, as the iron ball slapped the wavetops ahead of them and disappeared into the distance.

All was quiet now, save for the rush of water and the moan of hemp stretched to its utmost limit. Every man but the helmsman watched the vessel to windward as it rapidly closed the gap between them. There was nothing more to be done but urge *Independence* on, each of the crew with his own silent coaxing and promises to lead a better life. Squibb was doing his part, too, and held his breath as a second puff of smoke preceded the hum of a ball, this one higher and dangerously close to the rigging. If the next one found its mark, the game would be up.

The schooners were converging on a distant point in the ocean, but Squibb dared to believe that he could reach that point first and then put himself out of range.

"Touch her up, touch her up," he called, and Hiscock edged the bow even closer to the wind. Their opponent was now forced to sail with the breeze on his quarter, and was bracing his topsails around to keep the wind in them.

"Ease the sheets again, Mr. Salter." Another hint of speed, but he knew that he was sailing on a knife's edge. The jib leeches and foresail were feathering ever so slightly and another point to windward would rob the sails of their power.

Independence was clawing eastward at more than ten knots, her pursuer at roughly the same speed and bearing southeast to prevent her escape. But with every yard that *Independence* gained, the Yankee was losing its valuable windward position. Squibb knew that if he could draw even slightly ahead of the other, he would stand a fair chance of escaping *Coureur's* fate.

The privateer now fired its bow gun again, perhaps realizing that only a severed stay or halyard would slow *Independence*. The ball was low and struck the sea fifty yards short of its target. It hit the water, bounced, and then crashed through the larboard midship rail. Long splinters flew from the shattered oak and impaled two men, one grievously, judging from the blood that began to flow across the deck.

It ended the spell of the chase. The air was filled with shouts and running men as the wounded were carried below. Miller approached him, his clay pipe firmly clamped between his teeth.

"Return fire, sir?"

Squibb shook his head. The privateer's bow was pointed straight at the windward side of *Independence*—much too small a target for untrained gunners. And his own hull leaned to leeward, away from the Yankee, guns pointing upward. Even if they managed to fire, their only target would be an empty grey sky.

"Shall we give them a volley, sir?" It was Ethan, his sword unsheathed and his marines drawn up. Again Squibb shook his head. The range was too great, the motion of both vessels too erratic, for small arms fire to be effective. "Two minutes," he said aloud. Another two minutes and they would be ahead of the enemy, denying him the advantage of his topsails and perhaps forcing him to abandon the chase entirely.

"Deck there!" came a call from aloft. Squibb had momentarily forgotten the two men still at the masthead. "She's running out her larboard guns!"

Squibb looked at the privateer and saw her change course ever so slightly, her topsails drawing fully once more as she gathered speed. Moments later she crossed his stern at two cables distance, delivering a broadside as she went.

This time the guns released a screaming mass of chain shot—spinning lengths of metal designed to cut through rigging like a knife through pudding. At least one of the shots was true, parting lines aloft and alow in a final attempt at disabling *Independence*. The flying jib began to thunder but Greening and his crew had it in hand before Squibb could shout an order. A knot or two of the schooner's speed vanished, but the Yankee privateer had played her last card. *Independence* surged away while a second salvo passed harmlessly to either side. The enemy schooner kept her southerly course and made no effort to come about. In the distance and also heading south, the captured *Coureur* was under all sail.

As the crew were cheering their good fortune, the privateer fired a solitary gun to windward. Squibb's first thought was that she was signalling the prize, but there was no reply.

"By God, sir. I think he was saluting you!" Miller said in astonishment.

Squibb watched her go while around him the boatswain and carpenter rallied the crew to repair the damage. The quartermaster calmly kept the schooner on her course.

Squibb clasped his hands behind his back and paced the deck as his heart rate slowed. He paused near Salter, who wore an embarrassed look. "That was a very near thing," he said to the midshipman. "We've had a lucky escape."

"Yes, sir. I'm sorry if I was slow to—"

"Don't fret, lad. You will learn quickly enough, with enemies as lively as this one. She was well manned and well captained. The pity is, we can't even put a name to her." He heard no reply and turned to look at the young man, who seemed to be struggling with something he wished to say.

"Do you have an observation to make, Mr. Salter?"

"Sir, I may be mistaken. Although I think not."

"Well? What is it?"

"The Yankee privateer, sir. I can't be certain—she has been altered a great deal—but I believe she was once our *Egmont*."

THE CONVOY

St. John's, June 3rd

ndependence arrived in harbour as the eastern sky began to lighten. Squibb had waited half the night for the guard boat to lower the chain, the officer in charge refusing to do anything in the hours of darkness. He had used the time to write his report while the crew rove new lines for the standing and running rigging. It was dispatched to the governor before they picked up their mooring and a summons came within the hour. It directed him to a tavern called The Ship near the King's Beach.

The same well-tailored young lieutenant rose to greet him as he came through the tavern's door. Squibb had learned from Parker that the man was indeed the governor's aide, his flag lieutenant, that his name was Montague, and that he was the youngest son of an English marquess. Or was it a viscount?

Montague led him to a curtained booth at the back of the busy taproom, advising Squibb that the governor would join them shortly. Three pints of ale were brought and the two men lifted their tankards in salute.

Squibb sipped the warm ale while Montague briefed him on the situation in Carbonear.

The Church of England minister, he said, was being denied the use of the town's place of worship by the Methodists. The governor had issued a directive, but to no effect. The situation was part of a larger problem with the town, owing to the work of a Methodist preacher named Lawrence Coughlan. He and his sponsor, the Harbour Grace merchant John Stretton, had turned much of the population against the established church, setting two Protestant factions against each other. This was complicated, of course, by the Protestant-Catholic uneasiness that already prevailed in that part of Conception Bay. The situation was very like a tinderbox, Montague said, and could result in violence. A show of his majesty's authority was needed to cool a few heads.

Squibb was familiar with the ongoing quarrels of the Methodists and Anglicans. Their missionary clergy were less than diplomatic men, capable of starting an argument in an empty room. A few years earlier a Methodist preacher had visited Trinity, only to be taunted and tarred by a party of sailors—allegedly at the behest of a rival minister. Some of these missionaries were also great friends of the bottle. A line of Smollett's writing came to mind: "The fumes of faction disturb the faculty of reason," or something very like it.

"And then there is John Jones," the lieutenant was saying, "a Welshman and former artillery sergeant who preaches for the Dissenters at Placentia. He's been an aggravation for some time, as if we didn't have enough to occupy us."

Just then the curtain was flung back and the governor's large form filled the opening. "There you are!" he bellowed as he buttoned the fly of his breeches. "Damned queue for the heads this early in the morning. We must issue orders, Montague. Henceforth the outhouse to be kept clear for the governor, what? Ha! Ha!" He hobbled to the bench and dropped his weight onto it with a groan of relief. "Damn this pernicious gout! Do you have it, Mr. Squibb?"

"No, sir. I have been spared thus far."

"Damned painful business, I can tell you that." Governor Edwards took a deep draught of the amber ale in front of him.

"The lieutenant has been telling me about the situation in Carbonear, sir."

The governor stared at him for a moment. "Carbonear?" he cried. "The devil take Carbonear, man! I shall send Gardiner if I have to. It might keep him out of trouble, or at least keep him alive. He engaged to fight a duel, you know, with one of our American prisoners. I've put a stop to that, make no mistake. Another antic of that sort and I'll have him court martialled. No, Mr. Squibb. As of today, we have more important matters at hand. Now tell me about this Yankee privateer."

Squibb gave a verbal account of what he had already written, keeping to himself a suspicion that had been growing in his mind since yesterday. It had certainly been the Yankee schooner that he and his lookout had glimpsed through the fog off Cape Ballard, and it seemed clear to him that she'd been heading north in pursuit of *Coureur*. But was that pursuit mere coincidence, or had the Yankee known of the cutter's course and mission? And what of his own encounter with the privateer? Was it possible that, having taken the cutter, she was lying in wait for *Independence* as well?

"Yes," the governor was saying, "this Yankee captain is newly arrived and from what you say, he'll be making a damned nuisance of himself. If he continues south he may find *Maidstone* in his path. *Fairy* is on her way back from Placentia and may also come across him." The governor had kicked off his shoe and was examining a swollen toe. "But for now, Commander, I am sending you back to *Maidstone*." He glanced around the tavern and lowered his voice.

"You will inform Parker that we've just received a report concerning the French. They have bypassed St. John's and are heading southwest. The packet left here last evening to alert Halifax. De Ternay is most likely bound for New England but I remain suspicious. His new course may well be a feint. He could alter it and fall upon Halifax, or even return to take Newfoundland. I will send you back with written orders for Parker, but in brief I want the two of you to find this fleet and shadow it. We must know its intentions.

"You will leave this evening." The governor eyed his empty tankard. "But for now, let us have another pot of this excellent ale."

An hour later, with the ale sitting heavily, Squibb took his leave of the governor and went in search of tools and supplies. They were items of importance to the schooner but they were not to be had in the shops of the Lower Path, not for love or money.

Squibb returned to *Independence* with little of benefit and much on his mind. He needed to look in on *Amelia*'s caretakers, for one, but not before *Independence*'s food and water were replenished. He also hoped to have the less wounded of his two seamen returned and a spare jumbo boom located, if it were humanly possible. These and a dozen other concerns occupied him as he went aboard, although he was happy to see that a few of them were already in hand.

A brisk gun drill was in progress, with half the crew occupied in sponging, loading, and running out. Ethan's men were on the foredeck, sighting and cleaning their muskets, and Greening was aloft with a work party, finishing repairs to the rigging. Miller was waiting as Squibb moved aft, and he shared what he'd learned from his meeting with the governor.

"I think our cruise may be much longer this time," he added. "Ask the cook and warrant officers what supplies they need, though God knows where we'll find them."

"I'll attend to it, sir. And I thought I might nip over to *Amelia*, to see how they're faring." Miller, as always, was dependable and thorough. "And one other thing, sir. You have a visitor."

Montague was waiting for him in his cabin. The lieutenant seemed entirely at ease, lounging in Squibb's chair and reading from a small volume of verse.

"I am sorry to have kept you," Squibb said with some confusion. He could not imagine what Montague was doing here, so soon after their meeting at the inn.

The young man dismissed the apology with a wave of his hand. "I come unannounced, sir, and no courtesies are required. The governor wished me to deliver these orders for Captain Parker myself."

Squibb's look of surprise elicited no explanation. A lowly clerk would normally have conveyed the sealed papers that were now handed to him. And could they not have been given to him at their earlier meeting?

"Have you a general idea of where *Maidstone* may be found?" the lieutenant asked.

"Yes, of course. By now she will have reached the vicinity of Cape St. Mary's." He tapped the chart that lay on his desk. "The wind will not be in her favour for returning and so, with *Independence* sailing on the evening tide, we should meet in the vicinity of Mistaken Point."

"Excellent. That will be ideal for your purposes."

Squibb waited for some hint of what those purposes might be, but his guest merely picked up his hat and book of verse and moved to the door. "May I ask what you were reading?" Squibb enquired.

"Why, it is Walpole's latest. A thin volume. Do you have an interest in literature, sir?"

"Yes. Or perhaps I should say I did, in an earlier time. Of late I have been otherwise occupied."

Montague nodded in sympathy. "Of course. We are all taken up with more pressing matters in these uncertain times. Some of them less easily grappled with than others."

Squibb nodded. "It is difficult to come to grips with things when we cannot see them clearly. Rather like trying to find a ship in the fog, wouldn't you say?"

The lieutenant paused at the door and gave him a questioning look. "I am not certain that I take your meaning," he said.

Squibb had been thinking of the privateer. He was still bothered by how she had come to be at that place, at exactly that time, to intercept *Coureur* and then *Independence*. Was this the reason for the secrecy around the orders he held in his hand? "Forgive me," he said. "I was in a private muse."

"Then I will bid you good day, Commander." Montague turned to go. "And I wish you a fruitful voyage."

Alone in the cabin, Squibb stared at the sealed packet of orders and wondered why he hadn't been more forthcoming with the young man. But what could he have told him, aside from a vague suspicion with little basis in fact? He thought of the poet Walpole, half remembering a verse about uncovering truth. Yes, now he had it—

> *Both parties, I hear,*
> *Most freely declare,*
> *That 'tis not approv'd of by either;*
> *If 'tis damn'd, then, by both,*
> *It must be the growth*
> *Of somebody who is of neither.*

When evening and the stated time of departure arrived, the wind was easterly and foul for departing the harbour, but *Independence* managed to tack her way out with the help of the ebbing tide. Outside the Narrows, all sail was raised for the short southeast beat to Cape Spear. With the headland cleared, Miller put the wind on her larboard beam and settled the schooner on a southerly course. With luck they would not have to touch a sheet before Mistaken Point, sixty nautical miles away.

The night passed without incident. The next morning, Squibb was advised that an exercise had been arranged for his benefit, to demonstrate how the men had progressed in their training. While he waited for the summons, his thoughts turned, as they had the night before, to Miss Harriett Adams. He'd entertained hopes of seeing her before heading to sea again. The demands of getting the schooner ready had made that impossible, of course, and he regretted it very much. Her eventful dinner had left him with an impression of a quite remarkable woman. So bold and independent in inviting gentlemen to dine with her while her cousin was under arrest. It was not something he'd encountered before, though he was no stranger to women of confidence, his late wife among them. Just as he resolved to call upon her when he returned, the pleasant thought was interrupted by the invitation to come on deck.

Ensign Toope was the first to display the newly acquired skills of his men. Under his commander's watchful eye, and that of nearly everyone else aboard, he issued his commands in a strong voice. The marines presented and ordered arms, then Sergeant Parrell took them through a rapid load-and-fire exercise, every step of the sequence done with reasonable accuracy. Finally, the ensign gave the command to fix bayonets and repel boarders, which climaxed in a roar and a spirited charge along the length of the deck. Squibb was impressed, as were the sailors who witnessed the display. One was heard to say that now he'd seen it, all things were possible.

As noon drew near, Salter opened the gunnery demonstration. The gun crews eagerly took their places and tried to outdo the marines in diligence. The guns were swabbed, charged, loaded, wadded, and run out to the second mate's commands, hoarsely relayed by the gunner. The final order was followed by a series of bone-jarring blasts as the 4-pounders discharged a deadly volley of iron shot at an imaginary enemy. Long tongues of smoke and flame shot out from the schooner's sides and some in the audience clapped, cheered, and whistled until Miller gave them a warning look.

It was well done, Squibb had to admit. Not as flawless or as fast as some would have it, but well done. He knew that his officers and men would welcome his approval and he made certain to give it when the demonstration ended. But he cautioned as well that they must keep at it, for hard practice was the only guarantee of victory at arms. He knew, but did not say, that they had a long way to go before they were a match for any well-disciplined privateer. Still, it was an encouraging start.

The men were in good humour even before the reward of a noon ration of rum, and he wondered what rumours had come aboard regarding their mission. Certainly the visit of the flag lieutenant would have been noted. But foremost in their minds would be the prospect of prize money. Squibb knew from experience that most of them would already have spent their hoped-for riches, either in their imaginations or in the taverns. And now, having gained (in their own estimation) the skills to make it possible, they were eager to close with the enemy. Their morale was as high as any commander could wish.

The day passed with *Independence* galloping south in a moderate sea that required the pumps to be manned in the afternoon watch. Evening found her off Cappahayden and making five knots in a wind that was backing and dying.

Squibb sent a man to the masthead as he prepared to search for *Maidstone*. His intention was to sail southeast for a few miles, then run inshore on a southwesterly course, repeating the zigzag and covering as much sea as possible. If the frigate had passed Mistaken Point, they were certain to intercept her, as long as the wind backed no more than westerly and kept the fog offshore.

———o———

Less than twenty nautical miles southwest of *Independence*, the captain of HMS *Maidstone* paced his quarterdeck and glanced from time to time at the vessel hard astern. Both ships were beating southeast with little to show for it, and now the light easterly breeze was threatening to disappear completely. Treacherous Cape Race was not far off, and William Parker wished the wind would hold until they had put it safely behind them.

The smaller vessel astern had reduced her canvas in order to stay in company. HMS *Fairy* was a new three-masted sloop of three hundred tons or so, and George Berkley handled her with consummate skill. Parker stood with his hands on the stern rail and studied her. She showed little sign of having fought a warm engagement just the evening before. Her forestays had been replaced and a carpenter's crew was repairing damage to the starboard bow, but otherwise she was untouched.

Berkley had come across the Yankee privateer in Mutton Bay. The topsail schooner was sailing in company with *Coureur*, which she had evidently taken, and the action that followed had been sharp. The privateer and her prize were no match for *Fairy*'s sixteen long guns, however, and they quickly made off when *Maidstone* suddenly appeared. Parker was too late to do anything more than launch a futile chase, but at least most of *Coureur*'s crew had been recovered. The unwounded prisoners had been put in a boat and abandoned by their captors.

The privateer schooner had occupied his thoughts ever since. He had not seen her in more than a year, when she'd carried the name of *Egmont*. She was altered, to be sure, and had the look of a true predator, with her large crew and heavy guns. She was also well handled and swift—incredibly swift despite the guns, with her new rig and square topsails. And she had taken *Coureur*, in itself a bold and unusual move. The New England privateers generally avoided the navy's armed vessels, concentrating instead on fishing and trading boats. The other exception, of course, had been the capture of *Egmont* herself. But that had been an anomaly, thanks to what may have been Gardiner's negligence. Yes, Parker thought, this was not the behaviour of a run-of-the-mill privateer. According to *Coureur*'s people, the vessel had come close to taking *Independence* as well. The Yankee raider was no match for the squadron's frigates and sloops, of course, but she could outrun them any day of the week. It could prove to be an interesting summer after all, he thought.

The wind backed to the west as the morning wore on, allowing the two ships to pass Cape Race and finally turn northeast. *Fairy* parted company, setting all sail and flying along the coast, bound for St. John's and likely to arrive there in record time.

Maidstone was shaving past Cripple Cove in the afternoon watch, still in the loom of the darkly ominous coast, when her lookout hailed the deck. It was *Independence*, bearing rapidly down in the strengthening breeze. Mr. Squibb managed her beautifully, Parker thought, as he watched the schooner grow larger in the circle of his glass.

"Signal, sir," the midshipman of the watch informed the officer of the watch.

"Signal from *Independence*, captain," the officer relayed. Parker had seen the flags break out himself, but allowed the customary exchange to unfold.

"What does she have to say then?" The answer, that the schooner was carrying orders for *Maidstone*, was duly conveyed through the chain of command.

"Acknowledge," the captain instructed, "and have her come under our lee. Her master and commander to repair aboard."

Twenty minutes later *Independence* rounded up to leeward of the frigate and a boat splashed down. It rowed quickly across as the two vessels sailed slowly on. Parker met Squibb at *Maidstone's* entry port and led him below. "Welcome back, Jonah," he said when the steward had left them alone with their coffee. "I'm happy that you wasted no time."

"Thank you, sir. We passed *Fairy* on the way down. I see she's had a falling out with someone."

Parker told him about the brief engagement. "This is the second time that *Maidstone* has missed the action," he said ruefully. At Squibb's look of surprise, he added, "*Coureur's* crew are aboard. They told us about Toad's Cove."

"And the Yankee privateer, sir. Is she indeed our former *Egmont*?"

"She is, without a doubt. And sad it is to see her wearing that damned rebel flag."

"It may rankle, sir, but of more concern is her speed and how well she is handled. She very nearly had me, you know."

Squibb could see the captain's eagerness to hear the details, but the governor's orders were his first priority. He handed over the packet and

Parker immediately broke the seal. He read in silence, his face grave and his eyes squinting thoughtfully from time to time.

Squibb waited with as much patience as he could muster, until he was handed the papers and invited to read them himself. He scanned the lines greedily but saw little that he hadn't already been told. Details of the French fleet's speed and direction were scanty, but as the governor had indicated, they were tasked with finding it and determining its intent. *Independence*, the faster vessel, would then convey any intelligence to St. John's or Halifax, whichever was nearer. The future of the war in North America could depend upon it.

"What are your thoughts?" Parker asked.

"We must find the French, sir. It's as simple as that."

Parker picked up his cup and stared out the tall stern windows. The vast, seemingly endless ocean rolled away to the horizon. "Yes, my friend. As simple as that."

⎯⎯⎯⎯ ○ ⎯⎯⎯⎯

On the fourteenth day of June, storm-battered and running low on supplies, the two ships drew near one another on a rare calm morning to witness punishment. They were on the tail of the Grand Banks, some forty-six degrees north latitude, and about to sweep south yet again in their search for the French fleet. Ten days of gales and constant toil had begun to weaken the newly woven fabric of the schooner's crew. Squibb had been vigilant, heading off one crisis of discipline after another, but most of the men had little experience of long periods at sea and for many this was their first demanding voyage. A few were merely frightened and had refused their duty on the wind-lashed deck when the turbulent seas ran green across it. Others, the more seasoned sailors among them, had been willfully disobedient. On one occasion Greening had saved *Independence* only by driving these men to their stations with a knotted rope. It could not continue.

The frigate lay a few yardarm lengths away on the glassy water, her guns run out and her marines standing shoulder to shoulder on the quarterdeck. *Maidstone* had fared much better over the preceding days, her crew more experienced and her size giving her a decided advantage over the schooner in heavy weather. Only one man of her complement was to be punished, a mere six lashes for drunkenness. Squibb wished it could be the same for *Independence*. His crew numbered less than a sixth of Parker's, and yet there were five men who'd been marked down for insubordination.

The most worrisome case involved the gunner. Within Squibb's hearing, Tompkins had been insolent to the first mate, with Miller later admitting that it was not the first time. Squibb had spoken to the man and he was far from contrite, saying that Miller had no experience of a King's ship and had no right to tell him his duty. There was some truth in that, for Squibb had no reason to criticize the gunner's work. However, the two men had taken a dislike to one another and a captain was duty bound to support his first mate. Tompkins had been fined the loss of a week's wages and both men had been warned to guard their tongues when speaking to each another.

Then there was the troubling case of Crowdy, the marine private. Sergeant Parrell had revealed himself to be something of a bully and Squibb had observed him demeaning the men for small mistakes or lapses in their drill. He had turned a blind eye, so to speak, hoping that Ethan would take the initiative. He had not, and one of the marines had finally struck the sergeant after a particularly harrowing day. The man had to be punished, without a doubt. But neither Parrell nor his officer was blameless. It was Squibb's duty to take Ethan to task and this he planned to do immediately following the punishment.

At the call of the drum, the crew of *Independence* gathered on the foredeck, the officers to the stern and the marines and their prisoners amidships. Squibb took his place and felt the familiar abhorrence of the ritual. He had no liking for the lash and had always, as a young officer, sought other ways of instilling discipline. Those above him had not always approved and only now, as the commander of his own vessel, did he reluctantly acknowledge that a firm hand was often the only means of putting things in order.

The first to be called was Simeon Ballett, the cook, found hiding in the cable tier on one of the fiercest days of the past two weeks. He had refused his duty, saying his little cookshack was a coffin that was sure to be swept away. The carpenter assured him that it was sturdily attached to the deck, but still he refused and young Eli Bailey had been forced to do his best to feed the crew. Ballett was the only one of *Amelia*'s people to have disappointed Squibb. He would not see him flogged, but an example had to be made. He ordered his rum stopped for the rest of the voyage.

The next two cases were more serious. These were experienced hands, their long pigtails well tarred, who'd been sent to *Independence* at the governor's call for men. It was clear to Squibb that their former captains had been happy to be rid of them. One had cursed Salter for a bastard and worse, and now received six lashes and a week of cleaning the heads. His scarred back bore evidence of past felonies and he took his blows with no more than a few grunts of annoyance. The other sailor had negligently left the main boom's end lift unsecured, causing the fifty-foot boom to drop to the deck in a choppy sea. It had broken the arm of a sailor and come close to killing the quartermaster. The man took his dozen with a few gasps and curses under his breath. Squibb saw the glare of hatred that the culprit directed aft, and knew that the man would have to be watched.

Finally, the marine private, Crowdy, was brought forward. He was very young, even younger than Ethan. Squibb intended to be lenient, given the offender's age and his previous good conduct, and pronounced a sentence of six strokes and a stoppage of pay. Sergeant Parrell remained at attention but he was clearly astonished, his eyebrows having disappeared into his hat. The sentence was carried out immediately and with the whole unsavoury business concluded, Squibb instructed Ensign Toope to attend him in his cabin.

Ethan followed him down the companionway and they took their seats on either side of the desk. Squibb sensed that the young man was uneasy, as if he suspected that something were amiss. Ethan had given him no cause for complaint except on this one matter and had otherwise been conscientious in his duties. He had not summoned him to upbraid him for negligence, but rather to instruct and guide him if he could. Squibb had given a great deal of thought to what he might say, and now he went straight to the heart of the matter.

"I am sure you know, Ethan, that life under arms is often uncomfortable, and sometimes terrifying, for the ordinary soldier or sailor." The ensign nodded, his face revealing nothing.

"He has little control over his own life," he continued, "and it is important that his existence does not become soul-destroying as well. Injustice and petty tyranny must be eliminated as much as possible, and the only person who can do that is the man's officer."

Squibb shifted uneasily in his chair. He was not accustomed to making such speeches. His stepson was listening carefully.

"And so, if that officer takes care to look after his people, he will inspire their respect, and a man serving under an officer he respects is halfway to being happy with his lot. Do you understand?" Ethan nodded again.

"On the other side of the coin, an officer's career and possibly his life will depend on the conduct of his people in a crisis. If you are fair and firm you will earn and keep their respect, thereby ensuring your own success. Do I make myself clear on this point?"

"Yes, sir."

"Sergeant Parrell is mistreating your men and must be taken to task. And you are the one to do it. If I interfere it will undermine you and the regard that your men should have for you."

"I understand, sir."

"Good. See that you deal with this immediately. If you do not, I will have no choice but to relieve you of your command."

The look of shock pierced Squibb to the heart. His stepson stood, head bent beneath the beams and tears welling in his eyes.

"I am sorry to have let you down, sir. Once again." He saluted quickly and fumbled his way out the door.

Squibb sat at his desk for a long time afterward, trying to process those parting words. Did Ethan feel that he'd let his stepfather down before, after his mother's death? Had Squibb, in his grief and anger, made the boy feel that way? He could not say with any certainty, for he had little memory of that difficult time of mourning. He felt, he *knew*, that he had failed their boy, had not supported him as he should have, but what additional harm had he done? And now he had delivered another blow, as hurtful as if it had been laid across Ethan's face. And yet, what he had said just now could not have been put any differently. He was a father, but he was also an officer of the King's navy. *Independence* was his paramount responsibility, and her welfare came before all else, even his relationship with his son. He had long known that command at sea was the hardest service of all, and he wondered why in heaven he had chosen to return to it.

Later that day the wind rose to a faint breeze, coming from the southwest and bringing with it a fog as dense as any ever conjured on the Grand Banks of Newfoundland. Squibb despaired of ever finding the French. The last day or two had brought a gnawing fear that they had missed the enemy completely, but he'd managed to reason himself into a more optimistic view. The slow-sailing troopships would have encountered the same foul weather and would have been more likely to heave to and ride out the gales rather than push on. But now this fog could easily mask the entire French fleet.

The two vessels moved slowly northeast, *Independence* leading with two men aloft. It was a matter of faith that they were actually there, men and topmasts being invisible in the fog. From the deck Squibb could see no further than the bowsprit, but he knew that sound would travel far on such a day. He called for silence and the hours rolled slowly past, unmarked by the bell.

Late in the afternoon watch, the foremast lookout descended far enough to be seen as he gestured frantically. Squibb had heard the sound himself, what might have been a single, human cough coming from starboard. He stared intently but the fog was impenetrable. There it was again, this time a coughing fit, followed by a gruff, rebuking voice.

A short spell of silence came next, broken suddenly by a new sound, coming from somewhere ahead of them. It was an unmistakable thump of wood on wood and it preceded two voices raised in a short, muffled conversation. The cough from starboard came again, another thump from forward, and then the creak of a rope being pulled taut, originating somewhere on their larboard quarter. Squibb and those around him hardly dared to breathe. They were surrounded by ships but whether friend or foe was impossible to tell.

The mystery came to an end before Squibb had time to decide on a course of action. The fog began to thin, soon revealing half a dozen vessels near at hand. The partially obscured shapes of others could be seen in a wide arc ahead of them, rebel flags flapping lazily from several mastheads. *Independence* had sailed into a Yankee convoy and was now sandwiched among the rearmost merchantmen.

Squibb's first instinct was to fall quietly astern, but the other vessels were showing no interest in *Independence*. She flew no colours and her name alone might be her calling card, he thought. His schooner would appear to those around her as just another armed merchantman.

He ordered the few uniformed marines below while he and Ethan quickly removed their own coats. None of the others on deck wore clothing that would identify them as the enemy. Because of the fog, it took some minutes for Squibb to realize that the convoy was very large. No one could possibly know that *Independence* was an intruder. Thankfully there was no sign of *Maidstone*, still keeping her station a few miles astern.

It took several minutes more for Squibb to spot the frigates that were escorting the convoy. They were well ahead but they were French, without a doubt, and he pondered this while he looked around. Their nearest neighbour was a brig that was ghosting along on a parallel course. Her stout skipper was standing by the wheel, a cold leg of chicken in one hand and a mug in the other. Squibb was struck by the complete lack of suspicion in his manner and from this an idea came to his mind, fully formed.

"Mr. Salter."

"Sir?"

"Put our gig over the side with two reliable men. Give them fishing lines and compass and instruct them to slowly fall astern. They are to find the frigate and warn Captain Parker to stay where he is. Now hand me that speaking trumpet and bring us nearer to the brig."

He waited until the schooner had edged closer and then raised the trumpet to his mouth. "Ahoy, sir!" he called across the gap. The man looked over and raised his chicken leg in greeting. "I have some fine Demerara rum below," Squibb hailed. "It would go well in that mug of yours."

The man threw back his head and laughed. "A fine offer, sir. And I will bring the rest of the chicken to go with it." Squibb laughed as well and beckoned him over. The brig was towing a small boat, and having taken on the skipper and his chicken, it was rowed across by two of her crew. All three came aboard and with handshakes all around, were taken below for a glass of rum and an indefinite period of captivity.

The boat returned to the brig with Miller and two seamen dressed in the prisoners' clothes, with their pistols and swords well hidden. They knew there were another four men on board and as soon as they'd taken quiet possession of the deck, the remaining boat from *Independence* ferried two more of Squibb's men to complete the prize crew. Miller had orders to let the captured brig drop astern, to find *Maidstone* and to apprise Captain Parker of their *ruse de guerre*. Squibb, meanwhile, turned his attention to another merchantman, adding an offer of cold chicken to the enticement of Demerara rum.

The Newfoundland fox remained in the Yankee henhouse until he could not afford to send away another man. He had barely enough hands left to work the schooner and as evening approached, he too fell astern of the convoy. Not every offer to visit had been accepted. Several had declined for various reasons but overall he knew the merchant master's fondness for rum, news, and idle gossip. Ship visiting was common in calm weather and at no time had he detected a hint of suspicion. Now, somewhere close by, were four merchant ships manned by his men and loaded with valuable goods. He debated whether to return with extra hands from *Maidstone*, if Parker were agreeable, but decided that he'd pushed his luck to the limit. The fog had thinned a little and he saw that the French frigates, however unsuspecting, were closer than he might have wished.

The convoy was very large—nearly a hundred merchantmen was the figure given by his prisoners—and its destination was the French port of La Rochelle. Through his hospitable deception, Squibb had learned a great deal about the enemy's designs. De Ternay had made a rendezvous at sea with the American convoy and had detached two of his frigates to escort it. The French fleet had then carried on to New England. The governor would certainly be pleased to know this. Squibb was pleased as well, having picked up this valuable intelligence and made a tidy fortune for himself and his crew in the bargain. The men were naturally delighted and he was impressed with the way they'd behaved, especially Ethan. He was out there now, in charge of a valuable sloop with a marine and three experienced seamen for his crew. It was a fine day's work for one that had begun so badly. Four handsome prizes, laden with furs and tobacco, and not a single shot fired. It reminded him of why he'd returned to the navy in the first place. How well he remembered the thrill of bold enterprise on the high seas and the deep satisfaction of wiping the enemy's eye.

THE FORTUNE
OF WAR

At sea, June 17th

A grey, cool morning it was, with prizes and escorts on a westerly course, halfway to the shelter of St. John's. In the cheerful glow of success, Squibb was looking forward to seeing Miss Adams again. This time he was sure to have a few days ashore while the ships were victualled and watered. His hard-pressed crew was due a rest and *Independence* required a host of minor repairs. It had been a demanding cruise, but worth all the hardship in the end. Once they were safely away from the convoy, the prisoners had been transferred to *Maidstone* to prevent them from retaking their ships.

The newer hands were still congratulating themselves on their daring exploit. Those who weren't were watching the southeastern horizon and discussing with concern the warm, humid air coming from that direction. True to their predictions, the wind increased as the hours passed. By noon Squibb was studying the ominous line of dark cloud massing in the distance. He called Salter to his side.

"Have the topsails taken in at the next bell. Reef the main early as well. Perhaps in an hour."

"Aye, aye, sir."

"And check the lashing on the guns. Double everything if you have the time."

Salter went forward to muster the meagre watch while Squibb looked at the four prizes under his lee. He and Parker had discussed putting some of *Maidstone*'s men aboard them, but Parker wanted every skilled hand available to work the frigate and her guns. The threat of meeting a French or Yankee vessel was still very real.

Of the four temporary skippers, Squibb knew that Miller and Greening would have no trouble with their prizes in heavy weather, and Hiscock, the quartermaster, was competent enough. But the sloop with Ethan aboard caused him concern. As he looked at her now, he could tell that *Free Trade* was not a weatherly vessel. And with only four men as crew, Ethan would have his hands full if a real blow overtook him in the night. If Squibb was reading the wind and expanding clouds to the southeast correctly, the coming gale would be at its height exactly then.

The frigate led them onwards for the remainder of the day. The wind continued to build and the waves grew steadily until *Free Trade* showed only her topmast in the troughs. Squibb had signalled the prizes to reduce sail and stay in company as long as possible, and to raise lanterns aloft as darkness approached.

By midnight nothing could be seen from the deck of *Independence*. The lights had disappeared one by one, as the wind dispersed the prizes. Heavy rain obscured everything. Even *Maidstone*'s stern light, the highest and brightest and their primary beacon, was lost in the inky blackness. Wind thrummed the rigging and whipped the tops from the towering waves. *Independence* held fast to her course, though when he took the wheel, Squibb sensed her making leeway at a disturbing rate. By tomorrow, if the sun did not appear, he would be hard pressed to estimate his position.

The fore and main had been reefed to their utmost, a storm staysail had replaced the jibs, and all other canvas had been taken below. The stays and shrouds had been reinforced and the small crew was standing by with axes and hatchets, in case anything should go by the board. Wreckage would have to be cut away immediately, lest it drag the schooner beam-on to the mounting waves.

The gale that Squibb had foreseen soon surpassed his expectations. An hour after midnight he put the schooner's bow into the wind, shivering her sails while the crew took in the last of them.

Another hour and a full-blown storm swept all before it. *Independence* was forced to run under bare poles while dragging a warp—a long loop of heavy rope—to slow her and keep her stern to the wind. There was little that the skeleton crew could do, and Squibb ordered them to shelter in the companionways, where they could be called upon if needed. He stayed on deck with the helmsman and Salter, and throughout the long night they rode the monstrous waves that rose beneath their feet. It was a terrifying night for many of the crew, but no further crisis befell them, to the relief of all.

Independence herself weathered the force of the storm well enough, as Squibb knew she would. By dawn the wind was already abating; by four bells in the morning watch, the tired hands were spreading her sails again to resume their westerly course. Her commander climbed the mainmast with his long glass but could see nothing on the empty, white-capped ocean, save a few dark patches where torrents of rain added to the desolate scene.

The schooner overtook Greening's brig before noon. She was lying ahull, flying no canvas and threatening to toss her masts with every dreadful roll. Squibb was relieved to see that her small crew was carefully moving about, attempting to repair a great deal of damage. He approached from leeward but the seas were still too rough to come within hailing distance. Nor could a boat be sent across to assist them. Greening was the right man for the task, however, and he had several of the experienced *Amelias* with him. While *Independence* waited, they repaired her sufficiently to begin limping along in the schooner's wake.

Two uneventful but sea-pummelled days followed. On the third, *Maidstone* suddenly appeared out of a drenching squall, as big and reassuring as the land itself. The frigate's carpenter and his mates soon restored the brig to seaworthiness and the three ships carried on, with Squibb endlessly scanning the empty horizon for the missing prizes.

They came to anchor in St. John's on the afternoon of the summer solstice. Squibb stood in the bow as they passed through the Narrows, anxiously searching the harbour for *Free Trade*. Already there and in fine spirits were the quartermaster and his crew with their battered craft. Late that evening, in came Miller and his prize, men and vessel looking none the worse for the experience. Nothing had been seen or heard of the sloop with Ethan aboard.

Squibb and Parker made their way to Fort Townshend as soon as the prisoners had been escorted ashore. The governor saw them at once and listened intently to their account of the convoy. He questioned them in detail, seeking every scrap of information before sitting back and regarding them with a thoughtful eye.

"Now gentlemen," he said, "you have done well to learn of the French rendezvous with the American convoy—a fine piece of seamanship on Admiral de Ternay's part. It is also a relief to know that his fleet has carried on to New England. But news of this convoy is concerning." The governor considered in silence for a moment, his fingers forming a steeple under his chin.

"If the convoy's destination is *truly* La Rochelle, then you have struck upon a precious gem of information. They might have been headed anywhere in France, Holland, or Spain."

Parker and Squibb exchanged an uneasy glance. The governor's musing raised the question of whether the prisoners had given them false information. Had the Yankee skippers been instructed to give their destination as La Rochelle, when the convoy was bound elsewhere? The thought was uncomfortable, to say the least.

"La Rochelle," the governor repeated as he toyed with his snuff box. "Can it be so? It certainly has the advantage of a large harbour and ready access to European markets for their trade goods. At what latitude did you say the convoy was?"

"Forty-six degrees and nine minutes north, sir," Parker replied. "Or as near as we could make it."

"Bearing?"

"Dead east, sir," Squibb said. "Not a whisker off."

The governor nodded. "There can be no doubt then. La Rochelle is certainly the destination. It lies at just that latitude, bearing full east. The French have done just as I would do, were I charged with herding a parcel of damned merchantmen across the Atlantic. Half of them will be coastal traders and hard put to fix their longitude at Greenwich, let alone on the Grand Banks. But any lubber can find his latitude. Do you see?"

Parker and Squibb could certainly see, and they smiled with relief at not having been made the fool. The governor, chuckling and shaking his head, poured them each a glass of Madeira and hurriedly composed his report to the Admiralty. It was written, sealed, and dispatched to the waiting London packet before they had finished their second glass.

"Gentlemen, you have achieved nothing short of an intelligence coup," the governor declared as he capped his inkpot. "This knowledge will give England a strategic advantage at sea and on land, assuming these same vessels can be intercepted on the return voyage."

"Is there no likelihood of intercepting them as they approach the coast of France?" Squibb asked.

"Our Channel fleet will not have the news in time," Parker said. "But the return voyage is another matter."

"The importance of this convoy cannot be overstated." The governor tapped the desk with a blunt finger to emphasize the point. "It is essential that the rebels sell their cotton, furs, and tobacco to finance the war.

And in return they need weapons from their allies to pursue it. The real issue here is the return voyage, no doubt with holds crammed with arms and powder. Now that we know how many ships there are and from what port they will sail, we can dispatch a powerful squadron to surprise them at any point in the Atlantic. Truly a coup, gentlemen. Truly a coup."

With the governor's praise ringing in their ears, Parker and Squibb took their leave and walked down Garrison Hill to the harbour. Along the way they passed a row of taverns and through the windows they saw many of their own crewmen making merry. Like most sailors with a prize, these men were already spending against their expected windfall, and the harbour trollops were more than happy to help them do it.

On the Lower Path, a fight had broken out on the doorstep of one establishment. As they approached a ring of onlookers, Squibb saw John Cooper, one of his Trinity crewmen, trading punches with another man. He pushed his way into the circle, Parker roaring hell and damnation at his heels, and separated the two men roughly. They were quick to drop their fists when they saw who it was. The spectators, many of them sailors, were already drifting away.

"What the devil is this?" Squibb demanded. He turned to the other combatant. "And who are you?" The man kept his eyes down and mumbled a name.

"And what ship?"

"*Bonavista*, sir."

"Then return there straight away, if you have any regard for the skin on your back." The sailor hurried off and Squibb looked to John Cooper. "Well?"

Cooper shuffled his feet under the glare of his commander. His shirt was torn and his lip was split, but this did not subdue the anger in his voice. "The damned scrub was sayin' things about *Independence*, sir."

"What things?"

Cooper spat blood and wiped his mouth. "He was sayin' that we ran from that privateer, sir. At Toad's Cove."

Squibb looked at him in disbelief. "We were outgunned and out-manned, as you well know."

"Yes, sir. Only the word going 'round is that you ... I mean we ... that *Independence* is shy of a fight, sir."

"Get back to the schooner," was the cold reply. "Be there before I am or you'll regret this day."

Squibb turned to Parker as Cooper hurried away. He was about to speak but the captain was quicker.

"Pay them no heed, Jonah. Idle gossip in the taverns should warrant no attention. Good Lord, let them look at your prizes in the harbour if they want something to talk about."

Parker was right. Squibb would have dismissed the incident ... except the other sailor had been from Gardiner's ship. Had the gossip originated there? He pondered the matter as they walked on to the harbour, where he searched again for the overdue sloop. He found only disappointment and soon returned to *Independence*, where hope and anxiety visited in turns for the rest of the day.

———— ○ ————

That evening Squibb stood on deck and watched the solstice bonfires burn on the hilltops around the harbour. Since pagan times they'd been lit in the old country to banish demons, but Squibb's demons remained in his head, all that night and in the two days that followed. As he marked time in St. John's, awaiting new orders, he or one of his officers questioned every ship that came through the Narrows, but news of the sloop was not to be had. Alone, he fretted away the better part of one afternoon atop Signal Hill, searching the ocean with his glass. Eventually his orders materialized, but his stepson did not.

His new task was to patrol the approaches to the harbour, which meant a tedious daylight routine of sailing the unvarying route in all weathers. For the foreseeable future, *Independence* was to plough the same stretch of sea, from Motion Head in the south to Tor Bay Point, six nautical miles north of Signal Hill. The great consolation was that Squibb would be the first to see *Free Trade* if she were to appear. Another was that the schooner returned to port each night, giving him the opportunity to call upon Miss Adams.

And call upon her he did, within the week, paying his respects and expressing his hope that she was well. The visit was brief, owing mainly to his awkwardness, but a few days later he was thrilled to be invited to tea with her at The Rising Sun. Perhaps he hadn't been as awkward as he'd thought. On that second occasion they talked at length. She told him of her great interest in Newfoundland customs and dialects, and she listened politely to his account of the American prizes and prisoners he'd taken on the last voyage. He realized too late that his conversation may have been insensitive.

"Miss Adams, you must forgive me," he said in apology. "My manners have been dulled—"

"No, no, my dear sir. You have given no offence, I assure you. It is exciting to hear your news. I have little enough to entertain me here, aside from conversation. And chatting with you is most enjoyable."

He may have blushed at this. She was perhaps the most gracious and understanding woman he had ever met. Her next words seemed to confirm his feeling.

"Now you must tell me about your stepson. How distraught you must be, not knowing what has become of him." At his look, she quickly added, "Mrs. Edwards has been telling me of your misfortune."

This was a second surprise. "No doubt she heard it from her husband," Miss Adams explained, "who takes a great interest in all of his officers, I am told. Oh, sir, you don't object to my mentioning so personal a matter, do you? Or perhaps you are offended that I even know of it! Oh dear."

"No, Miss Adams, I am not offended. I am touched by your kind enquiry. I have no news to tell you, other than that my dear boy is still missing." At her gentle prompting he went on to tell her of Ethan, of his wife's death and of their years of happiness together. He did not speak of his current troubled relationship with his son, or of his growing fear that he might never see him again. She listened to what he did say with sympathy and offered words of true comfort. Squibb left her that evening with admiration firmly established in his heart. Aside from his duties and thoughts of Ethan, he could think of little more than when he might see her again.

The opportunity presented itself a few days later, when the carpenter discovered early signs of rot in the schooner's rudder. Replacing it would keep *Independence* in harbour for two days at least. Squibb had been casting about for excuses to spend more time with Miss Adams and he now saw an opportunity, based upon her professed interest in local customs. He quickly wrote her a note, asking if she might like to know more about tilting, that uniquely Newfoundland activity involving horse- or dog-drawn sleighs on frozen ponds. He regretted that it was summer, but if the subject caught her fancy, she might enjoy an excursion to a place where the sport was conducted. They would at least see the ice-free pond and enjoy a picnic. The invitation was accepted straight away.

At nine o'clock the next morning, on a particularly bright and pleasant day in the first week of July, Squibb and Eli Bailey, equipped with everything needed for the excursion, arrived at The Rising Sun. Miss Adams and her maid, whose name Squibb could not recall, were sturdily shod for the walk, as he'd suggested. He was relieved when, as they were setting out, her mistress addressed the maid as Sally. He noticed that young Eli also seemed attentive to the information.

The two women had little problem managing the well-trodden path to Twenty Mile Pond. They were accustomed to walking, Miss Adams said, as exercise was vital to maintaining a prisoner's mental and physical health. It took him a moment to realize that the comment was made, at least partially, in jest.

The large body of water—more a lake than a pond, Miss Adams observed—was situated about three miles northwest of the harbour on the overland route to Portugal Cove. It was a pleasant ramble, with Squibb and Miss Adams walking ahead and talking happily about the birds and wildflowers they saw along the way. The stroll was as nothing, and when they arrived at the pond he regretted the sight of it, for it marked the midway point of their outing.

Eli and Sally laid out their lunch on a square of canvas and all four of them sat down to bread, cheese, potted rabbit, berries, and a rare bottle of claret that had cost Squibb several days' pay. It was an unusual arrangement, dining with their servants, but neither of the women showed the least discomfort. Miss Adams was relaxed and in a cheerful mood and Squibb was delighted that the day was going so well.

"About this name," she said as she surveyed both the view and the feast. "Why is it called Twenty Mile Pond? As far as I can see, it is not twenty miles from anywhere in particular, nor is it twenty miles in length. Tell me your theory, Jonah," she demanded with a smile.

"Why, I believe the name indicates the distance around the pond—its circumference. I'd hazard that it was calculated by a sailor and no doubt it is quite accurate."

She laughed, the high, pleasant notes making him smile. "I am sure you are right, Commander. Now please tell me about this word tilt, or tilting. I know it from our old English, meaning to totter unsteadily."

"Yes, and that may well describe the sport, given its speed and the icy, slippery surface on which it takes place. Of course, we know the word from *Don Quixote*, as well. The old knight was keen to be tilting at windmills."

"Oh, yes," she said, giving him an appraising eye. "I'd forgotten. In that context it would mean jousting, on horseback of course. That may well apply to your island pastime. And Mrs. Edwards tells me there is a kind of log hut called a tilt?"

"There is. Further along this trail you would find one such tilt house. It is about halfway to Portugal Cove, on the other side of this peninsula, and is used by travellers as a resting place. And by parties who come here for the tilting."

"Then surely there is some connection. Does the sport of tilting come from the use of the hut when one is so engaged?"

"Why, you may be right. I hadn't made that connection before."

"No doubt the question will be debated and examined more closely in a later age." She smiled and added, "When Newfoundland society has the wealth and leisure to consider such weighty matters."

Eli and Sally, perhaps wishing to have their own conversation, asked if they might gather up the remains of lunch. The chore was quickly, if not hurriedly, completed before they casually strolled away to examine interesting stones along the shoreline.

Squibb watched them for a moment. "Your interest in our little island is very flattering, Miss Adams."

"Thank you, Commander. The governor's wife has been telling me a great deal about Newfoundland. She was born here, as you may know."

A large trout jumped near the shore. As they watched the ripples spread, she said, "And you, sir, have an interest in literature, if I am not mistaken."

"I confess that at one time I did. I would have gone to sea without a hat rather than go without my books."

"But what has changed? Books are still being written, you know." She smiled again and said, "Please tell me."

Squibb hestitated as he considered his reply. "I told you recently of my wife's death. I did not wish to impose the story of my grief as well. You see, it lasted a long time, and I suppose in that period I lost the pleasure that books had always given me."

"And now?"

"Now I am faced with another form of grief." He looked away. "The loss of my son..."

She reached out and touched the back of his hand. He felt it in every nerve as the skin tingled beneath her fingers. "You must stay strong for your son, sir. Promise me you will."

Nodding, he forced a smile and she withdrew her hand. When she spoke again her voice was brighter, as though she intended to banish his dark and fearful thoughts. "Now you must tell me what it's like to go a-tilting in winter. I think I might enjoy it."

If cheering him was her intention, it succeeded, at least for the time being. His forced smile became genuine. "Well, as for that, you must use your imagination. Picture, if you will, our pond frozen quite solid and surrounded by snow-covered trees. The charioteers are bundled in furs and warm clothing against the piercing winds. Their sleighs skim over the ice in all directions, sometimes spinning sideways but always flying over the glittering surface. It is quite a society event, you know."

At her skeptical look, he added, "Really it is. One commonly hears that Ensign Splatterdash or Captain Cobweb has gone a-tilting with the young ladies."

Her laughter sparkled in the clear afternoon air. When she looked his way, he thought he glimpsed something like fondness in her face. "And do the young ladies enjoy the outing?" she asked.

"Oh indeed. Why, tilting answers the same purpose as the pump room at Bath, or Hyde Park for the citizens of London."

She laughed again, and again he fancied that he saw some small measure of affection in her expression. "Now you must tell me something about yourself," he said. "You are quite a mystery to me, Miss Adams."

She told him quite frankly that her family was wealthy. Her father was a well-known Boston hotelier and a financial supporter of the war. "Father's distant cousin is a lawyer named John Adams," she said, "Perhaps you have heard of him?"

Squibb had not, but was interested to hear that the cousin had helped draft the Declaration of Independence.

"And yet," she said, "our cousin doggedly campaigns against anti-British sentiment. Peculiar, don't you think? He believes that we must maintain our cultural ties with England after we have secured our independence. Father thinks him quite eccentric."

"And what are your views of this conflict? You and I are on opposite sides of a very high fence, Miss Adams." He said it lightly, but it was a subject that concerned him a great deal.

"Oh, I find politics so very boring. I wanted nothing more than to tour Europe with cousin Winslow. But even as we tried to escape the war, we were caught up in it. I see this conflict as an extreme inconvenience, Commander, and I want nothing more than to see it end."

Squibb was about to tell her of his relief at hearing this and of his growing feelings for her, but Eli and Sally returned. The heat of the day was waning and the light breeze dying, and the changes were bringing swarms of hungry mosquitoes. The buzzing menace ended their leisurely time by the shore and hurried them on the homeward path, birds and wildflowers no longer as interesting. There was little polite conversation and much swatting and slapping and, sadly for all, the day ended less happily than it had begun.

During their evenings in port, the crew of *Independence* were kept busy with fitting out their prizes for the next convoy to England. There, the ships and their cargoes would be sold at auction. Discipline and morale had improved of late, because there was so little idle time. And occasionally the sound of laughter, concertina, or tin whistle could be heard.

One warm evening, as Squibb sat on deck to write in his log, the men gathered on the bow to mend a sail and sing their sailors' songs. He'd heard most of the tunes in his youth and one, somewhat altered to suit their location, he particularly enjoyed. A fine tenor voice led the way into it. To Squibb's surprise, he saw that it belonged to John Cooper. The other voices joined in on the chorus.

At the St. John's docks we bid adieu
To Kate and Polly and Sal and Sue,
Our anchors weighed and the sails unfurled
We're bound halfway around the world,
Hurrah, we're outward bound.

Five months and more we're out to sea
Them pretty young girls we long to see,
But it's no more Kate nor Polly nor Sue
And no more ale nor song, it's true,
Hurrah, we're outward bound.

One day the man who's on lookout
"A sail to windward" he does shout,
Then up on deck comes every man,
She's a fishing boat from Newfoundland,
Hurrah, we're homeward bound.

And when we gets to the Dog and Bell
There's plenty of ale, and girls as well,
Says one to the other, you hear 'em say
Oh, here comes Jack with his five months' pay,
Hurrah, we're homeward bound.

But when the money's all gone and spent
And there's none to be borrowed and none to be lent,
Then comes the landlord with a frown
Saying get up now Jack, let John sit down,
Hurrah, we're outward bound.

The days came and went in such routines, marked only by increasing worry about Ethan. Squibb himself wished he were outward bound, in search of his son instead of beating up and down the same stretch of coast. But the wish was mere fancy and *Independence* continued her monotonous patrols, day after day. Ships arrived from time to time, but never the one that he longed to see.

Squibb was thankful when the pattern was broken occasionally by invitations to dine aboard *Maidstone* or one of the other ships of the squadron. These he happily accepted, for besides offering a change of routine and company, they provided food that was usually better than his normal fare. Many officers did not have to rely upon their meagre pay, and their tables, if not sumptuous—given the limits of what was available—were often quite appealing.

His colleagues also kept him abreast of events, including the news that Governor Edwards was sending Gardiner and *Bonavista* to Ferryland. The town had recently been menaced by a privateer, and while the battery at Isle aux Bois had deterred the vessel, it was still in the area. Squibb heard nothing more of the events at Toad's Cove or the monstrous rumour that *Independence* had declined a fair fight. He hardly expected to hear such a thing among the officers, but he knew from Greening that the gossip still lingered in the rum shops.

News came to him, as well, of the war to the south, which appeared to be running in Britain's favour. Word had reached St. John's that the rebel army had suffered its worst defeat in years at Charleston, South Carolina, with the taking of thousands of prisoners and a great quantity of munitions. Now the focus was on loyalist New York, where the French troops transported by de Ternay seemed about to lay siege.

At sea, things seemed to be going equally well. Three new frigates of the Continental Navy had been taken in recent weeks, although the powerful British privateer *Watt* had been badly mauled in a vicious battle in June. It continued to be the subject of many a tavern debate. In mid-Atlantic the American ship *Trumbull*, 30 guns, had lured *Watt* within range by flying false colours. The British ship had twigged her game, fired first, and set off a two-and-a-half-hour fight. The ships hammered away at each other, most of the time yardarm to yardarm. So close were they that burning wads from *Watt* twice set the Yankee ship on fire.

In the end, with dreadful losses on both sides, small arms decided the day. *Trumbull*'s marksmen perched in her tops delivered withering volleys that cleared the British decks. *Watt* drifted away from the fight and the Yankee was too badly damaged to pursue. Barely a man on either ship had not been wounded. Dozens had been killed. The barstool strategists would not have seen it as such, but to Squibb the engagement was a metaphor for the war itself: prolonged, indecisive, and bloody.

One incident in particular stood out during the long days of July, and that was an unexpected visit by Lieutenant Gardiner. He came aboard from *Bonavista* shortly after *Independence* had returned to harbour one evening, politely apologizing for the imposition but requesting a word with Squibb. Squibb led him below and offered a drink, which was declined. Gardiner appeared unsure of himself and began with some small talk, which seemed out of character. As the lieutenant sat there, appearing uncomfortable, Squibb saw something in his face that he hadn't noticed before. When the man wasn't wearing his habitual scowl, there was a fineness, a sensibility, about his features. It seemed to be the face of a proud and honourable man who was also deeply troubled.

"My purpose in coming to you," Gardiner said at last, "is to request the return of Midshipman Salter to my ship's company."

This was a surprise indeed. "I see," Squibb cautiously replied.

"I am ordered to Ferryland. He would be very useful to me there."

The words did not have a ring of truth. Squibb considered them before saying, "Is the governor aware of your request?"

"No. That will not be necessary. The midshipman is hardly a naval prodigy."

"All the same, Mr. Salter has been of great value to me," Squibb countered. "And he remains so. I am sorry, Lieutenant, but I cannot grant your request. Mr. Salter is my second officer and I cannot part with so valuable an asset. If you strongly disagree, I suggest you put it to the governor."

Gardiner did not argue. He rose from the chair and said, "Very well. I have tried." He looked Squibb in the eye and appeared about to say something more. Instead he turned and said, "Good day to you, sir."

The brief encounter lingered in Squibb's mind as the July days came and went. There was more to Gardiner's request than he had revealed. Squibb was certain of it. He recalled his earlier suspicion, that Salter had been sent to *Independence* to learn something that would discredit her new commander. Did Gardiner want Salter back because the midshipman had failed to do so? Or was Gardiner no longer jealous of Squibb's appointment?

In the weeks that followed, Squibb was kept busy with his work and frequent visits to Miss Adams, sometimes alone and sometimes in company. On each occasion he felt his attachment grow stronger. One evening he was about to go ashore to play cards with her when Montague arrived on board with a bag of books. Aware of Squibb's love of reading, the flag lieutenant said he was only too happy to lend him a few volumes from his own collection. Among them was the text of Sheridan's latest play, *The Critic*, which had been performed at London's Theatre Royal just the year before.

As Montague left for an engagement of his own, Squibb glanced through the booklet and felt some of his old literary passion revive. But with it came memories of happier days with Ethan. The books, dinners, and conversation were welcome diversions, but always lingering in his mind was the fear that he would never see his stepson again. One passage from *The Critic* struck a particularly deep chord of sadness:

And thou my boy must needs want rest and food.
Hence may each orphan hope, as chance directs,
To find a father—where he least expects!

The lines made him think of both Ethan and his own upbringing, and when he arrived at The Rising Sun, Miss Adams seemed to know that something had lowered his spirits. At her gentle prompting, Squibb told her of his early life. He had been orphaned as an infant, when his parents' boat had capsized at the mouth of Trinity harbour. They had been travelling from the harbour of Ireland's Eye, taking their son to Reverend Benjamin Lindsay for christening on a particularly blustery day. Something had gone terribly wrong—Squibb had never learned the details. His parents drowned but their boy had miraculously survived, floating in the fish barrel his mother had placed him in for the passage. He was christened on the same day that his parents were buried. Unaware of what name they had planned for him, Reverend Lindsay had considered both Moses and Jonah—one an infant set adrift, the other a man delivered up from a savage sea. In the end he was named for the latter and adopted by the minister, to be raised by him and a succession of kindly housekeepers.

Miss Adams listened to all he said with an expression of sympathy. "Were you happy as a child?" she asked.

"I was," Squibb replied without hesitation. "Benjamin Lindsay was a good man and he gave me all that he could. There was little material wealth, of course, but we were rich in other ways. He taught me well and instilled in me the values by which I try to live my life. I think about him often and with great fondness." He looked at his hands and added, "I doubt that Ethan thinks of his own adoptive father in the same way."

"Why ever not?" she asked.

He blinked several times. "Another day, perhaps. Now then, are you prepared to lose this game of whist?"

———— o ————

It was late July when Squibb finally decided to call upon Captain Graham of the Newfoundland Volunteers. He had no doubt that the captain and his daughter would be as worried as he was over Ethan's absence, and he felt it his duty to see them. He knew he should have gone sooner, but with each new dawn, as he put to sea, he'd put the visit off, hoping the sloop would appear that day. And, if he were truthful with himself, he was dreading a scene of tears or anguish, uncertain if he would be able to keep his own emotions in check. But he was resolved to go at last, and even now he knew that he went for selfish reasons more than overdue courtesy. By speaking to others who cared for the fate of his boy, he thought he might draw some strength and renew his sense of hope.

It was a rare Sunday spent in port when he set out for Fort William. There had been a church parade that morning for the Anglican crew members, with the divine service conducted by Reverend Langman. His sermon, on the theme of the third commandment, had been piously listened to, and now the men were deep into their Sunday ration of rum. The commandment was to keep the Lord's Day holy, but it had its limitations.

The weather had been dry for several days and there were many people about, enjoying a Sabbath promenade without the usual nuisance of ankle-deep mud. Squibb spotted Harriett Adams among them and a smile came to his lips—until he saw that she was not alone. Gridley Thaxter, easy to pick out in his powder-blue coat, was her escort. They appeared to be enjoying themselves. He saw her take his arm as he gestured with his free hand, apparently relating something she found amusing. Squibb was aware that they were acquainted, perhaps even friends, but the sight of them alone together unsettled him. He was well aware that he could lay no claim to Miss Adams' attentions. And with that thought uppermost in his mind, he turned off the road and made his way by another route.

Half his life had passed since Squibb had last set foot in Fort William— eighteen years since he'd taken part in its recapture from the French in 1762. The walls and buildings seemed little changed, but the place had a general air of dilapidation and neglect. The British line regiments had moved to Fort Townshend earlier in the summer, reportedly happy to leave the old fort to the local Corps of Volunteers. A sentry directed him to the officers' mess, where he found Captain Graham eating his lunch. Squibb introduced himself and was received with a firm and welcoming handshake. He declined the offer of bread and butter but agreed to coffee.

The two men sat on benches by a window as the other officers left for duty. Graham was near his own age, with features tanned and rough. He was tall and broad, his red uniform coat stretched tightly over his shoulders. His eye was steady and his manner direct. Squibb took a liking to him straight away.

"Let me tell you, before all else," Graham said. "My family and I are very anxious for your son. My wife and daughter are wholly distressed and pray every morning that some favourable news will come."

Squibb thanked the captain for his concern and expressed regret that the Grahams should be put to such worry. "Still, it is heartening to know that others are praying for Ethan's safe return. I am in your debt, sir."

"You have a fine son, Commander. He came to my attention shortly after he enlisted. He has common sense and is honest and hardworking, which is why I urged his promotion. The same reasons, I suppose, that Nancy chose him as her young man. And," he added with a wink, "she and I are both excellent judges of character."

"I appreciate all that you have done for the boy," Squibb said. "In many ways, it seems that you have been standing in for me."

Graham said nothing and Squibb wondered how much he knew of his troubled relationship with Ethan. He ventured to add, "Things have not been well between us, this past year and more."

"Yes," said Graham, "I guessed as much."

"Then I will confess to you that I am as terrified as ever I have been. Both at the thought of never seeing the boy again and at the chance that we may never reconcile our differences." Squibb was unaccustomed to sharing such confidences and he regretted his words as soon as he'd spoken them. "Forgive me. I did not mean to burden you with my worries."

Graham shook his head. "Your worries are those of a caring father. They are no burden to one who understands what it is to have an only child. And I fully expect that Ethan will have the very same fear and regret."

"That is kind of you to say. Thank you."

In the hour that followed the two men talked of many things, including children, their service, the war, and what the future might hold. Graham was a Scot and had been a soldier all his life, for many years with the 71st Regiment at Halifax and Quebec. He and a few sergeants had been transferred to the Newfoundland Volunteers on its forming, to help train the recruits. He and Squibb saw eye to eye on most of what they discussed.

When Squibb was about to take his leave, Graham invited him to first meet his family. This he could not refuse and a few minutes later he was ushered into the kitchen of the captain's quarters on the north side of the fort. He was introduced to a short, energetic woman named Sarah, who was in the middle of her laundry chores. Kettles steamed on the woodstove and two tubs of soapy clothes sat on the stone-flagged floor. She was aghast and embarrassed that her husband would bring a visitor home on such a day, and she had no hesitation in saying so. The mess was one thing, she said, but washing clothes on a Sunday! What must the commander think of them!

Through all of this she held his hand in both of hers and was soon telling him how much she thought of his son and of her certainty that Ethan would soon return. Squibb was touched by her kindness and the three of them talked, until a young girl entered by the back door. She held an empty basket in her hands and her apron was stuffed with clothespins.

This was clearly Ethan's Nancy. She blushed and curtsied on being told who their visitor was. Squibb saw before him a girl of Ethan's own age, tall and willowy, with a pleasing countenance and hands that were no strangers to daily work. Her parents were obviously proud of her and he was conscious of the love that radiated among them. He felt his own sense of loss and emptiness more acutely, and when the time came to say goodbye he did so with reluctance. Their warmth was comforting. Squibb left with many good wishes and repeated assurances that his son would soon return. As he crossed their threshold, Nancy spoke. He turned to her.

She blushed again as she said, "Thank you for coming, sir. But you can't leave without knowing about the laundry. The woman next door had her baby last night and we're helping with the blankets and things. It couldn't wait, you see. It's all they have." Her voice was tremulous but determined, and he admired her courage. He smiled his understanding and turned to leave, then paused as he was struck by a thought.

"Would you do me a great kindness?" he asked. "When Ethan returns, would the three of you be my guests at dinner on board *Independence*?"

The invitation was readily accepted—with great pleasure, they assured him—and he walked away with a renewed feeling of optimism. It was as if Ethan's return, now needed to enable the dinner, was more likely to occur. A verse of Oliver Goldsmith's came to him unbidden.

Hope, like the gleaming taper's light,
Adorns and cheers our way;
And still, as darker grows the night,
Emits a brighter ray.

On his way back to the boat he passed The Rising Sun. His spirits had lifted after talking to the Grahams and he resolved to call upon Miss Adams, then and there. Hope glowed in his heart and he was determined to act upon it. This he did, but the old woman at the desk informed him that Miss Adams was out and not expected before evening. Undaunted, Squibb asked for ink and paper and wrote her a note, welcoming the opportunity to see her at her earliest convenience.

Two days of silence followed, during which he tried to divert his mind from Miss Adams and from worry over Ethan. He sent to *Amelia* for Henry Spurrell, being in desperate need of additional crew, however young. As soon as they were reunited, Henry and Eli set about trying to outdo each other. Squibb had devised what he thought was a judicious division of labour for the two boys, but they were intent on encroachment and their childish bickering soon became a constant annoyance. To keep them busy he gave Eli extra duties beyond his role as steward, general messenger, and cook's assistant. Henry was assigned to cleaning the decks and polishing the navigational instruments. In spite of the added work, they still found opportunities to squabble.

On the third day after Squibb had left his message at the inn, *Independence* lingered in harbour one morning for provisioning. The schooner's boats came and went from shore and Hogarth, the carpenter, returned in one of them with a note. Squibb recognized Miss Adams' hand immediately and was quick to unseal the folded paper. It was an invitation to take coffee that very morning and also, she wrote, to hear something that would surely be to his satisfaction. The unusual addendum sounded mysterious and only added to his anticipation, though he needed no urging to accept the promise of her company.

An hour later, washed and brushed, he was ready for his run ashore. He had endured the attentions of both Eli Bailey and Henry Spurrell in his preparations, the two boys competing in their devotion to duty. After ten minutes of this he'd ejected them both from the cabin and seen to the business himself.

He arrived at The Rising Sun at the time requested and was admitted to the familiar parlour by Sally. A small table had been laid for two and he was told that her mistress would be down shortly. While he waited, he wondered at how nervous he was. He'd been alone in Miss Adams' company before, but he still felt uncertain of himself each time they met. More like a courting youth than a widower nearing middle age. He squared his shoulders and told himself to buck up. He couldn't be certain that the advice would be heeded, but fortunately he did not have long to wait. Suddenly she was standing in the doorway, her hair shining in the morning sunlight slanting through the window. She smiled and he pressed her warm hand to his lips.

They exchanged pleasantries and took their seats, she pouring tea for him and urging him to sample the assortment of tiny sugared cakes that Sally brought in. Surveying these and other confections and savoury bites, he was struck, as he'd been before, by the richness of her table. The food shortages that came with the war seemed to have little bearing on Miss Adams and her hospitality. He nibbled a small cake and tried to surreptitiously brush the crumbs from his lap. It was plain, however, that Miss Adams' attention was his alone. She insisted that he tell her about his recent activities and to spare no detail. This he did, pleased at her interest and touched by her approval of his visit to the Grahams.

At the first mention of his stepson her concern became apparent and she laid her hand on his arm in a gesture of comfort. He dared to wonder if some deeper connection was not beginning to grow between them. She may have seen something in his expression, a look of tenderness perhaps, for she folded her hands in her lap and looked at her cup. He hoped he had not offended her. Were his face and manner so readable that she could know his thoughts? He wished he had her gift, that he might know something of her feelings.

"Jonah," she said with some firmness. It was the first time she had used his given name and it made him smile.

"Yes, Harriett."

"You will recall that I wrote of information that would be of interest to you." He nodded. He remembered every word of her note. "This information has come to me by a circuitous route and I cannot say what its origin is." She glanced at him before resuming her study of the cup.

"I can, however, assure you that it is true. Otherwise, I would never speak of it to you." She raised her head and looked him in the eye. "It concerns your stepson."

Squibb stared. Had he misheard?

"Your boy is safe, Jonah, and in good health." She looked away. He suddenly felt weightless. "You must not ask me how I come to know this. But there are a great many American prisoners here in St. John's, as you know, and more are brought in every day. News and messages are exchanged and that is all I can say." Her expression showed concern for his reaction.

"A host of questions crowd my mind, Harriett," he quietly replied. "The first among them is how can I be certain of what you say?"

"Oh, Jonah, you can only accept my promise that it is so. The prize with your stepson on board was recaptured a day after you last saw it. Apart from Ethan's survival, that is the only detail I possess."

Squibb said nothing as relief fought with caution in the turmoil of his mind. He wanted nothing more than to believe her, to embrace the promise that Ethan was alive and unharmed, but a small part of his heart remained guarded. He looked into her eyes and tried to read her intentions. His doubt slowly receded, then vanished completely. An involuntary surge of joy and deliverance rose up within him.

Tears blurred his vision and he turned his head away. "Thank you, Harriett," was as much as he could say. "With all my heart I thank you."

MERCURY

St. John's, July 24th

ugust was very near when the convoy to England prepared to sail. A dozen prizes and an empty troop ship were anchored in the harbour, along with a handful of merchantmen whose holds carried the first shipment of salted cod from the spring fishery. They would sail for Poole under the protection of *Cygnet*, captained by Commander Peter Baskerville, whose turn it was to provide the escort and to visit his family. For the first few days of the voyage, when the danger of attack was greatest, the little fleet would be accompanied by *Maidstone*, *Independence*, and *Fairy*, all under the command of Captain Keppel and his *Vestal*. The naval ships formed an impressive squadron. The two frigates and *Fairy* were a match for anything the Yankees had. The French were another matter.

Squibb knew that he ought to be pleased to quit St. John's. The summer heat was turning the harbour into a cesspool. Waste from the town and fishery floated thickly and the tide never entirely flushed out the reeking waters. Maggoty Cove, just below Fort William, had the worst of it. It was a wonder that the garrison there had not been struck down by the miasma.

He should have been happy, too, at the prospect of being productive—it would distract his mind from worry. There had been no further news of Ethan, and Squibb's revived sense of hope for his son's return had slowly faded. He had not returned to see the Grahams. As much as he wished to share what Harriett had told him, he felt it would be unwise to do so. There was a hint of duplicity about it all—of receiving intelligence from the enemy or of benefiting from contact with the other side. The only person he'd told was his friend William Parker, who'd advised him to follow his instinct.

There was a third reason why he might have welcomed a spell at sea. A busy patrol would ease the tension that had been building aboard the schooner. The crew's earlier contentment and good behaviour had gradually eroded; of particular concern was the behaviour of Tompkins, the gunner, and Sergeant Parrell, now in charge of the marines in Ethan's absence. Companions in drink, they had become quarrelsome, given to grumbling and questioning orders from the mates. Squibb had been obliged to speak sharply to both in the presence of the sailors and marines. This was unfortunate, as it was bound to affect good order and discipline. Their behaviour was also beginning to fray his patience.

But despite all the reasons why he should have been happy to leave, he was not. He and Harriett had seen each other often in July. There had been dinners, teas, and even a small ball at Fort Townshend at which they'd danced together for the first time. The governor's wife had arranged the event, inviting the unmarried navy officers and the town's eligible young women. Mrs. Edwards seemed to enjoy matchmaking, something he'd learned when he arrived at the ball.

"Oh, Commander Squibb," she called as he came into the room, the same in which he'd first met Harriett. Chairs and tables had been removed and a military band was tuning its instruments in a corner. Mrs. Edwards came sailing down on him, her generously proportioned figure trailing silk and a faint trace of scent. Her gaze was locked onto him, as if he might be thinking of escape.

"Good evening, ma'am," Squibb greeted her, giving a slight bow.

"It will be, sir, once we get things moving. Now here's what I want you to do." He was firmly instructed to go at once to the young ladies, who were gathering near the punch bowl, and write his name on as many cards as possible, preferably for each and every dance.

She looked meaningfully at Harriett, who had just joined the other young women. "I believe that some of our lovely guests would welcome the opportunity to dance with you."

He bowed again and moved off to do as he was told. Mrs. Edwards set a new course as another hapless sailor came through the door.

Squibb made straight for Harriett, who had overheard the exchange and was laughing behind her fan. "Do not feel obliged to fill my card, Commander," she teased. "Mrs. Edwards can be a force of nature."

"She is a wonderful lady," he gallantly replied. "And she has our best interests at heart." With that he took her card and pencil and filled as many spaces as he decently could.

Now, as he stood on the deck of *Independence* and awaited the signal to depart, Squibb knew that dancing the cotillion with Harriett Adams had sealed his fate—he had fallen in love, without a doubt. But did she have the same feelings for him? He could not tell, and the question never left his mind. Their leave-taking last evening had been tender and full of regret, and now the convoy was still in harbour, waiting for a change of wind. He could not go ashore, nor could he leave, and while he waited in limbo he was tormented by the thought of her being so close, yet so far from reach.

The favourable wind brought some relief, though he left St. John's with a heavy heart.

If Harriett Adams or anyone else had been watching the convoy put to sea that afternoon, one thing would have been evident. The trim schooner that led the pack was handled very differently than she had been on her first departure under the naval ensign. There were no shouted curses, no confusion on her deck, and no reason to think of her as anything other than a crack little ship of war.

As *Independence* passed through the Narrows, the boatswain's singsong voice rang out: *"Haul on the bowlin', the bully ship's a-rollin'."* Squibb stood by the wheel, part of his mind thinking that the mainsail halyard was not a bowline, strictly speaking, but that the shanty was serving the purpose. A dozen voices answered the boatswain with gusto—

"Haul on the bowlin', the bowlin' HO!"

The men heaved in unison on the word *Ho!* and the sail rose a dozen feet up the mast.

Haul on the bowlin', a long way to home then.
Haul on the bowlin', the bowlin' HO!
Haul on the bowlin', for Kitty is me old one.
Haul on the bowlin', the bowlin' HO!

With those three powerful heaves the sail was up and *Independence* took to her heels. She dashed through the Narrows with a following wind and was well off Cape Spear before the last ship in the convoy had cleared the harbour entrance. Signal flags appeared on *Cygnet's* halyards as Baskerville began the tiresome task of keeping his sluggish flock together.

Despite their ragged formation, they managed to keep the same easterly course for three uneventful days. No enemy vessels approached and none was seen, even by the wide-ranging *Independence* and *Fairy*. Humpback and minke whales were abundant, having pursued the deep schools of capelin northward earlier in the summer. Flocks of terns and gannets still fed on the remnants of those teeming masses, diving from great heights to gorge on the tiny fish. The skies remained clear and the steady rhythm of life at sea returned. Tensions on board began to ease once more and Squibb even heard the gunner thank Miller for helping move a gun carriage.

On the morning of the fourth day, with the sun rising crimson before them and the westerly breeze freshening, Keppel signalled his captains to come aboard *Vestal*. The squadron lay to while *Cygnet* and her charges continued sailing slowly eastward.

In the frigate's cabin, the four officers sat down to breakfast. Their ships were still well stocked, as well as St. John's could supply them, and they dined on eggs, fried squid, and potatoes and even experienced the rare taste of bacon. Half an hour later Keppel's satisfied guests sat back with pipes and coffee and watched as he ceremoniously removed his sealed orders from a strongbox.

This was the moment they had all been waiting for. They knew Keppel had been instructed to open his orders on the fourth day at sea and share their contents with those under his command. It was an unusual arrangement and the curiosity in the room was palpable. With his worn epaulettes shining dully in the light from the stern windows, Keppel's grave red face revealed nothing as he scanned the first page. Only when he looked to the second did his features hint at a rising interest. Squibb watched the slight but unmistakable transformation as the face of a dour, well-fed senior captain became that of a dour, well-fed buccaneer.

"Gentlemen," he declared at last, "we have a merry task ahead of us. A packet sails from Philadelphia this morning, bound for Holland, carrying a person of considerable interest to Great Britain. My orders are to intercept this vessel, named *Mercury*, and bring all aboard her to St. John's."

"Does the governor say who this person is?" Parker asked.

"He does not."

Squibb looked to his colleagues and saw the familiar eagerness that comes to those who love a chase. Berkley rose and took down a chart of North America's eastern coast. The breakfast things were pushed aside and four pairs of hands eagerly spread it on the table.

"We must assume that the governor believes the enemy to be unaware of our intelligence," said Keppel. "Otherwise, they would certainly take an evasive route and we would be fools to even attempt to find them. Now gentlemen, we are exactly here." He placed a stubby finger on a point three hundred nautical miles from Newfoundland. "If *Mercury* departs Philadelphia today and if we sail south immediately—"

"The packet is sure to be swift," Parker put in. "Allow her an average of ten knots or more."

"—and if we can manage six, or even seven knots—"

"*Independence* can range far ahead," Squibb interjected. "If it comes to a chase, she should nearly match the packet for speed."

"—then given the relative distances, we may well find her somewhere in the region of forty-two degrees latitude, forty-nine degrees longitude."

"I will calculate it more exactly," said Berkley, moving to the chart table.

"She'll be sailing fast on a northeasterly course," Keppel continued. "We will sail south, distributing ourselves as widely as possible and staying in signal contact with topmast lookouts. If we maximize how far we can see, we should cross her route and find her in less than two days."

Berkley's quill was rapidly scratching numbers.

"May I ask, sir, why you weren't given this information before we left St. John's?" Squibb posed the question that he suspected was on the minds of everyone else in the cabin. Berkley's quill stopped and the three younger men looked to Keppel. With only two days' notice, any delay now would allow *Mercury* to outrun the squadron and disappear into the Atlantic.

Keppel frowned and shook his head. "I haven't the foggiest, other than I suppose the governor didn't want us rushing off to find the packet and leaving the convoy too soon. No doubt he decided to remove the temptation."

Berkley turned back to his detailed calculations as Keppel bent to examine the chart more closely. Squibb cleared his throat.

"Is there something more, Commander?" the captain asked without looking up.

"Forgive me the liberty, sir, but may I ask who delivered your orders?"

Keppel's head lifted, his brow furrowed. "What a peculiar question. It was that young fellow, the admiral's flag lieutenant. Why do you ask?"

Squibb smiled in apology. "Forgive me, sir. It has no bearing on the matter at hand." It did, however, have a considerable bearing on what was running through his mind.

————— ◇ —————

A day and a half of hard sailing brought the squadron to the area of hypothetical intersection with the course of the Philadelphia packet. The officers knew, as did most of the men, that the calculation was by its nature inexact. Given the vagaries of wind and current or any delay in the packet's departure, it was at best an educated guess. Her heading and precise destination were also unknown, but any route to Holland would not vary by more than a degree or a degree and a half of latitude, given the many factors that Keppel and his captains had considered and reconsidered. These included the prevailing winds, the packet's intended port, and her primary goal of making a speedy passage. That variance, however, equated to as much as ninety nautical miles. It was an enormous distance and a long line through which the packet could easily slip, even with four ships well spaced.

For another day and a half the squadron sailed back and forth across the ninety-mile line through which the packet would likely pass. Sharp-eyed men were posted at every masthead.

Squibb was awakened the following dawn by a cry from the schooner's lookout. "*Maidstone* signalling!" He struggled into his breeches and emerged on deck to see his second mate aloft, one leg and an arm hooked into the rigging as he used both hands to steady his glass. Patches of fog blew across the ocean, obscuring Squibb's view of the other ships for minutes at a time. "Deck there!" came a cry from the masthead.

"Report, Mr. Salter!" he answered.

"*Maidstone* signalling that *Vestal* has seen a sail astern. All to wear and give chase." The squadron was sailing west in a light breeze, with *Vestal* at the rear of their line. *Maidstone* was ahead of her to relay signals to *Independence*. The schooner, in turn, now quickly passed the message to *Fairy*, leading the way westward. The wind was out of the southwest and the bows of all four vessels turned away from it, wearing ship until their sails filled on the starboard tack. They were now heading northeast with *Vestal* in the lead and the fog thickening. *Maidstone* came and went from view and from time to time *Independence* was sailing blind, relying on her compass or a glimpse of the frigate's topmast.

"Another signal!" Salter cried. Then a moment later: "Sail bearing east-nor'east. And another—general chase!"

Miller was standing nearby and there was unusual excitement in his voice. "That has to be her! By Christ, sir, it has to be her!"

"Alter course to join the chase," Squibb told the quartermaster. "East-nor'east."

"East-nor'east it is, sir."

Greening and his men had already trimmed the sails to the new direction and Squibb ordered every scrap of canvas set. The wind was variable and he found their uneven progress maddening. The thrill of the hunt was upon him, but the breeze and the mist came and went, hindering their speed and hiding their quarry. At last a localized gust propelled *Independence* forward, soon giving the schooner twice the speed of the other ships. *Maidstone*, her great weight a disadvantage in the uneven air, was passed ten minutes later and, although she was hidden, Squibb knew *Vestal* could not be much ahead.

He was straining to see something—anything—through the veil when one of *Vestal*'s guns gave a deep boom. Two more followed in quick succession just as *Independence* broke free of the fog and the packet was revealed, not two miles distant.

She was just as Squibb expected, small and lithe, cutter-rigged, and more like a yacht than anything else. He studied her through his glass and read the name *Mercury* on her stern. She was a handsome vessel, built for speed and no match for heavy guns. She had no need to be, if she could outsail them. One ball from *Vestal* had passed through her rigging, cutting a leeward shroud but failing to slow her. Squibb knew that the next one could shatter her to matchwood and he could see that her captain was trying for all he was worth to escape the frigate's fire.

Independence and *Vestal* were sailing on converging courses with the packet in their sights. The schooner was still favoured by the wind and was outpacing the frigate. Their prey was in danger of escaping and some of her crew could be seen aloft, working feverishly to repair the damaged shroud. The fickle wind was now rising steadily, the fog largely dissipated. *Fairy* was coming up fast from astern, but it was clear that *Independence* had the best chance of overtaking the fleeing vessel.

Squibb ordered the bow gun run out. The schooner and the packet knifed through the waves that were building with the wind, the schooner now starting to gain. On and on they raced, spray flying over their bows, with *Independence* steadily closing the gap.

A sharp crack from above broke the spell. All hands looked up. Squibb was standing at the windward rail, completely focused on the chase, and he felt the schooner lose her thrust. The main topsail was streaming downwind, the billowing mass of canvas snapping like duelling pistols. He saw at once that a cringle had torn through. *Independence* had slowed by half. Greening and Cooper were already climbing, knives flashing as they prepared to cut the sail away. Moments later, two others were manhandling a replacement up the shrouds.

Fairy surged past them. The schooner's crew worked like men possessed, but by the time the sail was in place they had been left well behind. *Vestal*, still closing on the packet, opened up with her 18-pounder carronades and was joined by *Fairy*'s guns.

It was all too much for the packet. Guns of any weight were a hazard to her light timbers, but an 18-pound ball would have meant the end of the vessel and all within her. It was a ploy on Keppel's part, as his short-range carronades were too far away to be effective. But the packet's master would not have known they were carronades. All he would have heard was the tremendous crash of the heavy weapons and he would have instantly feared the worst. *Mercury's* Stars and Stripes came down and she turned directly into the wind to await boarders from her British captors.

A few minutes later Squibb ordered *Independence* up into the wind as well. She lay close by as men from *Fairy* and *Vestal* took possession. *Mercury's* people were gathered on deck—about a dozen sailors and half as many passengers. Squibb counted two women and four well-dressed men, but nothing about them helped to identify the mysterious object of the governor's interest.

The passengers were waiting to be transferred to *Vestal* by boat. The crew of *Independence* lined the rail and watched the operation in glum disappointment. They knew they would share in the prize money for the packet, but they had lost their moment of glory. All because of a rotten sail.

As the last gentleman climbed into the boat, there was a shout from Eli Bailey, at his favourite perch on the bowsprit.

"There! Look there!" he cried and pointed. "That man! He dropped something overboard!"

In an instant the barefoot lad flung off his jacket and dove into the water. He was swimming strongly toward the packet before Squibb had time to speak. Shouts and cheers from all the ships followed his swift progress. The sea was slightly calmed by the surrounding hulls, but everyone knew—though the impulsive boy might not—that he was fortunate indeed. *Mercury* had been overtaken in the warm waters of the Gulf Stream.

All the same, as Eli neared the packet his luck seemed to run out. He suddenly disappeared beneath the waves. Squibb gripped a forestay to steady himself. Long seconds passed in breathless silence. Greening was stripping himself of his coat and boots when Eli's head popped out of the water, followed by a triumphant fist clutching a canvas bag. An approving roar erupted from every deck.

Within moments eager hands were fishing him from the sea. Eli was hauled onto the frigate's deck, where Captain Keppel took possession of the bag and clapped the boy on the back, calling for blankets and brandy as he led him below.

Eli's quick action was either brave or foolhardy. Squibb had not decided which by the time flags appeared on *Vestal's* halyards summoning captains to the frigate, post haste.

Squibb's boat arrived at *Vestal's* entry port just ahead of Parker's, and the two officers were quickly escorted to the cabin. There they found Eli sitting by the door, dressed in dry clothes much too large for him, shivering and sipping a sizable measure of brandy. Squibb would have ordered him out, but Keppel had obviously allowed him to stay as a mark of gratitude. Keppel and Berkley were standing at the desk, bent over rows of damp papers laid out to dry.

"There you are," Keppel said. "Help yourselves to that bottle. My word, Mr. Squibb, you have an enterprising boy there and make no mistake."

Eli reddened as Parker topped up his glass. "Yes," Squibb said, appraising the quivering hero. "So it would seem."

"Gentlemen, we have our man," Keppel announced. Exclamations of delight, raised glasses, and congratulations filled the cabin. The captain was beaming and all eyes were on him as he picked up one of the papers. His stern features quickly returned to their normal station. "His name is Henry Laurens and he is likely to be our greatest capture of the war. Mr. Laurens is no less than a former president of the Continental Congress. He is one of the richest men in America—certainly its largest slave trader—and also the rebel government's new ambassador to Holland."

"Congratulations, sir," Parker declared. "A successful day indeed."

"May I ask"—all heads turned to Squibb—"was the capture of Laurens the governor's sole objective?"

Keppel's jowls lifted in a brief smile. "A perceptive question. Perhaps so—perhaps not. Either way, we have much more than Mr. Laurens to gladden the governor's heart. As we know, this envoy was on his way to

Amsterdam. His purpose there," he said, indicating the damp pages with a sweep of his hand, "was to finalize a loan from the Dutch government, a loan of many millions that the Yankees would use to finance the war against England."

There were more exclamations as his audience realized they had hooked a very big fish indeed.

"Not only that," Keppel continued, "Laurens was carrying a draft of a possible treaty with the Dutch, which would bring them into the war. It is all here in glorious detail. It is possible that the governor had intelligence of this, but now we possess the proof. And we have this good fellow and his quick action to thank for it." Squibb turned and looked at Eli, who grinned foolishly back at him.

Questions and speculation now flew about the cabin. Everyone but Keppel seemed to speak at once, all elated by their success and the full import of their capture. There was ill-advised talk of official thanks and even promotion, and by the time they left the cabin, the brandy bottle quite empty, each man fairly glowed with self-esteem.

For Squibb and Eli Bailey, the heady thrill lasted only until their return to *Independence*. In the boy's case it ended when the secondary effect of the brandy took hold and he lost his breakfast over the leeward rail, much to the glee of his friend Henry.

Squibb's elation disappeared the moment he entered his cabin.

Miller and Greening were waiting for him, their faces grim. The boatswain was holding a square of canvas with the failed cringle—a thick ring of rope stitched into the sail. Squibb saw straight away that the cringle and heavy stitching had been partially cut through with a knife. The pressure of the wind had done the rest, and the heavy canvas had parted like linen.

"The sail was in good condition when I rigged it," Greening avowed, his beard failing to conceal the angry set of his jaw. "That was the day before we left St. John's. I inspected all the sails four days later, after we left the convoy. Since then, the main topsail has been in constant but easy use. And now it suddenly fails when the strain on it is increased. Just as we were closing on the packet."

Miller removed his pipe and added, "It could have been tampered with by any one of the topmen in either watch."

Squibb was already aware of this. The topmen were aloft more often than they were on deck, day and night, and all of them carried sheath knives. Privately he ruled out the *Amelias*, but that still left a dozen suspects. A few of them had been marked out as idlers and sea lawyers, but their skulking did not compare with the sabotage of a King's ship. This was a capital crime and never, to his knowledge, had a convicted man ever been pardoned or reprieved. Any rascal or rogue would think twice before committing such an act of suicide. Which was leading him to think that it was an act of political will, a deliberate deed of sabotage in a time of war. And carried out, he reluctantly reminded himself, on a vessel under his command.

He dismissed Greening and Miller with instructions to get the schooner underway. Their first priority was to beat a swift passage to St. John's with the squadron and its prize and prisoners. The culprit would be found, but for now the watchword was vigilance. His handiwork had been discovered and the felon was unlikely to attempt anything further. Which gave Squibb time to think.

——— ◦ ———

Titus Greening left the schooner's cabin in a state of mind that was only slightly calmer than when he'd entered it. The boatswain's anger was candescent but under control and he, too, needed time to process what had happened. That such a thing could occur under his nose would have been unthinkable an hour ago. Now that it had, he was livid. And it showed. He strode the deck, the sailors in his path quickly finding some urgent task to perform elsewhere.

Miller had just given his orders to the foremast hands when he saw Greening coming his way. "A word, mate?" he heard the boatswain call. Miller took his pipe from a pocket and waited.

"I've been at sea, man and boy, these fifteen years and never heard of such a thing," Greening sputtered. "Why, sails and their rigging are the very fabric of life at sea. The things that a ship and her crew depend on for their lives."

"Calm down, bo'sun. Mr. Squibb will see the culprit hanged, you can be certain of that."

"Oh, aye, but first the bastard has to be found. Now I've been thinking. That sail could only have been tampered with in the middle watch, sometime between midnight and four in the morning. Mr. Salter's watch. Any earlier and it would have failed before the chase.

"I was on duty until midnight, and by four there was light enough to see. The bugger must have guessed, as we all did, I dare say, that the packet would be found today or not at all. And that *Independence*, with her speed, would likely be the one to take her. There's no doubt in my mind that whoever did this meant to let that packet escape."

Miller rubbed his pipe thoughtfully. "Which means the ship is harbouring a traitor," he said.

"Exactly. Now, who made up the middle watch last night? Seven men, there were, with Sam Hiscock at the helm throughout the watch. Six men, then. The leading seaman was Francis Barnes, a good man and like my own right hand, as you know. Five men. One of the watch was a landsman, the most unhandy man in Christendom and never sent aloft. So there's four men left, all able seamen. Navy men. But even so, they were all banished to our schooner by their captains, weren't they?"

Miller was nodding his agreement. "It was a cloudy, moonless night," he observed. "And Mr. Salter wouldn't have seen what went on high above the deck."

"That's right, mate. He would have given his orders and Francis Barnes would have seen they were carried out." Greening had been talking intently; now he looked around and seemed to notice for the first time that they were already underway. He surveyed the deck: all was running smoothly, the men attentive to their duties but for a cautious glance or two thrown their way.

"I'll be back," he said to Miller. Francis Barnes was descending a foremast shroud and jumped the last few feet to the deck. He and Greening exchanged a few words and the two moved aft, where Greening told the helmsman to call down the open hatch if he was needed.

They drank their rum in a single draught, standing on either side of the gunroom table. Greening poured them each a second tot. Barnes, like every man on *Independence*, knew what had happened and had been waiting for the summons. "I'm d-damned glad it's only you," he said to the boatswain. "Mr. Squibb brings out my stutter s-something awful."

Barnes needed no prompting and quickly laid out the facts. "We was ordered aloft three times last night. The first at midnight when Mr. Salter wanted the f-foremast topsail doused, owing to the schooner gaining too much on *Fairy*. An hour later he wanted it set again."

"And each time the hands were on the foremast only?" Greening asked. Barnes nodded. "An hour before dawn, with the wind dropping, we was told to set the main t-topsail. Me, that awkward landsman, and Cooper stayed on deck to haul the halyard, while the rest went up to loosen the stops and gaskets."

"Three men, then." Greening was thinking aloud. "Just three men were in a position to cut that cringle. I know them by name and I know them by work, and none are overly troublesome. One is inclined to be lazy and another slow to learn, but all three are harmless enough. Or so I thought." He poured a last dram for them both and they returned to the windswept deck.

The ships of the squadron were running northwest, their positions staggered but close enough to maintain signal contact. Their much smaller prize, so sleek and swift, was officered by *Fairy*'s lieutenant and required shortened sail to stay in company. Speed and mutual protection were paramount, especially as night approached—and with it the fear that enemy privateers might undo the day's success.

While the squadron made its way to St. John's, events unfolded swiftly onboard *Independence*. Before nightfall the three men singled out by Greening had been put in irons. As darkness fell, Miller, Greening, and Salter were standing in Squibb's cabin.

"I found this knife on the deck last night," Salter said. "Just before I ordered the main topsail set. I didn't realize the significance of it until we realized the cringle had been cut."

"It belongs to George Mullins," Greening said, "The one who's slow to learn. It's his only knife, sir, and he must have gone aloft without it. It couldn't have been him." Miller nodded his agreement.

"Very well," said Squibb. "Release him and question the other two again." All three of the arrested men had denied any knowledge of the cringle being cut. It was an awkward business, Squibb had to admit. The evidence against them was circumstantial and without a witness he was at a loss to know which of them was guilty. It was no simple matter, since a man's life hung in the balance. Squibb was beginning to think that the affair would best be handled by the governor, although even that had no guarantee of a just outcome. He had known courts martial in which the presiding authority had punished all of the accused, rather than attempt to separate the guilty from the innocent. It was an awkward business indeed.

After two days of fast sailing, the squadron arrived intact at the Narrows. The wind chose to drop just as they approached the land. One by one the ships lowered their boats for the laborious task of towing into harbour. In the case of *Independence*, with only two small boats, it was an undertaking that lasted two hours. When the boats were moored at last, the exhausted sailors fell gasping on their oars. They hadn't the strength to hoist the boats in until after their noonday grog.

Noticeable in his efforts to assist, though not in drinking the rum, was Eli Bailey. Squibb had seen a change in the lad's behaviour of late. He seemed more serious and certainly more attentive to his duties since his exploit with the canvas bag. Squibb had not heard him squabbling with little Henry for two days now, and Eli appeared to be everywhere at once, lending a hand but never getting in the way. He also noticed that he was somewhat taller and heavier than when he'd joined *Independence*. More a young man than a mere boy. With two prime seamen in irons, several with injuries and others lost with the missing sloop, perhaps it was time for young Eli to take on a more responsible role. Squibb made a mental note to speak to the boatswain.

Even before she had taken up her moorings, *Vestal* received a visitor. Squibb watched Lieutenant Montague climb her side as handily as any man who worked the tops. Within minutes a line of signal flags appeared at the frigate's mizzen to inform the governor, waiting high above the harbour, of the mission's success. This was followed by pennants summoning the squadron's officers to the frigate.

Montague seemed very pleased, Squibb thought, as he took his seat in Keppel's cabin. Glasses appeared and a rare bottle of port made the rounds, creating something of a celebratory mood among the assembled officers. They listened cheerfully as Montague assured them that the governor was greatly pleased and would convey his congratulations in person when time and circumstance allowed. For the moment, however, there was much to occupy his attention, and here the young man's demeanour changed. He stood and looked around the cabin at their expectant faces. Not for the first time was Squibb struck by the confidence and composure of this relatively junior officer.

"I am sorry to tell you, gentlemen," he said, "that in the short term you will have little time to celebrate your achievement. We have received new information that suggests the enemy is about to change his tactics. And that, of course, means we must be prepared to counter them in haste."

His listeners leaned a little closer.

"The harassment of our fishing fleets and villages has reduced the value of the fishery, as you know. But it has not crippled it, and for this the navy may claim credit. The enemy is certainly aware of his failure, and of his own losses in privateers and other vessels. And now, we learn, he will be turning his attention to our military presence on the island itself."

Montague unrolled a map and spread it on the table. Eager hands reached to help as everyone rose to their feet.

"You are well aware that our forts and outposts are scattered, isolated, and largely unsupported. In theory, they prevent the enemy from seizing those settlements and harbours from which an overland attack might be launched on St. John's." He paused and looked at the map. "Very soon, gentlemen, the rebels will put that theory to the test."

The officers considered his words and Keppel, his face more severe than usual, was the first to speak.

"Are you suggesting that an invasion is imminent?"

"I thought we had passed that crisis," Berkley protested.

"The threat of some weeks ago remains," the lieutenant said, "though not from the French fleet. Our intelligence suggests that the rebels will use larger ships or small squadrons to probe our outer defences. They will certainly attack them if they are found to be vulnerable."

"How are we to prevent this?" Parker asked. "If indeed that is to be our intention. And where will the enemy strike?"

Montague smiled and nodded. "Very good questions, sir. Do we reinforce these outposts at the expense of our small garrison here in St. John's? Do we employ your ships in patrolling the approaches to these harbours, at the cost of reducing your presence elsewhere? Difficult decisions indeed, but the governor has made them. Your official orders are being written as we speak and will be delivered within the hour. You will put to sea after darkness this very evening."

"But that is ten hours away!" Squibb protested. "Why do we delay?"

The lieutenant looked up as a bump alongside was followed by loud voices on the quarterdeck. "There is your answer, Mr. Squibb. Troops, powder, and munitions are being sent to each of your ships. You are required to deliver them according to the instructions contained in your orders."

Squibb knew the ships could be loaded in three or four hours, perhaps less. A departure after dark was still a considerable delay. His thoughts turned to the possibility of an attack on the island itself. The news came as a surprise, and yet it was inevitable that the war here would escalate. As the squadron had proven so well, British vessels based on the island were a thorn in the Yankee side, intercepting its Europe-bound convoys and packets. It was only a matter of time before the enemy moved against the source of irritation.

The meeting ended and Montague quickly departed to report to the governor. The valuable Mr. Laurens and the other prisoners were transferred ashore, and Squibb returned to *Independence*. His task was to receive on board a large consignment of powder, several tons of 24-pound shot, and fifteen men of the 84th Regiment. His two shackled seamen were transferred to the gaol at Fort William, where they would remain until he returned.

His orders arrived within the hour, as promised. The bearer was an elderly clerk, clad in black, who reminded him of nothing so much as an undertaker.

A WILLING FOE

At sea, August 2nd

idnight, dark as any known, and *Independence* was beating southeast in a confused and unpredictable sea. She pitched, rolled, and heaved in a diabolical motion, threatening at every moment to throw Squibb from the hanging cot. Shortly after leaving St. John's, the schooner had sailed into the remnant of another tropical storm that had begun life far, far to the south. It had nearly exhausted itself on the journey north but still blew a near gale with air that was humid and oppressive. The watch above had stripped the light summer sails one by one and replaced them with the schooner's heavy-weather canvas. It would be the turn of the watch below to grumble when the system passed and the sails needed to be changed again.

Squibb had abandoned all thought of sleep hours earlier. It was not the motion that kept him awake, but his low, miserably low spirits and the prospect of the long, lonely weeks ahead. There had been no news of Ethan, and he had not made time to see Harriett before he sailed. He could have, but he could not in good conscience bring himself to go ashore when his crew were denied the privilege. Duty came first and duty had always been a hard master. He'd sent a note instead, explaining the situation and hoping that she would forgive him. With luck he would find a St. John's-bound vessel to carry a proper letter, sometime soon.

He tried to resign himself to the voyage and focus on the task that lay before him, yet with all his heart he regretted not seeing her. He sat up, lit the lamp in its gimbal, and forced himself to concentrate. He read his orders for the fourth time. Reduced to their essence, they required him to deliver men and munitions to the garrison at Placentia and then to patrol the bay of the same name. Should he encounter an enemy force of lesser or similar strength, he was to engage. Meeting an enemy of superior strength required him to retreat to Placentia and reinforce the defenders there. If that could not be done, he was to run like a hare for St. John's.

The directives were plain enough, yet he was still trying to rationalize the long delay in getting underway. It was not for the sake of secrecy. It was dark when they left, it was true, but the half-dozen vessels, each with a separate destination, had departed with top and stern lights ablaze. The explanation—adequate time to embark troops and supplies—was non-sense. Even the frigates with their much greater loads had been ready to weigh anchor long before nightfall. His pondering was interrupted by the marine sentry stamping to attention outside the door. He heard Miller's voice but before he could knock, Squibb called for him to enter.

"How goes the watch, Israel?" he asked as his first officer came dripping into the room. Miller's clay pipe was clenched in his teeth, the bowl upside down. His hands reached for the overhead beams as the schooner reared and plunged into another trough, defiantly beating her way southeast.

"All's well, sir. Canvas changed and stays all taut. Guns are double breeched and the boatswain has re-lashed the boats."

Squibb was glad to hear it. The schooner was taking a pounding and if anything came loose on deck it could be catastrophic. A thou-sand-pound gun rolling about in a heavy sea would destroy everything in its path. "How are the Highlanders faring?" His passengers, fifteen troops of the 84th Regiment, would have some experience of a rough sea but nothing like this.

Miller laughed. "Buckets have been issued, sir. The groaning should keep the watch awake."

"And pumps?"

"Three men just put to them, sir."

"Carry on, then. Southwest after you've weathered Cape Race. By then we should have daylight."

"Aye, aye, sir." Miller withdrew from the cabin, hand over hand on the beams until he reached the companionway ladder. A fair parcel of water came down the hatch as he climbed, but it made little difference to his sodden state. The drenched sentry at the bottom of the ladder shivered in silence.

Dawn arrived slowly, seeping through the darkness and rain as if through gauze. Squibb came on deck to see the great waves marching toward *Independence*, passing under her and falling astern. Long before it was time to change the schooner's course, he heard them smashing like thunder onto the granite breast of Cape Race. *Independence* tacked and flew southwest with the sun rising and the wind on her larboard bow until her master and commander knew that he had cleared Cape Freels. An hour later she bore off to the northwest. Putting the wind on her larboard quarter allowed the schooner to surf the wave crests for long minutes at a time. Often she outpaced them and surged impatiently ahead to catch other waves that would hasten her on her way.

Cape St. Mary's at last, to the certain relief of the soldiers. The schooner edged into the relative shelter of Placentia Bay amid the raucous cries of tens of thousands of gannets and other seabirds. The densely populated cape was one of the great wonders of Newfoundland. It would likely remain so because the birds had chosen a towering finger of rock on which to nest, where their eggs could not be reached by hungry sailors or other predators. Squibb stood aft of the helmsman, feeling the schooner rise and fall with the following sea. She had taken the hard passage south with confidence and hardly a lather. He felt some guilt at the thought, but she was the finest vessel he'd ever sailed. He would have to make it up to *Amelia* with a new coat of paint.

The mouths of the many little coves on the eastern shore of Placentia Bay appeared briefly to starboard and quickly fell astern. Before the war they had sheltered the shallops, tilts, and stages of hundreds of summer fishermen from England and Ireland. Now there was little to show that these seasonal workers had ever been there. The depredations of the enemy had forced the most determined of them further up the bay, closer to the fortified town of Placentia. Those less determined simply stayed away.

Later in the day, with the wind abating and the boatswain's voice ringing the change to lighter canvas, Eli Bailey knocked on the cabin door.

"Mr. Salter's compliments, sir. He says that Point Verde is in sight."

Squibb looked up from his desk. "Thank you, Eli." The youth made to withdraw but turned back when Squibb continued. "I have been meaning to ask—how do you like your new duties?"

Before leaving St. John's, Squibb had conditionally rated Eli as ordinary seaman. Whether he stayed as such or reverted to servant would be determined over the next few weeks.

"It's early days, sir, but I do love it. And thank 'e again for giving me the chance, sir."

"As I have said, there is no one to thank. You've earned the opportunity and it's up to you to make the most of it."

"I will, skipper—I mean, sir. And thank 'e. That is …" He flushed and hurried away. The commander's stern look became a smile as he returned to his paperwork. Eli would not let him down. Squibb knew that the lad could be depended on.

The deck was crowded when Squibb came up a few minutes later. The marines and troops, some of the latter a ghastly shade of grey, were arrayed in somewhat steady ranks. Both watches had been mustered as well, one standing by to reduce sail, the other manning the guns for a salute. *Independence* drew abreast of Point Verde and at Squibb's nod the wheel was spun. As her bow swung through an arc of ninety degrees, most of her canvas vanished. She wafted gracefully into Placentia's outer harbour under the inner jib and fore topsail alone.

A small crowd gathered on the beach and others looked up from the many moored boats as they moved quietly past. *Independence* made her salute on entering the Gut, the echo of her guns resounding from the stone ramparts of old Fort Royal, high above the town. The reply from Fort Frederick to starboard merged with that of the New Fort on the opposite side, creating an impressive hullabaloo. The schooner glided sedately on, through the smoke and the narrow channel that led into the sheltered inner harbour. Her remaining sails disappeared and the best bower plunged through sixty feet of water to grab a sandy bottom.

Squibb examined the anchorage while the boats were lowered. He'd been here before and was always struck by how finely situated it was. The entrance to the inner basin was easily guarded—on a clear day the old fort on the hilltop gave defenders a view of the entire bay and its approaches. The long, rocky beach was ideal for drying fish, its rounded stones making wooden flakes unnecessary. And the beach was backed by plenty of level ground for houses, gardens, stables, and pastures for grazing. All of these advantages, plus the abundance of cod in the bay, had made it the island's second-largest settlement, with some twelve hundred permanent residents. It was a prize worth having and the French, who had claimed it long ago, had fought long and hard to keep it—ultimately in vain.

The relieved soldiers were first over the side. The sailors rowed them ashore and returned with the surprised garrison commander, whom Squibb greeted as he came aboard. The ensign saluted and Squibb shook his hand before leading him below. Work parties began loading the boats with the hefty shot and kegs of powder. The young Scots officer arranged his sword to sit more comfortably in the little cabin, readily accepting the offer of a glass of rum. Squibb handed him a bundle of orders and letters from Fort Townshend and the two men exchanged the usual compliments before drinking a toast to the King.

After some minutes, curiosity got the better of him and the soldier asked what news there was of the war. His face showed his astonishment as Squibb told him that an enemy attack on the island's outlying forts was likely, if not imminent. The ensign ran a hand through his shock of ginger hair and shook his head.

"I've long feared such a thing, sir, for the outcome may not be good."

"Surely Placentia is more than capable of defending itself," Squibb said in mild rebuke.

His guest bristled. "My troops and I will do our duty, sir," he declared.

"Aye. But will it matter?"

"Why are you not confident that the town can be defended?" Squibb asked, puzzled. "I was told that you have the second-largest garrison on the island."

"The Lord help us, sir! Until you arrived it could hardly be called a garrison. I have a few artillerymen, aye. Enough to work a couple of guns, but the rest are old men—pensioners. Subtracting the sick and infirm, and adding those you brought, I canna' parade more than thirty. Not enough to man the heights of Fort Royal. At best a lookout might fire a cannon or two and hopefully deceive the enemy."

Squibb could hardly believe his ears. "And it's no different elsewhere," the ensign went on. "Unless something has changed, there was only a garrison of two dozen in Tor Bay, half that at Bay o' Bulls and maybe five in Petty Harbour. And as for Harbour Grace and area—nowt!"

Squibb had no reply. His own vessel was certainly undermanned, as were most of the naval ships, but he had no idea the situation was so dire. The governor had not drawn attention to it either, perhaps out of concern for morale. All the same, the rebels were sure to possess the same facts, hence their change of tactics. Governor Edwards was doing what he could to bolster his defences, but it seemed a forlorn hope. Any well-manned privateer could put forty or fifty men ashore and still have enough crew to lie in the offing and bombard the town. Squibb now understood why he'd been ordered to remain in the bay. If or when the enemy appeared, all would be lost without naval backing.

He expressed his sympathy for the ensign's plight, gave him strong assurances of support and saw him over the side. The young man was rowed away, sitting morosely in the stern of a boat that was sunk to the gunwales, loaded down with shot for his cannon. If nothing else, his few gunners would have plenty of ammunition, Squibb thought.

He returned to the cabin, concerned and preoccupied with making the best of a difficult situation. He was studying a chart of the bay when Salter knocked, reporting the return of the boats and asking for orders. Squibb had decided to spend the night at anchor and told the second mate to allow the crew ashore in small groups, each for a couple of hours. The men had not had leave since they'd departed St. John's with Baskerville's convoy. They would head straight for the rum shops and tippling houses, he knew, but he needed them sober and satisfied in the days and possibly weeks ahead. Salter left him and Squibb returned to his thoughts, chief among them the task of defending Placentia from an attack by sea.

Squibb slept soundly that night, oblivious to the commotion of men departing and returning, until he was awakened by the officer of the watch. Miller reported that Salter had gone ashore with the boatswain and two sober marines in search of three men who'd failed to return on the final boat.

Squibb was not surprised. Nor was he concerned. There were always a few who became overly cheerful once on shore. After a hard day's work with a hangover and no grog for a week, they usually saw the error of their ways. He returned to sleep with instructions that he be notified when the boat returned.

He was dressed and shaving by the day's first light when Salter came to the cabin. He looked tired and discomposed after his long night, as indeed he had a right to be. His shore party had come to grief at the hands of a rock-flinging gang of Irish children. A few bruises aside, he had both good news and bad to report. The absconders had been rounded up and were now on board. One, a seaman found drunk in a shebeen, had been given extra duties and the usual fines and stoppages. The other two, he reported, were confined to the gunroom to await the commander's orders. Squibb paused in his shaving.

"The gunroom?"

The young man's eyes focused on a point beyond Squibb's shoulder. "Sergeant Parrell, sir. And Mr. Tompkins." The tip of his tongue darted nervously over his lips.

Squibb took up a towel and carefully wiped the blade of his razor before folding it into the handle. He dried his face and buttoned his shirt, calmly and deliberately. There was a slight edge to his voice, all that betrayed his irritation, as he called for Henry Spurrell. The boy came immediately and both he and the basin of water quickly disappeared.

"Where did you find them?"

"On the beach, sir. I followed them from a drinking den not far away."

"Dead drunk, I suppose?"

"Not quite, sir."

"Warrant officers, for God's sake!" he breathed as he picked up his coat. "The very backbone of a ship!" If he were not in desperate need of every man aboard, he would suspend their warrants and put them both in irons. A court martial might not see them out of the service, but it would be a damned good lesson in naval discipline.

Salter cleared his throat and Squibb turned to him. "Is there something more, Mr. Salter?"

"I wish to say, sir, that they claim to have taken a wrong turn to the boat."

"And do you believe them?"

"No, sir."

"Exercise your judgment, Mr. Salter. Do you think it was their intention to desert the ship?" The second officer's reply was not immediate. "Well?"

"I do not, sir. There may have been some other reason, but only they know what it was."

"Which I will shortly discover. Whatever it may be, it does not alter the fact that their conduct is grossly irresponsible."

"Yes, sir."

"Tell them to attend to their duties, if they are able. Otherwise, I will find someone who is. And make it known that I will deal with them later."

"Aye, aye, sir."

"And get us underway. Shape a course for the southern end of Merasheen Island."

Salter departed, shouting orders before he reached the companionway. Still seething, Squibb took up his chart of the bay and tried to give it his full attention. Bare feet drummed on the deck above him as men ran to their stations. A moment later the schooner began to move, even before the anchor was catted home. A light easterly breeze brought *Independence* slowly out of harbour and into the bay. He sent Henry to fetch the boatswain and a few minutes later Greening's powerful form filled the cabin doorway. A discoloured lump stood out from his forehead, evidence of the children's mischief.

"Parrell and Tompkins," Squibb said, "where did you find them?"

"At the far end of the beach, sir."

"And they claimed to be searching for the boat?"

"Yes, sir."

"Do you believe them?"

"Not for a minute, sir. They'd taken drink, to be sure, but they were sensible enough. And a man can't walk that fast when he's in drink."

"What do you mean?"

"Why, sir, they were heading out of town, and at a fair trot, too." Squibb weighed this new piece of information. The boatswain was looking him squarely in the eye. "May I speak freely, sir?"

"You may."

Greening stroked his beard. "I've shared the gunroom with them two from the start of this commission. I don't trust 'em, sir, though I know it's not my place to say so. Devious is what I'd call 'em. Mind you, I don't know what their game is, but I'd say they knew just what they were up to last night. They were . . . purposeful. Yes, that'd be the right word. Purposeful." Squibb was considering this when a cry from above drew their attention. "That's my mate, sir. I'd best go up."

"Yes, go. And my thanks for speaking your mind." The boatswain knuckled his forehead and was gone.

An hour later the ship's gunner, sallow and sweating, stood in the cabin. Before him sat the commander and the first mate, the latter taking notes. Parrell swayed on his feet beside him, locked at attention and letting his accomplice do the talking. "No, sir," Tompkins said in a low voice.

"Speak up, man!" Squibb was rapidly losing patience with the answers he was hearing. The gunner could not be mistaking his mood for anything but anger, nor could he be naive about where that anger might lead. He and Parrell had colluded in a version of events that saw them disoriented and trying to find the boat in the dark, but Squibb was having none of it. His mood was becoming blacker by the minute, and the two men were likely to end up in chains or something worse.

"I will ask you again," Squibb said slowly. Miller scratched a few words onto a page, an official-looking activity that seemed to rattle the gunner as much as the questioning. "Why were you at the far end of the beach and where were you going?"

He glared as Tompkins hung his head and tried to appear contrite. The man was a damned poor actor and Squibb could read him like a book. He suspected an attempt at desertion, always a possibility in remote places where a man or two could disappear into the woods, or else be hidden by sympathetic locals. Men had been known to steal a fishing boat and quietly head south to find a Yankee ship. Many sailors, pressed into service or not, had had a bellyful of the King's navy and were all for liberty and freedom in the land of plenty. But it was a suspicion only, for the proof was lacking.

Tompkins jumped as Squibb slammed his hand on the desk. His nerves seemed to have suffered a good deal since last evening. Still, Squibb could see that he had his wits about him and he hadn't lost his skill as a liar.

"We was seeking a woman, sir," Tompkins mumbled.

Miller's quill stopped scratching and Squibb leaned toward him. "Did I hear you say a woman?"

Tompkins nodded and shifted his feet. "Aye, sir. A woman."

The two officers exchanged a glance, Miller with an expression of disgust. "We heard there were a woman out that way, sir. Who did favours for sailors, like."

Squibb sat back and shook his head. Parrell swayed and remained mute, his good eye staring straight ahead. He might have been on parade. The gunner lifted his sagging shoulders and warmed to his tale.

"It were wrong, we know, sir, with orders to be back on board and all. But with a drink or two a man can lose his reason when it comes to…"

His voice trailed off and he set his pale features in a show of shame and remorse.

Squibb pushed back his chair and rose to his feet. "Get out of my sight and get back to your work." The two men were already underway but they caught his parting shot: "And don't think I'm done with you!"

Squibb watched them go, exasperated. "What do you make of this, Israel?"

Miller shifted his pipe and sat back. "I agree with the bo'sun, sir. I wouldn't trust either of them. Still, a woman could explain why they were there and in such a hurry."

"Yes, it sounds plausible enough. The first story about going astray was plainly a lie, then."

"Plainly, sir."

Squibb frowned and shook his head again. "I need to think about this. For now, dock them two weeks' wages and see that it appears on their record of conduct."

"Aye, sir."

Squibb went on deck a few minutes later and saw the sea churning on the rocks of Merasheen Island, off the starboard bow. The schooner's position was where he'd expected it to be and he walked forward, his hands behind his back as *Independence* eased along in a following breeze. He retraced his steps, knowing his face must be as dark as his mood, judging by how quickly the seamen and marines made a lane for him. Twenty minutes later the schooner came abreast of West Head, with the leftover swell from the recent southern storm climbing up its face. When the cliff was astern, Squibb ordered Salter to bring them onto a heading of thirty degrees.

To the newer hands, the skipper seemed lost in thought and not at all aware of Isle Valen slipping away to the west or the maze of surf-pounded rocks that made up the Ragged Islands in the east. Sugarloaf, Crane, the Three Docks, Jean de Gaunt—the old *Amelia* hands counted them off as they passed. They had sailed these waters many times in the skipper's little schooner and they knew that he was wide awake to where they were. He could navigate this bay with his eyes closed, having charted much of it with Captain Cook himself when he was still a boy.

Squibb's pacing took him to the wheel again and those nearest heard him say, "A touch north, Mr. Salter. Keep us off the Brandies Shoal if you can." The *Amelia*s exchanged knowing smiles, made all the brighter by the look on the midshipman's face.

Squibb turned and resumed his pacing. As he was walking forward yet again, he suddenly stopped. For a long moment he stood stock-still, staring at the base of the mast in front of him. Those who were watching saw his chest suddenly expand as his lungs took on a mighty cargo of air. The order that followed was heard by every man aboard, on deck or not.

"About ship!" he roared. "Cast off and haul!"

Independence swung immediately into the easterly wind and her sails began to shiver. Lines were let loose to larboard and brought home on the starboard side, even as the main boom swung across with force enough to kill a tall man. The massive pine spar and the smaller fore boom were arrested by the men handling the main and fore sheets and quickly belayed. The schooner, as though sensing the urgency in the bellowed command, carved her way through the oncoming waves, leaning from the wind on the larboard tack.

Squibb resumed his pacing and said nothing. Salter had been given no course and no destination, and the watching crewmen suspected that he had no desire to ask, after the embarrassment of the Brandies Shoal. The schooner tore east, close-hauled, with every line stretched taut. Their commanding officer was like a man removed from the world around him, wrapped in unapproachable solitude as he walked the pitching deck with never a lurch or a stumble.

Squibb's mind was fully occupied, not least with the knowledge that he had nearly made a strategic mistake. He had intended to take *Independence* north of Merasheen Island, to patrol the western side of the bay and look into its harbours and anchorages. But the likelihood of an enemy already in the bay was small. What purpose would it serve a privateer to lurk among these empty islands and treacherous shoals? Especially as few captains would be familiar with the area and fewer still would have accurate Royal Navy charts. No. If a raider came into the bay, it would be for the sole purpose of putting Placentia to the torch.

"Southeast, Mr. Salter," Squibb ordered, to the second mate's relief.

As the schooner tore southeast, a plan began to take shape in his mind. A vessel entering the bay on a direct approach to Placentia would sail to the east of Long Island. The distance between that island and the town was no more than twenty miles. Just south of Placentia was a small cove, a sheltered notch in the coastline. It was there that *Independence* would go, and it was perfect for what he had in mind.

———————o———————

"Signal, sir," said Henry Spurrell, peering through a glass toward the crest of a nearby hill.

Squibb, sitting on a stool just abaft the wheel, was absently carving a deadeye from a block of wood. He waited.

"Blue flag above, then white. Nothing to report, sir," the boy proudly announced. The schooner was moored fore and aft in Gooseberry Cove, with a thin mist enveloping all and the birds singing sweetly in the tall grass behind the beach.

"And who is reporting?"

"Oh. Sorry, sir. Blue flag is…Mr. Greening, sir."

Squibb stretched a leg forward and looked up at the signal station on the hill. He had used the same arrangement long ago, when Colville had retaken St. John's from the French. It had served its purpose then and was doing so once again. The station, consisting of two signalmen, a flagpole, and his ship's most powerful spyglass, relayed messages to *Independence* from the schooner's two boats out in the bay—simplicity itself.

Greening was in charge of the blue boat today, Miller commanding the yellow. Signals were hoisted regularly as they patrolled the bay, white meaning nothing to report and red announcing that a vessel had been sighted. The two boats plied the waters around the clock, with regular changes of crew. At night or in a fog, a single shot from a swivel gun would raise the alarm. In heavy weather *Independence* took over the patrol, though Squibb preferred to keep her hidden from view in the snug little cove. He hoped, and needed, to have the advantage of surprise if a hostile visitor were to enter the bay.

They'd been following this routine for more than a week, watching and waiting for an enemy who might never materialize. Squibb had begun to doubt the governor's information and was growing concerned as the schooner's supplies dwindled. Placentia, he knew, had barely enough to feed its own people and soon his crew, like the town residents, would be eating fish three times a day. Beneath their keel the salt beef bones had formed a small reef of their own.

With so little to occupy his mind, the fate of his stepson had become another daily worry. Ethan had been missing nearly two months now. Even if he had been able to stay in good physical health, Squibb had seen the effects of prolonged captivity before and feared their toll on him. He knew it was hardest on young men. The weight of that fear made his own days feel like imprisonment, and there was no end in sight.

The worry and monotony of the past week had been broken twice with small celebrations to boost the spirits of the crew. Little Henry's birthday had been one, with the boy embarrassed and delighted to have the ship's company sing him out of his bunk. An extra ration of rum had made it something of an event, with a fiddle or two on the deck that evening. The other was a slightly late nod to Lammas Day, marking the midway point between summer solstice and fall equinox, and traditionally the time of year for the first harvest of wheat in England. The practice went back a thousand years, it was said, and Squibb had the cook bake Lammas loaves from their small store of flour. To the crew's delight he made them in the shape of tiny owls, with salt for eyes. Once again, extra grog had helped lift their morale.

"Jesus and Mary! Yellow and red! Yellow and red!" Henry's high pitch rang out like a noonday bell.

Squibb was on his feet, shouting orders even as he made a mental note to cuff the boy's ears for swearing. The hands rushed to their stations, one party bringing in the stern anchor as others scrambled aloft. The bow anchor had been set beyond the mouth of the cove and now the crew clapped on to the hawser, winding it down into the forepeak as it came aboard and moving *Independence* out to sea. The two signalmen ran pell-mell down the hill and jumped aboard a small raft, even as the anchor was hauled short. Deck and rigging swarmed with hurrying, climbing figures. Sails appeared and wooden wheels rumbled as the guns were run out. The raft came alongside and the two men clambered aboard just as the anchor came home and the canvas snapped to the southeasterly wind.

"Make her fly," Squibb told the quartermaster. "Spare nothing." The schooner gathered speed on the misty, white-capped bay. Her two boats ran to her like seaborne chicks to their mother.

———— ◇ ————

Some twenty miles to the west, the privateer schooner was already in the bay. Her square topsails caught the southeasterly wind to good advantage and she was soon inside the channel west of Merasheen Island. The vessel ran on with speed and assurance, with little regard for the breakers and sunkers that lined her course, the Brandies Shoal among them. Her captain stood by the wheel, wrapped from eye to heel in an old naval cloak and with his hat pulled low. He was a little below the common height and slight of build. An observer might have taken him for a youth, but when he spoke to the helmsman there was no mistaking the voice of a man accustomed to giving orders.

Below the deck on which the captain stood, Ethan Toope sat on a coil of heavy line, his customary seat. He was spooning warm oatmeal from a small iron pot into three wooden bowls. It was the morning meal, unvaried these many days past and often uneaten by himself and his two companions. The boy who'd brought it stood waiting to take the pot away, saying nothing.

"What news today, Caleb?" Ethan asked. The boy shook his head as he often did, fearful of disobeying his captain. "Come now," Ethan gently coaxed. "Heard anything from home?"

The boy's eyes darted to the bolted door. "The glass is dropping," he blurted.

"Indeed?" Ethan replied. The boy grabbed the pot and hammered on the door to be let out. The three prisoners watched him go and took up their meal. It was tasteless, as always. They longed for a piece of figgy duff, but more than anything they longed to know where they were.

The schooner's former storeroom had been their cell for fifty-two days, as many days as there were scratches on the bulkhead. The storeroom had no hatches, save a scuttle high up in the hull that let in a tiny square of light. They were rarely allowed to leave the dark, dank place except to draw water from the casks in the hold or to empty their slops bucket, always in the dead of night. The sailors had orders not to talk to them, although the prisoners did experience small acts of kindness from time to time. Sharing the news of a coming change in the weather was one of them. It made little difference to them, but it was something on which to focus, aside from their captivity.

It was a painful existence for three active young men and they were beginning to experience signs of mental and physical decline. Seaman Cyrus Oldford had begun mumbling to himself and Private Crowdy, the marine who'd shown such pluck in standing up to Sergeant Parrel, was often very low. And all three of them spoke of headaches and other pains.

Nevertheless, the greatest threat to their mental well-being was having no word from, or knowledge of, the outside world. Were they still in Newfoundland waters? Why had they been so long at sea? When would they be put ashore or exchanged? The three prisoners debated these questions endlessly, but without information they talked themselves in circles. They had survived both the storm at sea following their raid on the convoy and the retaking of *Free Trade*. Whether they would survive their captivity was another question.

Ethan had devised a few strategies to try and keep himself and his companions active and alert. Pushups, arm wrestling, and a contest of lifting the heavy coil of line were daily events. There were quizzes and riddles, drawn from memory, and each man took it in turn to give a lesson on some aspect of his trade. As carpenter's mate, Cyrus Oldford was due that day to explain the use of adze and plane in shaping a futtock.

It was all helpful, but lately they had begun talking about their shipmate who'd gone overboard in that terrible gale and the other who'd been shot dead by boarders the next morning. Were those men better off? For each of them, every new day was a struggle to face and a struggle to fill, but face and fill them they did, one after the other. Ethan did so with as much good humour as he could manage, because as their officer, the others looked to him for strength and for leadership. And that was the hardest part of all.

———— o ————

Down through the cool, thin mist came word from the masthead that the Yankee schooner had entered the western channel beyond Merasheen Island. Squibb had known her identity since the boats had returned. She was the Yankee privateer they'd encountered at Toad's Cove early in the summer. What he didn't know was her reason for continuing north through the confined and dangerous strait. If she survived the passage she'd be at the head of the bay and could only turn south again, though there would be a choice of three channels when she did. Perhaps that was it. Her captain hoped to recover the element of surprise, supposing, of course, that he had experience in these waters or possessed a reliable chart. Either was possible, but a working knowledge of Placentia Bay made him a far more dangerous adversary than one who could simply read a map.

Salter was driving *Independence* hard but Squibb knew they would not catch the privateer, not with a following wind in her big topsails. In fact, it would be foolish to try. But she would have to come south, sooner or later, one route or another, and the best he could do would be to meet her on his own terms. The three routes that her captain would choose from were defined by the two largest islands in the bay. There was the channel west of Merasheen, which the privateer had taken to go north, the wide-open water east of Long Island, and the narrow passage between the two islands.

Squibb decided to put the schooner's boats to work again, to watch the first two waterways. The open reach to the east was the most likely choice for the privateer, given its sea room, relative lack of hazards and proximity to Placentia. *Independence* would be waiting there, hidden in one of several places and, he hoped, in a position to intercept the enemy before he reached the town.

"Heave to, Mr. Salter."

"Heave to it is, sir. All hands! All hands to heave to!"

Squibb had been deep in thought for some time and had failed to notice the general air of expectancy on board. The crew had been prepared for a fight and now that it seemed unlikely, their faces showed either relief or disappointment. A few even dared to whisper that it might be true, that the skipper was shy of a fight after all. Others said they would gladly fight the doubters as well as the enemy.

Squibb retreated to his cabin, calling for the two mates to follow. There, with the schooner lying quietly with her bow just off the wind, he outlined his intentions. There was agreement all around and the business was concluded in minutes. The boats were underway soon after, provisioned once more with powder, shot, sails, oars, small arms, food, water, and men. The plan left the schooner even more woefully short of manpower but Squibb was aware of the risk. He knew that if his plan failed, it would fail completely. It was not something he intended to dwell upon.

Under cover of darkness *Independence* rounded the southern end of Long Island and continued north along its eastern shore. In the first light of morning she stood outside a cove called Haystack and Squibb took the wheel. He knew the tiny inlet—not well, but enough to require just one man in the bow to sound his passage in.

As a grey dawn unfolded, the crew moored the schooner stem and stern and Squibb went below to check his barometric glass. The mercury had been falling for hours. He lay in his cot, unable to sleep; as the day wore on, the southwesterly wind lessened, and at noon the water was flat calm. By then Squibb knew exactly why the privateer had gone north and stayed there, and what he must do himself.

The falling glass and the calm air heralded one thing only—a change in the wind. Most likely a new breeze would arrive by dawn the following day and from the opposite direction as the previous one. A nor'easter was on the way. His opponent had foreseen this and taken his ship north, knowing he'd be able to run like lightning down the bay when the wind changed. If any adversary lay in his path, the Yankee would have the all-important weather gauge, the windward position that would allow him to control any action. Squibb was now certain that the privateer would take the eastern passage. To do anything else would rob him of that advantage and the shortest, swiftest route to a surprise attack on Placentia.

A short time later, on a hill high above Haystack, Eli and Henry ran up their signal on a makeshift mast. Through the powerful telescope Eli could see the pinnace rowing slowly in the still air between Merasheen and Long Islands. He watched as the tired men bent and pulled, bent and pulled, until he saw Mr. Miller take up his spyglass and put it to his eye. There was no danger that the barely stirring air would make the flag unreadable, for the skipper had told them to hold it out if they had to. Eli held his breath as the first mate, after a long moment of staring straight at him, snapped shut his glass and spoke to the crew. The oarsmen came to life, putting their backs to the task of alerting the distant gig.

Just after dark the two boats reached *Independence*, their men weary and thirsty. Squibb had been running scenarios through his mind for hours, considering every eventuality, and now, with a dozen men restored to the schooner, he was prepared to meet what the daylight would bring.

The watch changed at midnight but no bell was struck. Calm air and silence prevailed. Two hours before dawn the first stirring of a breeze was felt and by first light the wind was pushing hard from the northeast. Squibb was pacing the starboard deck when a lookout hailed him. All eyes followed the skipper as he calmly took a spyglass from the rack and made his way aloft.

Squibb's heart was pounding, but not from the climb. The lookout made room for him, and from his high perch Squibb sighted beyond the northern spur of rock that enclosed the anchorage. There, in the circle

of his glass, was the Yankee privateer, square topsails set and coming like
fire and brimstone down the bay.

The privateer looked to be making more than ten knots and keeping
to the middle of the passage. *Independence* was still hidden by the spur of
rock but that would change very soon. He handed the glass to the lookout and slid to the deck on a backstay, where the officers were waiting.
His senses were fully alert, his pulse had calmed, and his mind, like the
schooner's deck, had been cleared for battle.

"Mr. Miller, buoy the anchor cables. Mr. Salter, stand by to hoist main
and fore."

Small barrels were soon bobbing from the cables—preparation for
leaving the anchors behind. Lines of men stood, halyards in hand, waiting for the order to haul away. On the afterdeck Squibb visualized the
unseen privateer moving rapidly south. His own intention was to remain
where he was as long as possible, hoping the enemy lookouts would not
see his topmasts until they were south of his position. Then he would
emerge from his hiding place, fall in behind the other vessel and claim
the weather gauge.

Minutes passed before the enemy came in sight, sailing past the spur
of land. She continued south, all hands aboard *Independence* watching
and holding their breath. She was nearly abeam the cove, three or four
miles out, when her bow suddenly swung toward them.

"Cut and run!" Squibb shouted. "Up sails and heave!" Axe blows followed as the cables were cut. The deck slanted as the sails clattered up
and caught the wind.

"Topsails!" Men aloft cast off the gaskets and others on deck pulled
the gaff lines taut.

"Pinch her, quartermaster," Squibb ordered. "Put us above that
damned Yankee." *Independence* shot out from her hiding place, gathering
speed as her sails caught the wind beyond the spur.

"North-nor'east," Squibb directed. They were on the starboard tack
now, close-hauled to get above the privateer. The Yankee had braced

around her topsail yards and now had the wind dead astern. On she came, the big topsails driving her fast and throwing her bow wave high.

"Full and by, full and by," Squibb cautioned the man at the helm. The quartermaster carefully adjusted the wheel, attempting to point higher than the oncoming privateer and steal the windward advantage. The Yankee was now much, much closer. A puff of smoke preceded the hum of a ball that passed a few yards astern.

"Forward starboard gun!" Squibb called. "Fire away!"

Though rapidly closing the gap, the enemy ship was still a small target as she came bow-on toward them. Their own 4-pounder gun with Salter in charge barked once and a plume of water rose close to the downwind side of the approaching vessel. The gun crew was rapidly reloading when the privateer altered course unexpectedly and presented a line of black muzzles from her starboard side. Flame and smoke belched from them. *Independence* shook as two shots came home, somewhere near the waterline.

"Starboard battery. Fire as she bears!" Squibb called. "Carpenter's crew below."

Salter was there and one by one the guns roared. They did little damage, as far as Squibb could tell. The privateer had abandoned her quest for the windward position but was still coming on to leeward. Squibb saw that her captain had dispensed with manoeuvres in favour of pounding *Independence* at close range. Within minutes the two schooners came abreast and the guns of both vessels roared again. This time, shattered blocks and lengths of cordage rained down on the deck of *Independence*. Men fell under the debris and Squibb felt his ship slow.

"Repairs aloft!" he heard Miller shout. "Bosun's party aloft!"

"Reload and wear ship," Squibb ordered.

The schooner turned sharply south, answering her helm despite the damage. The Yankee turned north in the same instant, protecting her vulnerable stern from the next broadside. She was slowing too, her square topsails losing the wind. Squibb saw his chance as the two ships turned in a clockwise circle. His own forward momentum had given him a slightly better position and the Yankee's starboard quarter was under his guns. But before he could give the command to fire, the other's 6-pounders roared again.

The gig, secured amidships, went to pieces in a storm of splinters. The foremast groaned horribly and leaned to leeward, with only the stays and shrouds holding it upright. Greening was running with a broad axe and men were scrambling to lower the sails before the mast went by the board. Squibb hurried to the guns.

"Make every ball count!" he shouted. "It's now or never, lads! A reward for every shot that finds its mark!"

In quick succession the smouldering match was laid to the touch-holes. He moved down the line, sighting along the barrels himself and hardly pausing to look as one by one, each 4-pound ball went home.

When the smoke cleared, every man could see that the privateer had suffered at least as much as *Independence*. Her main boom was in two pieces, the foremast was damaged and the running rigging was a shambles.

Her momentum carried her out of range, due east of them, where she lay with smoke pouring from her forward hatch. Her crew could be seen running to fight the blaze. Squibb knew they would be desperate to keep it from reaching the powder magazine.

As he watched, three figures appeared at the stern of the stricken vessel. A small boat that hung from the aftermost davits dropped into the sea and the figures jumped after it, swimming briefly before pulling themselves aboard. Then, to the wonder of all who were watching, they took to the oars and rowed straight for *Independence*.

A SEA OF TROUBLES

Placentia Bay, August 13th

he crippled privateer soon managed to raise a sail and began drifting out the bay on the dying northeasterly breeze. Events aboard *Independence* received far more of her crew's attention, however, than the slow departure of the enemy. A few heads lifted when she fired a single gun to windward, but they quickly turned back to witness the strangest sight—the skipper with tears in his eyes. The boat from the Yankee had come alongside but all hands knew who was in it long before it reached them.

When the three young men were helped aboard, there were three thunderous cheers of welcome and a great deal of backslapping. They were all deathly pale and Ensign Toope seemed thinner, if that were possible. All three laughed and cried with the emotion of the moment, but it was the reaction of the skipper that everyone was amazed to see. Their stern, unflappable skipper, standing back and wiping his eyes, watching his stepson return.

Later, in the privacy of Squibb's cabin, once Henry had finished fussing over a tray of coffee and brandy, father and son regarded each other across a low table. Squibb knew his emotions were likely showing in his face. He could not conceal the happiness, love, and concern that were written there. Ethan's expression was less easy to read. Exhaustion was evident, to be sure, along with relief and a measure of awkwardness.

"Welcome home, my boy." Ethan nodded and looked at the coffee, which Squibb quickly poured for him. "I have been so afraid—" The words caught in his throat and Squibb checked himself. "We have much to talk about, Ethan. Perhaps when you have eaten and rested."

"Yes, sir," was the reply. "You will want to know the state and strength of the enemy."

For a long moment, Squibb was too hurt to reply. "Right now, Ethan, I want to know how you are and how you have fared. And I want to talk about the two of us and how we are to put things right between us."

The young man drank his coffee greedily, his hand shaking slightly, and Squibb refilled the cup. When Ethan had finished, he laid the cup aside and studied his trembling hand, seeming to gather his thoughts.

"If there is any benefit to being a prisoner," he said at last, "it is the time it gives you to think. And it has given me time to realize that I was wrong, father. That I have been unwilling to forgive. You have acknowledged your mistakes after my mother's death, which is more than I have done." He looked up, remorse showing clearly in his face.

"I have been hoarding my anger at her death, and at you. It was childish, but after a while it seemed to become a part of me. Now my only wish is that we can be what we were before."

Squibb leaned across the table and awkwardly pulled his son toward him. The embrace was returned, and the two men remained that way for some time, before sitting back with an emotion that was never so deeply felt. Squibb, determined to let nothing stand between them again, had more to say.

"Ethan, I must tell you something. It has been a long time since your mother died, and now I find ... " He hesitated over the choice of words. "I find that my affections are taken by a certain lady. I believe that she is aware of my feelings and has done nothing to discourage me. And so, you see, I have hopes of speaking to her soon, to ask—"

The look on Ethan's face froze the words on his tongue. They had not been spoken rashly. He had wrestled with them over the weeks of his son's absence, planning what he would say when, and if, Ethan were to return. He had hoped, even expected, that the news would be received with approval. He was not prepared for his son's reaction. The look of disbelief was a blow in itself and the shocked silence made the pain more sharply felt.

"Ethan," he pleaded. "I felt I must tell you. You have a right to know and we should have no secrets between us. Talk to me, please. I am sorry if—"

He did not finish, for his son had stumbled out the door.

Squibb sat alone for a long time, trying to deal with the tangle of guilt and regret, even as he felt the familiar weight of loss and despondency settle upon him again.

Repairs to the schooner began even before the burial of the one man killed in the skirmish. Josiah Goldsworthy, late of the *Amelia*, had been slain by the same ball that wounded the foremast. He was widely regarded as a good soul, though given to profanity, and he'd known as much about splicing and gammoning as any man aboard. His loss was certainly felt, especially now, when the crew of the damaged schooner had much need of his skills. Squibb said a few words over him before his friends sewed the body into a sheet of old canvas. He would be buried at Placentia if they could reach the town in a day or two.

It was pure luck that many more had not shared Goldsworthy's fate. Two men lay below in their hammocks with serious wounds, and others were going about their duties in bandages. The carpenter reported that the mast was beyond repair and that it would take a dockyard hoist to replace it. There was every likelihood, however, that the shot holes could be plugged and the schooner made seaworthy by the following day. The boatswain had already begun work on the rigging. Greening reported that she would have a chance of reaching St. John's, but he gave no promises about her speed or appearance.

The schooner limped back to Haystack under a jury-rigged sail, where the sounds of heavy work disturbed the evening and carried on into the night. There was little sleep for anyone, save the liberated prisoners. After as good a meal as *Independence* could offer and a generous portion of rum, the three young men slept for twelve hours straight with never a twist or a turn. They were only roused the next morning by the lookout's voice, piercing the working din to announce a sail on the horizon.

The first collective thought was that the privateer had returned—or worse, a new enemy was in the offing. But within minutes the mystery vessel was identified as a King's ship, coming in their direction. A cheer went up when Salter, after a long study with his glass, declared her to be *Maidstone*. She was the answer to many a prayer, with her surgeon, materials, and large carpenter's crew, not to mention the protection of her heavy guns. Squibb ordered flags and pennants raised so they would be spotted, then went to his cabin and awaited a signal to go aboard the frigate. Breakfast had been laid for him, but his concern over Ethan had taken away his appetite.

The signal did not come. Henry surprised him when he breathlessly announced that Captain Parker was on his way to *Independence*. Squibb met him as he came over the side, grasping his offered hand and telling him what a welcome sight he was.

Parker had obviously studied the damage on the pull across. After returning Squibb's greeting he shouted down to his boat's midshipman. "Return to the frigate. *Maidstone*'s carpenter, boatswain, and surgeon to come across and lend a hand. Tell them to bring what men and supplies they need."

Squibb led him below, where before anything else he told him of Ethan's escape. Parker's surprise and delight at this filled the small room. Well acquainted with his friend's anguish over the boy, he demanded that the young man be summoned. When he came, the captain's good cheer and hearty congratulations served to ease the tension between father and son. It was a small but welcome relief for Squibb, despite Ethan's determination to avoid his eye.

Parker was eager to hear about the events of the previous day, and everyone's attention was soon focused on the privateer. Squibb provided details of the action and Ethan related what he knew of the enemy ship. It was clear that *Independence* had badly damaged the Yankee and that one of her shots had started a fire that threatened the powder magazine.

"An iron hand was needed to keep her crew fighting that blaze," Parker observed. "The threat of explosion is a terrifying thing."

Long before now Squibb had realized that the privateer's captain was no ordinary, opportunistic skipper.

"Yes," he agreed. "The discipline of her crew is remarkable, along with the rate and accuracy of fire from her guns. The captain's skill and confidence in these waters stand out as well, along with his enterprise. They make his vessel a match for all but our largest ships."

"I have no doubt of that." Parker nodded thoughtfully. "Now, Ethan," he said, switching tacks, "tell me the details of your imprisonment. How were you treated?"

The older men listened closely, exchanging a glance now and then as they came to the same conclusions. When the young man began to tire, Parker phrased the question that Squibb had been longing to ask.

"Given the care with which the privateer was managed, and the close confinement you were kept under, how did you escape?"

"Well, sir, when the guns fell silent and smoke was filling the lower deck, we heard the bolt to our door being drawn. We waited but no one came, so I tried the door and found it unlocked. We made our way out and up the aftermost companionway as fast as we could, unchallenged. All hands were forward, it seemed, fighting the fire. Releasing the boat was simple enough and before anyone was the wiser, we were rowing for all we were worth."

Squibb and Parker said nothing as they pondered the questions that came immediately to mind. Considering what they knew of this captain, how was such a thing possible? How—or *why*—had the boat come clean away with never a cry of alarm or a volley to stop it? It made little sense, and they discussed it briefly until they realized that Ethan had not had his breakfast. He was sent away to eat and Squibb turned their talk to other matters, foremost among them the question of how the frigate came to be here.

"The governor ordered *Maidstone* to Placentia in support of you," Parker answered. "Why he did so, when there are so many demands on the squadron's resources, is puzzling, as I am sure you agree. Nevertheless, I am here now and my only regret is not arriving sooner. My best course, as far as I can see, is to remain in the bay while you make your way to St. John's. I cannot leave Placentia undefended. You can deliver your report to the admiral and return with orders when the schooner is repaired."

It seemed a sensible plan and Squibb readily agreed to it. The privateer would not make a second attempt on Placentia with a frigate lying in her way. The two men went on deck to see how the work was progressing. The foremast was already stabilized, with lines rigged to allow the use of the big main topmast staysail at deck level, in place of the unusable jibs and foresail. It was not an inspiring sight, nor did it promise much in the way of speed, but in theory it would allow *Independence* to raise St. John's in three or four days. The threat of another attack was Squibb's biggest concern, but he had his guns and his crew had proven they could use them.

That evening, before the ships parted company, the anchors were retrieved, Goldsworthy's body was sent to Placentia, and the badly wounded were transferred to the frigate. *Maidstone*'s surgeon had judged it best to keep them under his care and to spare them the unpredictable journey.

It was well that he had. Scarcely were they out of Placentia Bay when Crowdy, the young marine so recently liberated from the privateer, lost command of his reason and tried to kill Sergeant Parrell. Evidence of provocation was lacking and no motive could be attached to it by any of the crew, other than the widely held view that his captivity had unhinged his mind. The sergeant escaped injury and his attacker, in his madness, was believed to have thrown himself into the sea at night. There were no witnesses and he was never seen again.

Cyrus Oldford and Ethan, by contrast, soon returned to duty, having regained much of their strength. They had need of it, for on the second day of the voyage the wind rose unexpectedly and forced *Independence* far out to sea. Her jury rig was no match for nature's whim, and she ran for a full, clamorous day with only her main gaff topsail to prevent her from broaching to. The sea rose to monstrous heights and ran deep across her deck, breaking bones and concussing one man, who lay delirious in his hammock for the rest of the voyage.

At the height of it all, Squibb was on deck and struggling to belay a loose and defiant jib stay when he felt another hand on the heavy line. It was Ethan's, and together they were able to wrestle the thick, twisting python of rope until Squibb could secure it with a rolling hitch. It was a temporary knot but it would do for the moment, and with a hold on each other, they staggered below and out of the grasping wind. Clinging to the ladder, they caught their breath. Ethan spoke to him for the first time since they'd left Placentia Bay.

"Father," he called in gasps, above the howling and moaning in the rigging, "Your news. About your lady friend. It was a shock."

Squibb shook his head and tried to speak, to apologize for his tactless blunder. "No, father. Let me say this. It took time to digest. That is all. Mother's ghost has been laid to rest. And lovingly, I know, after so long a period of mourning. I am happy that you have found someone to care for. And, I hope, to care for you."

Ethan paused for breath, Squibb threw an arm around his son's shoulders, and they swayed together as the schooner plunged and reared over the next fearsome wave. Icy water came down the hatch and onto their heads, and only then did they turn back to the business of staying alive.

When the wind finally abated, the schooner began to recover the miles she'd lost, slowly and in a constant state of repair. Fresh water was now added to their anxieties, several of the large casks in the hold having been stove in during the blow. Rationing was ordered, even as the late summer sun reappeared and parched the men working long hours to keep themselves afloat. It was another trial of will, of mind over adversity. When Signal Hill was sighted at long, long last they had spent nearly two harrowing weeks upon a spiteful sea—on a journey that should have taken a few days.

The fight with the Yankee privateer and the ordeal that followed had wrought a further transformation in the crew of *Independence*. In fact, Squibb had begun to notice the changes earlier, in Placentia Bay. His men had grown initially from a collection of unwanted sailors to individuals united in the cause of prize money. Now they had become a team, strong and united, the bond forged in battle and cemented in one more trial of life and death at sea. Nearly every man worked for the good of the whole. Even Tompkins and Parrell were behaving well, though their motivation may have had more to do with appeasing the skipper's still-evident displeasure. But overall, he thought, his crew had become all that he could hope for. He was proud of them.

Long before they arrived at the Narrows, the state of their vessel had been observed and someone in authority had ordered a train of boats to tow her in. Squibb was grateful indeed, for he had doubts that enough men could be found among the spent and dehydrated hands to row their one remaining boat. He had hardly slept in the past two weeks and was unsteady on his feet as their anchor plunged to the harbour floor. But even here, in calm and safety, rest was not at hand. After seeing to the crew and drinking as much water as he could hold, he went ashore with Ethan, who went straight to Fort William and Nancy. Squibb made his slow and breathless way up the hill to Fort Townshend, determined to see his duty done before all else.

Upon his arrival at the governor's office, Montague looked up from his desk. "Good Lord, sir!" he exclaimed, and urged Squibb to sit. He did so without protest, thinking how dirty and dishevelled he must appear next to the lieutenant in his elegant uniform. He informed the young man that he had something of importance to tell the governor. He was admitted to the inner office without delay, allowing him to think that he might be in his cot within the hour.

Governor Edwards was at his desk and he greeted Squibb in his usual hearty manner, though his sharp eye took in every detail of his appearance and manner. Montague lingered to hear the report delivered. It did not take long and once finished, Squibb felt his mind begin to wander, despite his best efforts to concentrate. He could not remember if he'd given Miller orders about the damaged casks. And what had he said to Salter about the foremast? His eyes were burning and he closed them for a moment, a restful sensation that may have lasted longer than he intended. Someone coughed politely and he started, alarmed to discover the two men staring at him.

The governor gave a powerful heave and rose to his feet. He came from behind the desk and his large hand gripped Squibb's. There were words of congratulation, something about the successful defence of Placentia and teaching the Yankee knaves a thing or two. Then came decanters and glasses and the governor loudly insisting on hearing every detail of the skirmish.

A couple of redcoats who were waiting in the anteroom joined them, and soon Squibb was at the centre of a confusing prattle of tactics and logistics and how best to twist the enemy's tail. There were other things spoken of, news that had come by the London packet, but exhaustion and a single drink rendered him unable to make sense of it. The babble grew louder and less coherent, every mouth seeming to move at once, and Squibb felt a growing sense of disconnection from his surroundings. He was faintly aware of the room revolving before Montague appeared at his side and took him firmly by the elbow. They emerged from the building arm in arm and walked onto the parade square, where he was handed into the governor's waiting carriage. It was his last vague recollection of the day. A short time later the driver tried in vain to shake him awake. Finally, four strong sailors appeared and lifted him gently into a boat.

———————— ◇ ————————

During Squibb's long and restorative sojourn in the hanging cot, the damaged foremast was lifted and replaced, along with its rigging. The schooner was careened a few degrees and the two shot holes at the waterline were permanently repaired, while new water butts were filled and stowed securely in the hold. The work did not disturb him in the least, which caused Henry to check his breathing at every bell.

Montague arrived in the early afternoon to find Squibb up at last and eating a plate of boiled cod and biscuit. He had come, he said, to assure himself that the commander had recovered and to bring him an orange. Squibb took the gift and held it to the light, enthralled at the sight of it. He had not laid eyes on an orange since the start of the war. An entire barrel of them had been taken from a recent prize, the lieutenant said, and the governor's staff had benefited to a small degree. Montague also brought with him a great deal of news, including word that the Admiralty was assigning Keppel a new frigate.

"He is to have *Aeolus*," he said, "32 guns, as a reward for the capture of *Mercury*. And for *Fairy*'s part in the action, Berkley is to be promoted captain. He will take command of *Vestal*." Squibb saw the embarrassed look as his guest hastened to add, "Of course, he has been due the step for some time." Montague was well aware of that day's events and Squibb knew that he was trying to spare him any further disappointment.

"I am pleased to hear it," he told him. "I will be sure to congratulate Berkley." He felt no envy or malice. What had happened that day could not be changed.

"That is good of you, sir. May I add that *Mercury* has been bought into the service and is to be commanded by Lieutenant Prescott, Berkley's first officer."

Squibb nodded. "The honour is well given. I know the man, and I am pleased for both him and the service."

The lieutenant went on to explain, to his listener's great surprise, that St. John's was in an uproar. That very morning the governor had called out the troops and put the town under martial law. The reason was a widespread mood of uncertainty and disquiet that had taken hold after the arrival of yesterday's London packet. The vessel had brought disturbing news, which Squibb vaguely recalled hearing at the governor's office the day before. He had made no sense of it then because of his exhausted state and now he listened carefully as Montague related the details.

Parliament had recently passed legislation giving additional rights to Catholics. Among these, owing to the pressing need for manpower in the navy and army, was the elimination of the Protestant oath for new officers. Lord George Gordon, head of the Protestant Association, immediately predicted Catholic treachery in the armed forces of the nation. His words had been too much for the mob. Some fifty thousand had gone on a rampage in London, burning the homes of wealthy Catholics and attacking the carriages of members of the House of Lords. The prisons and the home of the Lord Chief Justice had been destroyed. Only the presence of fifteen thousand troops had prevented the Bank of England from being breached. The rioters had been fired upon and hundreds were dead. The monarchy itself was under threat and London was paralyzed by what the press were calling "King Mob." The situation was perilous there, and now that news of the riots was known in St. John's, the governor was preparing for any outcome here. All naval ships in the harbour, including *Independence*, would be receiving orders to assist in maintaining the peace.

Squibb had listened in silence and was ready to bombard Montague with questions but the lieutenant held up his hand.

"There is more. The packet has brought other news that could well add fuel to the fire. The governor's office has been the subject of an important legal decision brought down by the courts in England. You may remember that last year a merchant was fined by the governor for a customs infraction—a criminal conviction. A group of his fellow merchants immediately mounted a legal challenge to the governor's authority to do so. And now, to everyone's surprise, we learn that the merchants have won. The courts have ruled that the Newfoundland governor has no legal authority other than the jurisdiction granted to naval officers by King William's Act of 1699. And that jurisdiction extends only so far as civil proceedings, not criminal cases." Montague paused for breath.

"But who will be the final authority in such cases, if not the governor?" Squibb asked in disbelief. "He has always been regarded as the highest legal power in the land. Good Lord, this leaves the island in a state of judicial limbo!"

"Exactly," Montague replied. "Imagine the implications. Disquiet among the town's Protestants over greater Catholic rights, fear of Catholic treachery, and the Catholic majority realizing that the governor's sentences and decisions are invalid in law and cannot be upheld."

"And all of this in the middle of a war with the town full of American prisoners and Irish sympathizers," Squibb said. "A perfect recipe for riot and mayhem."

He assumed he had heard it all. Then Montague dropped his exploding shell. Squibb listened in stunned silence to the news that the Corps of Newfoundland Volunteers was to be disbanded. The British government had refused to pay the enlistment bounty, the monetary incentive to which every serving man was entitled. This had created such dissatisfaction within the Corps that the governor could no longer trust its loyalty. When invasion seemed likely and civil unrest about to take hold, several hundred troops were going to be disarmed.

Squibb could not believe his ears. It hardly registered when Montague said that Ethan and his handful of men could be officially re-enlisted as marines if they chose to do so. He was still trying to take it all in when the lieutenant said that he must be off, that the governor would be waiting for him. Squibb saw him into his boat, remembering too late that he'd meant to bring up the matter of his two men still in gaol at Fort William and awaiting trial for sabotage. His mind had been entirely taken up with what he'd been told, and it was not until he returned to the cabin that he realized he was still holding the orange.

Before Montague's arrival Squibb had been thinking of several things that needed to be done, including a visit to Harriett. She had likely seen *Independence* at anchor and would be waiting to hear from him. Despite the morning's many distractions and with so much to do, Squibb had no intention of staying away a moment longer. Half an hour later he was at the front door of the inn, smoothing the wrinkles from his coat and scraping the mud from his heels. The forbidding matron sent a boy to inform Miss Adams of her visitor.

He waited in the small lobby for what seemed an age. The boy did not return and the old lady watched him narrowly. Guests and tavern customers came and went and still he loitered. He was beginning to feel self-conscious under their curious glances, when suddenly the object of his impatience appeared at the top of the stairs. The time spent waiting was forgotten.

Harriett was dressed in a laced mantua gown that matched her blue-green eyes, with a yellow petticoat just visible below the skirt. Her hair, uncovered as always, hung freely to her shoulders. If the sight were not enough to plant joy in his heart, her bright smile and expression of unaffected delight assured it. She lifted her skirts and skipped down the stairs like a schoolgirl. Instinctively he opened his arms and she rushed into them. He was on the verge of kissing her but remembered the watchful sentinel and settled for a brief embrace.

It was a moment of pure happiness, certainly for him and, he had no doubt, for Harriett as well. They laughed at nothing other than the ridiculous pleasure of seeing one another again. She took him by the hand and led him, half running, to the privacy of the salon. The door was left discreetly open but behind it she kissed him for the first time. It was a mere peck on the cheek but it was a kiss: as sure a sign of her affection as any he could imagine.

They sat and talked, hand in hand. He could not have repeated what was said, although their words were warm and tender. An hour passed in something of a blur, as it had at his last meeting with the governor. But this time it was happiness, intoxicating happiness, that addled his senses.

———o———

The following morning, Henry found Squibb out of bed before dawn and sitting at his desk. He greeted the boy with a lively "Good day" and told him to fetch the cook straight away. While he waited, Squibb took up his quill and wrote a hurried note to Captain Graham. He could not remember feeling more alive. His stepson was returned, his love for Harriett Adams was reciprocated, and there was nothing to dull the shine of his enormous good cheer. He was determined to celebrate with a dinner as grand as *Independence* could manage. The constraints were, of course, the size of the cabin and the availability of food for the guests. The first of these he intended to address by having his desk, sea chest, and other impedimenta removed to the hold and his hanging cot trussed up to the beams. The second would be left in the hands of Simeon Ballett, along with several shillings.

Harriett had already agreed to come, and a favourable reply from the Grahams set the wheels in motion. For the rest of the day the cabin was the scene of intense preparations and that evening, at the appointed hour, father and son stood together on deck, dressed as smartly as their tired uniforms would allow, and waited for their guests to arrive. It was strange indeed, Squibb thought, to be here with his stepson as each awaited the object of his affection. Strange and joyful, for he remained happy and buoyant, his cares and responsibilities packed away like the furniture in the hold.

The Grahams arrived first. He and Ethan had arranged for the captain to be piped aboard in ceremony with the marines presenting arms. They were technically Graham's own men and it was not, strictly speaking, something that was due his army rank. But he certainly seemed pleased by the compliment, and amazed at the men's precise drill and confident bearing. Mrs. Graham and Nancy, blushing to her shoulders, came aboard with cries of happiness and embraces for Ethan, who beamed with pleasure.

Ethan led the Grahams below while Squibb waited for Harriett. Her boat arrived within minutes and once she was safely on deck, he embraced her then and there. She was certainly surprised and the crew were certainly entertained, and he wondered what had come over him. He was not impulsive by nature, but the sight of her seemed to loosen all constraint. A radiant smile was her only reply as he escorted her to the cabin, where Ethan was answering questions from all three of the excited Grahams.

Harriett and Ethan appeared to take to one another immediately, a relief to the man who loved them both. The meal was a great success as well, for the cook had secured a rare leg of pork and carrots and potatoes, newly and perhaps prematurely harvested. The cost had been high but there'd been a few pennies left over to buy the makings of a pandowdy pudding. Another precious bottle of claret had been found, and when it was empty they drank their toasts with rum punch or Madeira, according to their taste. Graham, flushed and cheerful, proposed one such toast to the young couple, handsomely promising them every support in their future lives together.

"That is," he hastily added after a nudge from his wife, "if they should decide upon that course."

It was all good fun and everyone laughed. They laughed as well at the captain's anecdotes of army life, one of which involved an eccentric senior officer.

"He was of the first order when it came to being cool and decisive," Graham said. "But at the same time, he would say and do the oddest things. One day he took his pet pig with him when he went to instruct the troops in musketry. He told them that to ensure a perfect aim, one ought to shoot first and call whatever was hit the target." The captain laughed. "The men would follow him anywhere, though mainly out of curiosity."

Nancy also told an amusing story of her own about a governess she'd had when her family was stationed at Halifax.

"We were studying arithmetic and the governess asked me a question. If five blackbirds are sitting on a fence and a gamekeeper shoots two of them, how many are left? My reply was none. This annoyed the governess very much and she asked me how I had arrived at such a conclusion. I told her that the other three had naturally flown away at the sound of the gun!"

Squibb was struck by the girl's unaffected manners and simple sincerity. He could not imagine a better match for Ethan. The stories and conversation flowed freely until it was time for the guests to leave. Darkness had fallen when the Grahams, accompanied by Ethan, were helped into the boat for the trip ashore. While they waited for the pinnace to return, Squibb and Harriett strolled the deck, she with his coat over her shoulders against the damp. She'd been very much a part of the evening but once or twice he had noticed her fall silent and thoughtful, perhaps even a little sad, though only for a moment. She shivered in the darkness and he put an arm around her, drawing her closer.

"Harriett," he said, "you know I will be sent to sea again, perhaps very soon." She looked up at him but said nothing, her eyes catching the light from the binnacle lamp. "Before that happens, I must speak to you about something of great importance."

"Importance?" she replied. She looked away and pulled his jacket tighter. "It cannot be so urgent as all that. Surely it can wait."

He smiled. "You must know that I have strong and tender feelings for you, Harriett. What I wish to ask you, before I leave again—"

"Hush. Let us not dwell on parting. We have had a wonderful evening and such friendship can stand any short period of separation, can it not?"

"My dear, surely we are more than friends. Is there no love between us?"

"Why, of course there is. It is a fact, well established, that no friendship can exist without love as its basis."

"That is, Miss Adams, one of the boldest statements ever made. You seem to deny the very existence of friendship. All is love, according to your reasoning."

"Perhaps that is true, for I believe that no friendship can thrive where there is no love. And further, no friendship can exist where no affection is returned."

Squibb nodded as he studied her face. "That I will concede. You cannot be friends with a person who has no regard for you. But love?" He wondered if she had guessed at what he was trying to say. Was she avoiding his question?

"Love is implied, or inherent, in the very concept of friendship," she said. "Even a man must see that."

Squibb laughed. "In that case we must define degrees of love, and types of love, for the love of two friends differs from the love of a mother and child, or of a husband and wife." The conversation continued thus, bantering and affectionate, until he returned to what he had intended to say.

"My dear, forgive me but I must ask my question. I must ask it before I go to sea." He gently turned her toward him and she searched his face before looking away.

"Harriett, my feelings for you have become more than I could have imagined. I know in my heart—"

"What was that?" she cried.

"What?" he asked, startled and listening for something out of the ordinary.

"That sound. There it is again!"

Squibb recognized it, in dismay. It was the splash of an oar, heralding the return of the boat. He sighed and accepted defeat, though only for the moment.

———o———

The next day's sunrise brought with it a terrible thirst and a dull ache behind Squibb's eyes, made worse by Henry and his immediate chattering. Last evening's dinner had been the grandest of occasions, Henry chimed. It ought to be done more often, by his reckoning, and with cheese the next time. Squibb let him prattle on as he dressed and shaved while drinking two cups of scalding coffee. By the time he came on deck he was feeling better, though his mood was not improved by the sight of several men with their heads together on the forecastle.

"Mr. Salter," he snapped. "See to that party of clucking hens and report to me."

Salter dashed away, dispersing the seamen with oaths and orders. Squibb looked around as the rest of the crew suddenly made themselves busy. Salter returned, full of apologies, and received a brief lecture on his duties and the need to keep the hands active. An order to clean ship followed, beginning with the sleeping quarters. Everything movable was to be bought on deck and every plank scrubbed with vinegar.

"Fall is approaching, Mr. Salter," his commander reminded him. "Grippe, ague, and fever must not be given a chance to take hold and thin the ranks of men so tightly packed together. Not when their numbers are precious few to begin with. And in case you have forgotten, there is a war on and every man must be fit and ready to do his duty." Salter saluted and hurried away.

Squibb realized that he was out of sorts. It was not just the combination of rum punch and pandowdy. He had parted from Harriett without speaking frankly. He wondered now, in the cold light of morning, if it were not for the best. Perhaps she had felt this as well, for she had certainly avoided his question. They were, after all, on opposite sides of a war that had gone on for six years with no end in sight. Harriett had told him of her dislike for politics and they rarely discussed the war, except when she wished to hear about what he had seen or done at sea. Still, the conflict was always there, in the room but never coming between them.

As he paced the deck, Squibb reprimanded himself for this line of thinking. Love could transcend anything, he told himself, even a revolution. It might take longer for affection to blossom into love and marriage, but he knew it was possible. He also knew how he felt about her and he refused to be disheartened.

He concluded these reflections and was beginning to consider breakfast when the first visitor of the day appeared alongside. Major Pringle of the Volunteers arrived without notice and came aboard without his hat or sword. Squibb hurried to greet him but Pringle, it seemed, did not stand on ceremony. He asked that Squibb assemble his senior people straight away, and there on the deck he unrolled a large sketch of the harbour and laid it on a hatch cover. The squadron's ships were drawn in at several locations and as Miller, Salter, and Ethan gathered around, Pringle told them that *Independence* was required, without delay, to move into the position indicated on the plan—just off the harbourfront with her starboard battery facing the town.

"For what purpose?" Miller bluntly asked.

"This is in keeping with the governor's preparations," the major replied, "in the event of public disorder."

"Is the situation so serious?" Ethan asked. Like the others, he was alarmed at the idea of bombarding the town and their own people.

"Not as yet," Pringle replied. "The rabble-rousers have been making speeches in the taverns and we have detained two or three of the most inciteful. Our troops are patrolling, and a display of naval resolve should be enough to keep the mob under control."

With that he gathered up his plan and told them to be in position within the hour. As he stepped into his boat, he handed Squibb a note. "From the governor," he said. "Another council of war."

The repositioning of the schooner was a strange and humorous sight, as evidenced by the catcalls and laughter from the other ships of the squadron. *Independence* was moved under tow to her new mooring, her crew in a state of vexation and embarrassment. The move had been ordered in the midst of the skipper's call to clean ship and now here she was, an armed schooner manoeuvring to uphold the governor's authority with her decks piled high with barrels and bags, boxes and sails, hammocks and chests—even a couple of cats that the men had smuggled aboard since their return to St. John's. These newest crew members were now high in the rigging, adding their own expressions of displeasure to the shame of the crew. All hands were mortified at the spectacle they made, but the tow was at least done quickly and the schooner was scrubbed and made shipshape again in record time.

Shortly before noon Squibb was standing on deck when the London packet came limping into port. She was clearly damaged and word spread quickly that she had only just managed to outrun a privateer on the nose of the Banks. It was also said that the Yankee had been a square topsail schooner with several prizes under her lee. It was an interesting piece of news on many fronts but Squibb noted in particular how quickly the privateer had been repaired, and so far from friendly ports.

The next day, the first of September, the governor's council gathered as before, though with fewer naval officers. Many of the ships were patrolling at sea or, like *Maidstone*, still protecting the outlying settlements. As the handful of lieutenants and the usual army men took their seats in the spacious office, Squibb was surprised to find himself, aside from the governor, the most senior naval rank in the room.

Governor Edwards lost no time in opening the meeting, having settled himself into his chair with a glass of wine at his elbow. The first item of business was news from the south. Lord Cornwallis had won a great victory at Camden, South Carolina, in August, routing a numerically superior force under the rebel General Gates. It was the first favourable report since early summer and the governor hoped it would raise the morale of the town and garrison.

He went on to summarize the reports of the naval patrols, Squibb's included. The enemy was certainly active, but there appeared to be no concentration of force. Thus far only one attempt had been made on a town, if the encounter in Placentia Bay could be counted as such. The more pressing concern for the moment, he warned, was St. John's itself. The danger of trouble from within was very real, and all officers were to remain vigilant and prepared to suppress any hint of civil disorder. The large number of prisoners in the town, many of whom were paroled, was to be reduced straight away. A cartel carrying more than a hundred would sail to New England the next day for a prisoner exchange. Murmuring filled the room as the governor paused to drink.

"Now gentlemen," he resumed, his expression dark and troubled. "We come to what I consider a matter of utmost urgency. As you know, our former *Egmont* is under enemy colours and making a damned nuisance of herself these three months past. I have lost count of the number of vessels she has taken, including our *Coureur*. Her captain has also been destroying fishing premises from Fogo to Burin. Commander Squibb very nearly had him last week but he slipped away and is now back to his goddamn tricks. I want this man and his vessel taken, and taken soon!"

The governor drank again before eyeing each of the naval officers in turn. "I have an additional reason for wanting an end to the career of this enterprising fellow. Our spies in Boston have identified him, without question. And what of it, you may ask? One traitorous Yankee is much the same as another, eh? But no, gentlemen. Not this time."

The governor had everyone's full attention now, even the army men. "This man is more than a common rebel. He is a former officer of the Royal Navy, a turncoat who seeks to kill, maim, or capture his former shipmates in the service. The service, I may add, that trained him, looked to his welfare, and paid him the King's wages for many years. Such a thing is hard to believe and hard to accept. And yet there is no doubt that it is true."

Squibb was nodding. Now it all made sense. He had known all along that the privateer was in the hands of no ordinary skipper. The man acted as he would have acted himself, and the discipline and skill he'd witnessed could only have come from long naval training and experience. But who was this turncoat?

"The man in question," the governor was looking straight at Squibb as he spoke, "was a senior lieutenant who in fact served on the Newfoundland station some years ago."

Good Lord, Squibb thought. He must at least have heard of him. And this would explain the man's confidence in the waters of Placentia Bay.

"The ships on which he served include *Northumberland* and *Liverpool*."

Squibb felt a sudden wave of nausea. He'd spent years on the old *Northumberland*, and the *Liverpool* frigate was well-known to him, too. It might even be an old friend or messmate.

"And his last ship was HMS *Serapis*, which was captured at Flamborough Head last year."

Squibb felt as though he had lost his breath. As his mind reeled he was distantly aware that the governor was still watching him. Was he gauging the effect of his words? Did he know what impact they would have?

"And the man's name, sir?" a young lieutenant asked impatiently.

The governor looked down at the paper in front of him, even though it was a name he was unlikely to forget. "The name is Froggat. Friday Froggat. He was listed as killed in *Serapis* during her capture, no doubt a ploy by the Americans to disguise his treachery."

The governor sat back and regarded his officers. "Now let me be clear. I want this man. I want him so badly that I am putting a reward of fifty pounds on his head. Bring him to me, gentlemen, and give me the pleasure of seeing him hang."

———o———

Squibb remembered nothing of his return to *Independence*. He was in a daze or, more likely, a state of shock. His old friend Friday Froggat, not only alive, but a deserter and a traitor? He could not believe it. Alone in the cabin he stared through the high stern window, seeing nothing. When had he last seen him? Six years ago? Seven? It was certainly before the war, when *Liverpool* was at Bonavista. Froggat had sailed a ship's boat up the bay to call on him at Trinity. Ethan would remember that visit. The boy would also remember the stories he'd been told over the years, about Squibb's adventures with Froggat in the Seven Years' War. And the time they trekked into the island's interior in search of the Red Indians. And how Froggat had saved his life, and vice versa, on more than one occasion. That he was now a traitor was too much to comprehend.

How could it be? How in God's name could a brave and honourable man throw aside his convictions and his good name to join a cause that was so fundamentally opposed to everything he had lived by? It made no sense.

Squibb wanted to be thrilled at knowing that his friend was alive, but instead he was struggling with confusion and doubt. He needed to talk to Ethan. He would have to be told before the knowledge became general. Perhaps by talking, Squibb might make sense of it all himself.

Ethan was summoned and came straight away, and as soon as he saw his stepfather's expression, he knew that something was wrong. His own youthful face clouded with concern.

"Father? What is it?"

Squibb tried to compose his thoughts. It was difficult to repeat, but he told him what the governor had said. Ethan sat himself on a locker, speechless and shaking his head. Squibb could see that he was trying to come to terms with what he was hearing. He would be thinking of his weeks of imprisonment and attempting to reconcile his treatment at the hands of a man who'd been his father's dearest friend. There had been gifts for the boy when Froggat had come to Trinity. He carried a folding knife from him that he cherished. How was it possible?

Squibb saw his stepson's confusion, a mirror of his own, and moved to sit next to him. Their closeness helped to calm his mind and focus his thoughts.

"There may be an explanation," he said after a short silence. Ethan looked at him. "Perhaps he is not of sound mind. If he was wounded at Flamborough. If he hasn't recovered properly. I have seen it before." Squibb knew he was grabbing at the wreckage, trying desperately to keep the last fragment of his loyalty afloat.

Ethan looked down and said nothing. They both knew that treason was a heinous crime and a capital one, with no clemency even for a man who'd lost his reason. Outside the cabin, the marine sentry stamped to attention, breaking into their thoughts. A sharp knock was followed by Miller's head looking around the door.

"Boat approaching, sir. You and Mr. Toope had best grab your hats and come on deck." Squibb stood and followed him reluctantly, wishing he could be left in peace.

A barge was approaching the schooner and at its stern flew the broad blue pennant of a rear admiral. Miller had already mustered the marines and a few of the warrant officers. Henry Spurrell appeared from nowhere and neatly clipped Squibb's sword to his belt. The governor rarely visited the ships in harbour and the idea of his coming out to a mere schooner was unthinkable. It could only be a surprise inspection of the ships moored with their guns trained on the town, but even that seemed unlikely. All the same, the barge was about to hook on to *Independence*, and her commander was thankful that everything had been thoroughly cleaned and tidied just the day before.

Greening sounded his boatswain's whistle as the governor came up the side. He was surprisingly agile for one so large. The marines presented arms and Squibb saluted while their guest stood for a moment to catch his breath. He scanned the deck with a critical eye, returned the salute, and then, to everyone's amazement, threw his arm around the skipper's shoulder. In doing so he deftly turned him toward the stern and, with Montague close behind, the three of them made their way below. Once inside the cabin, with the governor tightly wedged into the chair behind the desk, Squibb offered his guests a drink. The offer was politely refused, to his surprise, and the governor came straight to the point of his visit.

"You will excuse my stopping by like this, but I have something to ask of you and your vessel. And I wished to make the request in the flesh, so to speak." He pulled a large red handkerchief from his pocket and blew his nose.

"*Independence* is yours to command, sir."

"Wait until you hear what I have to say, young man. Then you may agree or not. I told you this morning that a cartel will be sent to New England with American prisoners. Well, I have other prisoners, much more important ones, who will not be going home so soon. These I am sure you know of. Henry Laurens, the American envoy to Holland, and Winslow Warren, son of Washington's paymaster. These are men whom their lordships in England would like to examine more closely. Now is an opportune time to send them to London, given the local turmoil and the fact that a convoy will leave Halifax within the week. I am asking you to take these prisoners and rendezvous with it. You will transfer your charges to the convoy's flagship, HMS *Invincible*, and return to St. John's when you have discharged your duty. If you are agreeable, of course."

Squibb knew full well that there was no such thing as a request from an admiral, much less one who was also a governor. It was merely a polite form of issuing an order. "I will be happy to do so, sir."

"Excellent!" the governor boomed, rubbing his hands with satisfaction. "Your orders will be sent to you in due course. I expect you will leave shortly thereafter." He turned to Montague. "When shall we send the prisoners?"

"Tonight, sir. After dark."

"Yes, of course. And my thanks for your attention and cooperation, Commander," he said as he struggled to remove himself from the tight-fitting chair.

The visitors departed and Squibb was suddenly too busy to brood over Froggat. The marines' berth would have to serve as quarters for the prisoners, with the red-coated "boiled crabs," as the sailors called them, moved with their hammocks and dunnage to the seamen's berth. The new arrangements would not be popular, for the space was already crowded. The carpenter would have to install a strong lock on what would become the prisoners' cell, while general matters of security had to be discussed and arranged. The two gentlemen would also need a few creature comforts, and their baggage would have to be searched and securely stowed.

Evening and darkness came quickly and with it two boats from the *Proteus* hulk. One carried Henry Laurens, whom Squibb had last seen at the capture of the *Mercury* packet. The man was at least sixty, though he looked much older than he had on that day. He moved slowly, with a quiet dignity, as if confinement and the failure of his mission to Holland weighed heavily upon him. Squibb greeted him politely and Laurens was taken immediately to his new quarters while Miss Adams' cousin was brought aboard. Winslow Warren's only value to Britain seemed to be his parentage, Squibb thought. He certainly did not appear to be a man of worth in his own right. More of a powdered, rattle-headed dandy who fussed and exclaimed over his baggage until he was hustled aft. What their lordships hoped to learn or gain from so frivolous a young man, Squibb was at a loss to say.

The night passed quietly, but the schooner's commander enjoyed no rest. The little sleep he had was wracked by nightmares of a court martial in which the defendants were dressed as chimney sweeps and enormous ravens sat as the officers of the tribunal. They squawked and pecked at the prisoners throughout the proceedings. When dawn brought with it a pallid, black-garbed clerk from the governor, Squibb wondered if he were still in the grip of his dream. His orders were handed to him and the dour messenger went away, but it was some time before he could set his mind to reading them.

When he finally did, he immediately did so again. It had been a terrible night and he was slow to comprehend. He was required to do exactly as the governor had asked—that was clear enough—but he was not to depart the harbour until the following morning, fully twenty-four hours from now. He did not understand. Nor had he understood an earlier delay some weeks before, when the squadron had been ordered to reinforce the outlying forts and settlements. He also read that he was to allow the prisoners to receive visitors. What in God's name was the governor thinking?

Squibb knew, however, that Harriett would want to see her cousin. The delay at least allowed her that chance, and gave him another opportunity to speak to her. A quick and tender note informed her that a boat would bring her at any time she chose. Her swift reply was that she would be ready within the hour. Eli Bailey was sent to escort her from The Rising Sun.

Squibb came on deck when he heard the boat's hail a short time later. Despite his excitement at the prospect of seeing Harriett again, something cold touched his heart when the boat pulled alongside. Sitting next to her was Gridley Thaxter, smiling up at him and excusing himself for having "hitched a ride." Squibb ignored the apology and the strange American expression, so annoyed was he with the unexpected arrival. Still, he was determined to be civil. He'd been issued no restrictions on who might visit the prisoners. He informed Thaxter that the marine guard would have to search his person.

The unwelcome guest was led aft, leaving Squibb alone with Harriett. She began to explain that Thaxter happened to be at the inn when the note arrived and had insisted on coming along. What was she to do? Her evident embarrassment softened his ill humour and he assured her that it was a kindly gesture on her part. She seemed relieved at his pliant tone and favoured him with a smile and a fleeting brush of her hand upon his cheek. He knew full well the spell that she cast upon him, but he was no less happy with the knowledge of it. He gestured with his hand to invite her aft and she teasingly asked if she was to be searched as well. He laughed and gently took her arm as they walked to her cousin's cell.

The visit would have to be conducted in the presence of an officer and he assigned Ethan the duty. An hour later coffee was sent in to them. Squibb continued to pace the deck, growing ever more impatient to speak with Harriett. He had finally decided to finish what he'd started to say on the evening of their dinner with the Grahams. His proposal had been left unsaid and since then, doubt had begun to take hold. Could such a woman be happy in his house at Trinity, he wondered? It could certainly be improved upon, and in any way she wished. But would she choose to live in Newfoundland or in Boston? Once the war was over, they could spend time in each. Perhaps he would sail *Amelia* between the two whenever she chose.

When the visitors came on deck, his daydreams ended, and with them his hopes of speaking to her. Harriett was clearly distressed. She sobbed into her handkerchief and was supported on either side by Ethan and Thaxter. When she did look up, her tear-filled eyes were red and swollen.

Squibb felt a stab of pain at the sight of grief in one so dear to him. Fully conscious now of being her cousin's keeper, he could do nothing but say how very sorry he was and that he would personally see to Winslow Warren's comfort and safety. She dabbed at her tears and thanked him for his kindness before expressing her wish to return to the inn. There, she said, she would shut herself away from the war and its cruel use of the innocent. Squibb kissed her hand as she departed, and without a word or a backward glance, she was carried away by the boat.

THE VIRGIN ROCKS

St. John's, September 3rd

t was not quite dawn when *Independence* floated free of her mooring, despite the governor's orders. The sky was no longer pitch black, it was true, and that was near enough for the man who'd been waiting restlessly for hours. The pinnace was sent ahead to ensure the chain boom was down, and the boat was hoisted aboard as the schooner ghosted through the gap. A fiery red light illuminated sea and sky until the sun's crescent broke the eastern horizon.

After setting a course to rendezvous with *Invincible* and her convoy near the Virgin Rocks, Squibb turned his thoughts to entertaining his passenger-prisoners. He called the cook and they undertook a review of the ship's provisions. It proved to be a disappointing exercise. There was little they could offer beyond the sailor's standard fare of salted meat and dried peas and biscuit. The cook said he would put a few hooks and lines over the side in hopes of having something fresh to serve that evening.

At mid-morning Squibb called upon the two men. He was surprised to find Winslow Warren indisposed, suffering from seasickness. It said something about the man, he thought, for the wind was steady and the sea as restful as ever it could be, aside from a long easterly swell. Henry Laurens was not affected by the motion and in fact seemed improved in his health. The sea air or the change of confinement evidently agreed with him. He greeted his gaoler in a courteous and gentlemanly manner, inviting him to sit in the small and sparsely furnished space. Behind a canvas wall that divided their cabin, Winslow Warren groaned as if he were at death's door.

Squibb declined the offered stool and invited Laurens to walk the deck with him, which the prisoner gladly accepted. They set out side by side, Laurens managing very well despite the ship's ten-degree heel and the occasional plunging twist. He smiled quite cheerfully and nodded to the sailors, as if he were not on his way to London to be tried as a traitor to the Crown. They paused at the forechains to watch a whale surface and blow, not fifty feet away.

"Such a wondrous sight, Commander!" the older man enthused. "One of God's great creatures and here we are to witness its majesty."

Whales were as common to Squibb as bread on the table, but he agreed out of politeness. Was he mistaken, or was his passenger a little more animated than his situation could warrant? The question was soon answered when Laurens turned to him and smiled.

"I must take this opportunity to express my thanks to you, sir."

Squibb gave him a puzzled look. "Forgive me, sir, but I can think of nothing that can deserve your gratitude."

"Oh, but sir, you are providing me with transport to England. Although I confess that I am confused about our southerly direction. But I'm sure you know your business. The important thing is that I am on my way to stand trial in London, where I will put voice to the injustice that your government has visited upon the people of America. The world will know of it, sir."

Squibb shook his head and smiled, "In that case, sir, you are most welcome."

"Are you a political man, Commander?"

"I am perhaps the least political man you will ever meet. But I do have my opinions."

"I am sometimes envious of those who have no strong political convictions. It can be a curse, you know, the compulsive need to be involved in the fray. But this will be my last battle. My last and greatest battle, I have no doubt. The times are changing quickly, and younger men have opinions and ideas that must be heard."

Squibb regarded the aging, doleful face, framed by grey hair and whiskers. Before he could ask him what he meant, the prisoner spoke again.

"My son, you know, is an aide-de-camp to General Washington. John is adamantly opposed to the institution of slavery, as are many of his generation. You will find it incredible, but he proposes to enlist slaves for the war effort, in return for their emancipation."

Squibb did indeed find it incredible. He knew that the man before him was one of the largest slave traders in America, tens of thousands of the poor wretches having passed through his hands. But now, with the family fortune secure, his son was comfortable enough to voice his moral opposition.

"I know what you are thinking, Commander," Laurens continued. "But I have not traded in slaves for a decade now and even when I did, I abhorred it. I was not the man who enslaved them. We may thank England for that institution."

"And yet you saw no contradiction in profiting from their misery?" Squibb had no intention of entering into a debate, but it was hard to say nothing. Henry Laurens opened his mouth to speak, but the conversation was interrupted by the first mate.

"Begging your pardon, sir, but there's a sail coming up astern."

"Mr. Miller, take our guest to his quarters," Squibb ordered as he moved to the windward shrouds and began to climb. From the masthead he could just see the land to starboard, no more than a dark line between sky and sea. The lookout passed the glass and said, "One of ours, sir." Squibb took it and watched the distant ship for half a minute.

"*Fairy*," he said, "on the same course."

He climbed down and went to his cabin, thinking little of it. He hadn't learned the name of her new commander, with Berkley promoted to *Vestal*, but whoever it was, he would be under his own orders and have little interest in *Independence*.

A short time later Squibb realized that he was mistaken. Salter was at the cabin door, reporting that *Fairy* was flying the signal to heave to. Before he could acknowledge the extraordinary message, Miller was there as well, saying the sloop was coming up fast and about to put a boat in the water.

Squibb went on deck and ordered the mainsail scandalized, easing the peak halyard to spill the wind rather than lower the sail entirely. It slowed the schooner but was easily reversed, and he was impatient with the unusual demand. *Independence* continued to crawl forward as *Fairy*'s boat was cast off. The quartermaster handed him a glass and he lifted it to his eye, there to behold the startling sight of Captain Keppel sitting beside the coxswain. A file of stiff marines sat between four pairs of oarsmen, their bayonets glinting on the barrels of their muskets.

Lines were thrown and the boat made fast before Keppel climbed aboard. Greening's whistle sounded and Ethan's marines presented arms. Squibb lifted his hat to the senior officer and Keppel returned the compliment before leaning in to speak.

"Let us go below."

The cabin door was barely shut behind them when Keppel held out a sealed paper. "Another surprise for you, Commander."

Squibb quickly broke the governor's seal, scanned the lines of writing and looked up. "But—" was all he managed to say before Keppel held up his hand.

"I can tell you very little beyond the instructions you see. The governor wishes you—orders you, I should rightly say—to relinquish your prisoners to me. My orders are to transport them to London in *Fairy*. Straight away."

Squibb was baffled. "But why?"

"Only the governor knows the why, sir. But no doubt it has something to do with my role in capturing both of these men. And I have been given *Fairy* for the task, owing to the governor's reluctance to do without my frigate."

"Yes, of course. I understand the custom, but why send them with me in the first place?"

Keppel's jowls lifted in a brief and unusual smile. "No doubt the reason will be revealed. You know as much as I do."

Squibb looked again at the paper in his hand. "As you can see," said Keppel, "you are required to continue on your course to intercept the Halifax convoy."

"This is absurd. To what purpose? I will have no prisoners to transfer. Nor is any other objective stated or implied."

Keppel shrugged his heavy shoulders and moved to the door. "I am not without sympathy, Commander. But I really must be underway. Kindly have the prisoners readied."

It was done straight away, to the confusion of the two gentlemen and many of the crew. Salter in particular seemed dismayed when told to take charge of the transfer. Even Henry Spurrell stared, speechless, when he was instructed to see to the gentlemen's baggage.

As the boat departed with Henry Laurens and a miserable-looking Winslow Warren sitting between the marines, Miller came up to Squibb and asked for orders.

"Resume your course," was the answer, after a lengthy pause. Miller's broad face showed no surprise and with little more than a glance at the departing boat he turned away to shout his commands.

Wind and weather continued fair, apart from a low haze on the water and an increase in the swell. On the following day the officers took their bearings at noon. Their sextants, lunar tables, and observations of the previous night's sky confirmed that they were in the region of fifty degrees West longitude and forty-six degrees North latitude—very near

the Virgin Rocks and their rendezvous with the Halifax convoy. All that
remained was to circle the dangerous shoals and wait.

Squibb returned to his cabin, where Ethan and Eli Bailey were waiting for him. With the abrupt departure of the prisoners, the two young
men had been enlisted to help eat the meal that the cook had prepared.
The prime halibut would not be wasted.

The hungry youths were standing awkwardly in the small space when
Squibb entered. Eli appeared somewhat nervous, for the summons to
dine with the skipper was not a common one. In fact, as the cabin's former steward, he knew that Squibb rarely dined with anyone, excepting
one of the mates or Captain Parker, on rare occasions. His concern was
eased by the offer of a glass of brandy, which he accepted in spite of his
last experience of it.

Squibb had decided to invite Eli as a mark of his satisfaction with the
lad's progress. He had spoken with the warrant officers and senior hands
that morning and they were unanimous in their approval of his work
and general conduct. He was a fast learner, deft and nimble in the tops
and better than most when it came to knotting and splicing. He was also
attentive to his duty and quick to lend a hand, often before he was told.
He had, in fact, seized the opportunity he'd been given and was making
the most of it.

Henry Spurrell waited on table and Squibb was glad to see that the
childish rivalry between the two Trinity boys had given way to a more
mature friendship. Eli thanked his friend when his plate was laid before
him, with Henry looking pleased and replying that he was most welcome. Ethan mimed a look of shock and his father tried not to smile.

"Now then, Seaman Bailey," Squibb said as he reached for the salt.

"Sir?"

"The quartermaster tells me that you do very well at the wheel. Under
his eye, of course."

"Thank 'e, sir. It's one of the best duties, sir, to handle the ship.
Especially when we're under all sail. She's a beautiful thing, sir, and to

have her under your hand…that…that is to say…" His voice trailed off, as though he feared he was talking too much.

"I am also told that you are doing well in your other duties. You are a quick learner, it seems, and at the end of this voyage, if all goes well, I intend to rate you able seaman."

The boy's look of surprise gave way to a wide smile of delight. "Able seaman, sir! Thank 'e, Mr. Squibb!"

The smile was infectious. Ethan grinned and said, "He will expect you to work that much harder, you know."

The boys laughed and Squibb passed the food that had come hot from the galley. Eli, no longer nervous, was almost too excited to eat his fish.

"Where exactly are we, sir?" Ethan asked as he helped himself. "Presumably near our rendezvous?"

"Oh yes, very near. If this swell gets any larger, I daresay we will see the Virgin Rocks themselves."

"Do tell us about the rocks, sir!" Eli exclaimed. "I've heard so much about them."

Squibb nodded, pleased that the boy had a sailor's curiosity about his watery environment.

"Well, let us see … their position was first laid down about the year 1520. The Portuguese, I believe. The rocks lie less than a hundred miles south of east from Cape Race, and they are famous for two things—as good fishing ground and as a hazard to ships. Some of the shoals are no more than three fathoms deep in a calm, and the Main Ledge shows white water in heavy weather."

"And how far do they stretch, sir?" the boy asked. "And what is their nature?" Intelligent questions indeed, Squibb thought.

"They are a mass of protrusions, rising like carbuncles from the ocean floor. At their widest span they cover about three miles from east to west and six or seven, north to south. It is possible for a small vessel, even our schooner, to sail right over them in fair weather. But a sober captain would stay well clear, especially with a swell like we have today. A large ship with a deep draught should never come near."

Ethan was nodding politely, more interested in his dinner, but Eli was paying close attention. "And their position, sir?"

"The Main Ledge lies at the centre of the shoal, forty-six degrees twenty-five minutes North and fifty degrees forty-nine minutes West, give or take a few seconds." He could see the boy committing the position to memory.

"The rocks are known individually?" Ethan asked out of mild curiosity.

"Oh yes. They have all acquired names over the last two and a half centuries."

"And all their positions are written down?" asked Eli. "Like the Main Ledge?"

"Yes, but the accuracy of those positions is another matter. The sun is rarely available for a fix on this foggy bank. You seem very interested in these details."

Happy enthusiasm lit the youthful face. "Oh yes, sir. I should like to know everything about my profession, sir."

Squibb smiled and shook his head. He was reminded of another lad at that age, a newly made midshipman whom a sailing master had taken under his wing more than twenty years ago. The man had taught him nearly everything there was to know about navigation, triangulation, and accurate chart-making. James Cook, the last and the greatest of the navigating explorers, was exceptional in his desire to pass on his knowledge to youngsters like himself. News of his tragic death in the Hawaiian Islands had reached Newfoundland in March, and Squibb still mourned the loss of so great a man. "Would you care to learn trigonometry, Seaman Bailey?" he asked.

The boy's reply was drowned by a cry from the masthead lookout. It came down to Squibb like a physical jolt, bringing him to his feet with knife and fork still in hand. A sail, visible in the northwest. Cutlery clattered to the table.

Ethan looked up in surprise. "That will be the convoy, will it not?"

Eli was quicker to grasp the meaning. "Northwest, Mr. Toope," he said in a hushed voice. "The convoy is due from the southwest."

Squibb did not hear the exchange. He was already on deck. The low haze was still present, the light northwesterly keeping *Independence* idling north-northeast under topsails and jibs. The shoals were no more than a mile to leeward, the Maloney Ledge the nearest off the starboard bow. From the deck Squibb could see a square topsail above the haze.

"Deck there!" the lookout hailed. "Schooner she is, on a sou'east course."

Ethan was now standing beside him, his napkin still tucked into his waistcoat. "Is it the Yankee?"

"None other," Squibb replied. "Beat to quarters!"

The rattle of the marines' drum brought men pouring from the hatches. Squibb stared at the topsail as it moved steadily toward him with the following wind. Whatever Friday Froggat had become and whatever the next hour would bring, he could not help but admire his old friend's cunning and seamanship. He had caught *Independence* at a grave disadvantage with a hazard to leeward, and with the wind so light, never a chance of beating around it before she was intercepted. The schooner would be engaged and boarded before she could clear the Deepwater Bank on the northern edge of the Rocks.

"Cast off your breechings," Miller cried as the gun crews found their places.

"Mr. Greening," Squibb called, "preventer chains to the gaffs and double your stays where you can." A minute later the boatswain was aloft with his lines and crew.

"Fore and mainsail, sir?" Miller asked.

"No. Speed will not help us now. Mr. Toope, place half your marksmen in the starboard shrouds. The rest to stand by. Mr. Tompkins, grape for the starboard guns and ball for the bow chaser. Mr. Salter, steady on this course and be ready to tack on my signal."

The privateer's hull was now visible and her jib-boom was pointing straight at him. It was a matter of minutes before she opened her fire and Squibb's mind was working furiously.

"Silence fore and aft," Miller called. There was little need for the order, as most of the men were quietly watching their old foe approach. Most knew that the privateer held the upper hand, but they had fought her to a standstill once and it stood to reason that they could do it again.

The first shot came sooner than expected, a 9-pound ball from her bow gun. A thunderous boom preceded the sight of it, a dark blur skimming low and lethal across the water. The elevation of the gun had been off and the ball fell short, bouncing a few times before punching a hole in the swell.

Squibb paced the length of the deck, watched by the gun crews as he coolly ignored the second shot, which passed overhead two minutes later. The whoosh of that ball was clearly heard, but by a miracle it missed the spars and rigging. The men at his own bow chaser knuckled their foreheads as he came up to them. The gun protruded forward on one side of the bowsprit and was pointing at nothing but open sea.

"Ready now, lads," Squibb said. "Fire as she bears." He raised his hand and looked aft, catching the quartermaster's eye. His hand dropped and *Independence* began turning into the wind, allowing the gun to bear and after it, the line of starboard 4-pounders.

The sails began to shiver. And an instant later he realized that the turn had stalled.

The gun crew knew it, too, and with just a sliver of the privateer's bow in their sights they put the slow-burning twine to the touch hole. The powder exploded and the blur of the ball flew clean past the bow, missing it by inches.

The manoeuvre had been bungled. Squibb looked back at the helm in angry disbelief, only to see Salter struggling with the quartermaster at the wheel. The sight was bewildering but he had no time to consider it. The privateer had moved to within two hundred yards and a boarding party was gathering in the bows. *Independence* fell back to her previous course but further off the wind, giving the larboard battery a clear target.

"Prepare to fire!" he shouted to the men crouched beside their guns.

Above his head, the marines in the rigging were already peppering the enemy's deck and Squibb saw one or two of the boarders fall.

"Fire!"

The smouldering hemp was laid to the touch holes of the larboard guns and every man waited for the explosions.

They waited in vain. No grapeshot swept the privateer's men from their perch on the rails. No voices cheered a blow for King George and England. There was only shocked silence, then a mighty roar as the enemy realized what had happened—victory was theirs and their own bow gun roared in triumph.

Squibb shouted "Reload!" and looked aft. Salter had taken the wheel and the quartermaster lay in a widening pool of his own blood. A round-shot passed close by Squibb's shoulder, staggering him as he grabbed a cutlass from the rack. The gunner, standing by the mainmast, saw him coming and ran like a rabbit. He did not get far. Greening brought him down with the barrel of a pistol as he passed, the gunner's body dropping like a rag doll.

On seeing this, Sergeant Parrell seemed to be seized by his own fit of panic. He was standing forward of the wheel, next to Ethan. He lifted and drove the butt of his musket at the young man, catching him on the neck or jaw, Squibb could not tell which. The musket discharged with the blow, hitting one of the marines in the rigging. The man cried out as Ethan dropped his sword and fell to his knees.

Parrell looked wildly about and saw Squibb coming. It was Salter that Squibb was intent upon, but Parrell stood in his way. The sergeant faced him with bayonet levelled and there was no mistaking the stance of a man who'd been charged before.

Squibb approached him at a trot, though he knew how hard it was to get a sword under the long barrel and bayonet of a rifleman. He had no need to try. Eli Bailey, serving one of the guns nearby, stood squarely behind Parrell and brought his ramrod down like a man splitting wood.

The privateer was now so close that the grappling hooks could be seen in the hands of her crew. Swords and pikes bristled above the tightly packed mass of men who were waiting their moment to board. Every second brought them closer to *Independence* and Squibb knew he had one last chance to save his ship. Salter would have to wait.

The powder in the larboard guns was being drawn and reloaded with desperate haste. Ethan's marines kept up their fire but the enemy was responding and two men fell from the rigging.

"Fire when ready!" Squibb roared. Number three gun was the first to answer. Its canister of musket balls exploded across the gap. The range was too close for the shot to expand fully and so its effect was concentrated. A narrow lane appeared in the mass of men but was instantly filled by others. The extent of Salter's treachery was clear as he spun the wooden spokes and the schooner turned sharply, denying the other guns their target.

The privateer's jib-boom passed over Squibb's head as she rammed *Independence* amidships. Grappling hooks flew through the air and the boldest of the boarders leaped for the schooner's rail. Pikes and ramrods interlocked as Squibb's crew struggled to repel them. A few of the enemy fell screaming between the vessels but more and more appeared, roaring and slashing as Squibb joined the fray.

He knew the situation was impossible, even as he stood shoulder to shoulder with his men. They parried and hacked at the pointed and edged weapons that were thrust at them. Pistols cracked here and there and smoke mingled with the smell of sweat and fear. They were outnumbered to begin with and they were fewer now as men cried out and dropped to the deck, Miller among them.

Squibb lost sight of Ethan as a pike thrust tore the skin above his eye. Blood began to flow and soon he could scarcely see. He and his men were being forced back and back, and the first terrible thought of surrender entered his mind.

Step by faltering step they gave way under the crush until, as if by a signal unseen and unheard, the din and tumult began to lessen. Within seconds the press of men had eased until there was only the cursing and crying of the wounded and the gasping breath of those who were still standing.

Squibb wiped the blood from his eyes and saw a man in a uniform jacket leap across the gap between the schooners. This boarder paid no heed to the struggle or its victims but went straight to the nearest hatchway. He disappeared below, seeking what was no longer there. *Independence* had served as she'd been intended, as a deception, and the enemy had swallowed the lure.

The man reappeared and shouted across to the privateer. A moment later another figure stepped across to the schooner's rail. He paused there a moment, eyeing the scene and steadying himself with a hand on his own bowsprit. He was short and lightly built, with an old cocked hat and a naval cloak that had seen hard use. His sharp gaze searched the crowded deck and came to rest on Jonah Squibb. Squibb stared back at the unhandsome face of his former friend and comrade, for whom a short week ago he would have sailed to the ends of the earth.

———o———

The privateer's cabin was spartan. It said much about the man who lived there, Squibb thought, as he pressed a rag to his forehead. Froggat had never been one for trifles or frippery. There was a spare chair on which Squibb sat, but every other item, save the cot, was concerned with the running of the ship. The usual rack of swords and pistols, a chart table, desk, weather glass, sextant and compass, volumes of lunar tables, and the *Articles of War*, but nothing of a personal nature. Squibb lowered the cloth. The bleeding had stopped, as had the blood from a deep slash on his left forearm, though the wound throbbed with every heartbeat.

"Forgive me," the other man said as he turned from the wide stern windows. "I rarely entertain and I have little to offer you." There was a coolness, a distance about him that Squibb had not seen before. As a boy, Froggat had been quiet and shy, an underfed Marine Society orphan sent to sea to earn his daily bread. As a youth he'd been open and talkative, too much so when Squibb had been trying to sleep or to concentrate on a logarithm. As a young man he'd shown a certain reserve, but nothing like that of the person who stood before him now, as remote from human contact as any captain Squibb had ever known.

"You know they will hang you."

The prematurely lined face showed no concern. "They will never hang me, my friend. I will see to that." His two front teeth were of polished ivory, an improvement on the yellowed whalebone he'd relied on for years. The red hair was faded and streaked with grey.

"I am no longer your friend," Squibb replied as he dabbed at the wound. "I am your prisoner, and yet I must ask a favour of you."

The other man lifted his shoulders. "Aside from restoring you to your command, you have only to ask."

"I need to know if my son is alive. This is the second time you have given me cause to wonder."

"He has a fracture of the collarbone and a few cracked ribs. My surgeon has bandaged him and says he will heal with time."

"Why did you keep him a prisoner so long? And so ill confined?"

Froggat stood at the desk and regarded Squibb impassively. "I could not put him ashore, near any settlement, without endangering my crew and vessel. And I had no desire for him to know my identity or my purpose here. I released him when I thought the magazine might explode."

"And what is this purpose of yours? It can hardly be to rescue Winslow Warren."

"My orders are simple. To receive information and to act upon it." He turned a paper on the desk.

"Information that comes from the office of the Newfoundland governor, if I am not mistaken."

The shadow of a smile appeared on the other's lips. "You were always very clever, Jonah."

Squibb was not so sure of that. It had taken him a long time to work through his suspicions. The man who stood before him had known when and where to find *Coureur* in June. He'd known that *Independence* would be alone in Placentia Bay in early August. The outcome of that encounter had not been what he'd hoped, but how many other ships had he captured by knowing where to find them? He remembered the occasions on which Montague himself had delivered his orders. Occasions when nothing had gone wrong. Which meant the governor had suspected that a spy was at work.

"How did you receive your information?"

Froggat shrugged. "I don't mind telling you, since you will not be returning to Newfoundland anytime soon. Information from the governor's office was passed to one of our many patriots detained in St. John's."

"But how did it come to you?"

"Fishing boats come and go from the town and nearby harbours. A rendezvous is easily arranged, in darkness or in some hidden cove. The same arrangement may be made for provisions and repairs. Not every fisherman is a loyal subject of the Crown, Jonah."

"Nor is every officer of his majesty's navy," he shot back. "Are you going to tell me why? You owe me that much."

"I owe you? You are a prisoner of war, Commander Squibb. You are owed nothing."

Squibb threw up his uninjured arm and looked away. "You are not the man I knew. If you do not appreciate the value of loyalty, you can never know the cost of betrayal."

"You were always one for the pithy quote. Here is another—an honest enemy is better than a false friend." Squibb looked up. The tone was reminiscent of their bantering in happier times, but the hint of a smile had disappeared.

"Please tell me."

The man turned away with a sigh, either of annoyance or resignation. Squibb waited, his head and arm throbbing painfully.

"I was harbouring doubts," came the answer after a few moments, "even from the first days of this endless, senseless war. You and I have always believed in the principle of a just war, Jonah. If we are to fight, it must be in a just cause, with right intent. I could not find that justice in a King's war against his own people."

"And so you chose to fight for a cause that was conceived as an act of treason? Where is the justice in that?"

Froggat turned, temper flashing in his eyes. "There can be no betrayal without wholehearted loyalty! I was a faithful servant of the Crown until I was asked to do the unconscionable, to fight my own countrymen." He took a breath and said, more calmly, "Should Englishmen, even those who live in America, be denied the right to choose their own destiny? Should they be forced, at the mouth of a gun, to submit to a monarch and parliament that refuse to do what is right?"

"That is a lofty ideal, Friday, but human motives are always mixed motives. Surely there is more to your decision to betray your country than some notion of what is just and right!"

"There is no moral ambiguity here, my friend. Betrayal, if that is your word for it, is not ambiguous and it is not done lightly."

"Yes, and now I have learned that betrayal never comes from one's enemies! You call me your friend but have you not betrayed your friends as well as your country?" He paused, aware that their voices had become very loud.

Froggat shook his head. "All a man can betray is his own conscience. And my conscience is very clear. Don't you see? I cannot betray England if it is no longer my country. I fight for what I believe to be right and I had hoped that you might come to see that, too."

Squibb looked at him in disbelief. "You thought I would join you?"

"Think of it, Jonah. A Newfoundland free of England's domination. Think of the immense riches of the land and sea, all for the people of your island. Such wealth! It would stay where it belongs and not enrich men who have never set foot in the place. Imagine that! Working together, united in a just cause, there is no limit to what we might achieve."

"So that is it? You envision the island as one of your rebel colonies? One of your united states?"

"And why should we not? It would serve all of our purposes. Wealth and freedom for Newfoundland as part of a new nation that will one day eclipse England and all the old powers of Europe. Many of your people are in favour of it already and prepared to rise up."

Squibb said nothing. From beyond the silence of the cabin he heard a heavy object splash into the water. Another followed.

"Your dead are being buried," he said quietly. "May I be allowed to go across and bury my own?"

The two men looked at each other. A friendship forged long ago through hardship, struggles for survival, and earned respect had been broken forever. Nothing would change that now and each saw the sadness and regret in the face of the other.

"Yes, of course. I will send the surgeon across to look at your wound."

Squibb stood and winced as pain shot through his forehead. He moved to the door and paused with his hand upon it. "I don't remember who, but a poet once said that it is easier to forgive an enemy than to forgive a friend. I hope that is true."

He opened the door and stepped into the passageway. As he did, he heard the voice behind him say, "You surprise me, Jonah. The poet was William Blake."

———o———

The schooners had been separated and the remnants of Squibb's crew were sitting or lying amidships when he was rowed across from the privateer. Armed rebels stood over them and five bodies that lay in a neat row, swathed in canvas like cocoons that would never open to new life. Only Henry Spurrell moved about, sniffling as he swabbed at the blood-stained deck with a dirty mop. A few broken remnants of a clay pipe rattled into the scuppers.

Squibb moved among the men, touching a shoulder here and speaking an encouraging word there. Many were wounded, a few seriously. He told them they had done well and there was no dishonour in losing to treachery and deceit. They had indeed done well, he thought, in spite of their unpromising beginning. They had found a sense of honour and a deep store of courage, and it was something that every man could be proud of.

He made his way to Ethan, who was propped against a gun carriage with an arm firmly bandaged to his chest and side. Hogarth, the carpenter, lay beside him, breathing with difficulty. Greening stood over them like a protective apparition, his clothes torn, his head roughly bound, and his beard clotted with blood. These were his only remaining officers. Israel Miller lay in his canvas shroud next to Hiscock, the quartermaster. And as for Salter, Parrell, and Tompkins, he had no idea of their fate, but hoped they were already in hell.

The dead had to be buried and Squibb rallied the crew as best he could for the difficult task. It was a physical challenge as much as an emotional one, with so many weak and wounded. The guards refused to help and the bodies were tipped over the side for want of a process more dignified. Squibb spoke their names and committed them to the deep, "To be turned into corruption, looking for the resurrection of the body when the sea shall give up her dead." The shrouded figures, weighted with shot, slipped beneath the enormous swell and were lost to everything but the memories of those who knew them.

While they waited for the privateer to get underway with its prize and prisoners, the cook was permitted to fire up his stove and Greening passed around a small keg of rum. Squibb went below to make a final entry in the log, only to find the cabin plundered and the logbook missing. He was about to leave in disgust when a party of armed men came down the companionway, Salter among them. The young man left the others outside, removed his hat, and entered the cabin. It was as if he were still the second officer, coming to report to his commander.

Squibb turned away, anger rising at the sight of him. Through the high stern window he saw white water foaming over the Main Ledge, not more than a quarter of a mile away. Salter cleared his throat and spoke, the hesitating midshipman's voice no longer there.

"I have been given command of this prize and I am making sail. Your crew is being moved below and you will have to join them."

Still staring through the window, Squibb drew a deep breath and exhaled slowly, containing the outrage that heated his face like a furnace blast.

"If it should ever lie within my power," he said in a calm, tight voice, "I will see you hanged for a traitor and a murderer. You may depend upon that." There was no reply and a moment later he heard Salter walking away.

"Wait!" he said as he turned from the window. "It was you, was it not, who tampered with *Egmont*'s powder? It was you who caused her to be captured?"

Salter met his gaze. "Yes. I hardly thought it would work a second time. But of course, I had Tompkins and Parrell to help."

"You knew they had intended to desert in Placentia. You held that over them and they were forced to do your bidding. Am I right?"

"I'm impressed, Commander. Your hindsight is exemplary."

"And when we were in pursuit of *Mercury*, the topsail cringle was not cut by any of the men in your watch. It was you who did it. Because we were the swiftest and most likely to take her. Your task was to prevent Henry Laurens from being captured."

Salter shrugged. "Not every strategy succeeds."

"And what of those awaiting trial for your crime? Would you see innocent men hanged for what you did?"

"I would see my enemies hanged, if that is what you mean."

"Your craven schemes will not win you this war, you know."

"If it moves my country one inch closer to independence, one inch further from the grasp of your King, it will be a victory. However small."

The two men stared at each other.

"Now, if you will excuse me, I have a vessel to command."

Over the days and weeks that followed, there would be many who made much of that brief conversation between Squibb and his betrayer. Some said that the commander had drawn the meeting out, to delay Salter long enough for events to overtake him. Others claimed that it was an act of God that caused the traitor to tarry so long, for wasn't God on the side of England and its gracious King? There were other theories too, but the truth, as it usually is, was much simpler. Squibb was as surprised as everyone else at the unexpected sound of a gun. And everyone knew that the sound came from a gun much larger than anything fired that day.

Salter and his men ran on deck, followed by their prisoner. Like them, Squibb could hardly believe his eyes. The privateer was making sail as fast as she could, for out of the low-lying mist came the looming shape of *Maidstone*, her forward guns firing again as she bore down on the two vessels. Squibb saw at once that she had the privateer in her grip. Just as he had been cornered by the privateer, Froggat had no hope of escape except through the maze of the Virgin Rocks. *Independence* was as good as retaken, with not a sail on her and the prize crew alarmed and confused.

Salter shouted and struck his men with the flat of his sword, trying to bring discipline to their panic. He succeeded in having them get the pinnace off the booms and over the side. Even as they were doing it, a boat from the frigate was being lowered, her marines ready to board.

The rebels abandoned their prize and tumbled into the pinnace, Salter the last to go. They rowed for the Yankee privateer, which was heading for the shoals in a desperate bid to escape. The pinnace followed, disappearing and reappearing in the heavy swell as her men plied the sweeps for all they were worth. Minutes later, Parker pulled his wind a short way from *Independence*. As the frigate came about, a full broadside exploded from her ports. One ball clipped the pinnace as it rose on the swell, sending splinters and pieces of plank high in the air. The boat sank in an instant and on the following rise there were only a few heads to be seen in the water. On the next there was nothing at all.

Another of *Maidstone's* shots had hit the privateer squarely astern and at the waterline. It was clear that her steering was gone, for she fell abeam of the wind and the fearsome swell. She heeled dangerously to leeward, even as her dark hull was lifted and pushed toward the white water that marked the Main Ledge. Frantic efforts were made to lower her sails and to get the boats into the water, but her lee rail went under, tumbling men into the sea. Her foremast went by the board, forcing her over even further, until it looked as if she would capsize. In a final, prodigious lift of the swell she was cast onto the foaming rock and her back was broken. When she rose again it was in two yawning halves joined only by a tangle of ribs and rigging. A few men clung to the bow and stern sections but then they, too, were flung from the wreckage and into the churning sea.

The frigate and schooner stood quietly by, the chance of picking up survivors too small to risk further life. As Squibb watched the terrible scene, he felt a hand on his arm. It was Ethan. All who could stand or be helped were gathered around him. The last moments of a ship and her crew, no matter if they be friend or foe, are moments of horror to every sailor. Squibb and his men, and the two hundred men of *Maidstone*, paid respect to the dead with their silence.

Friday Froggat had been right. He would never be hanged.

A GLEAMING TAPER'S LIGHT

St. John's, September 10th

M ontague was setting down a tray with three glasses upon it when Squibb entered the tavern. The governor looked comfortably settled before the fire, his fingers interlaced across his ample stomach. The day was cool and damp, but Squibb had taken little notice of this on his walk to The Ship. His mind had been occupied with the events of the last few days and how they fitted into the larger picture of the previous three months. He took a seat at the fire and Montague handed him a glass of wine.

"A toast," said the governor, holding up his glass. "To a successful summer." He drank, smacked his lips, and sighed contentedly. Sitting back, he regarded Squibb with a benevolent gaze.

"You may well ask why I consider it successful. The answer is that we have survived it. There were times, I confess, when I had my doubts. But in a month, the season for fishing and war will come to an end. The autumn gales will be upon us and the last convoy will leave for England.

204 · THE YANKEE PRIVATEER

Our struggle is as good as over for another year, Commander, and perhaps there will be peace before spring arrives. If not, as my dear wife says, what cannot be cured must be endured."

Squibb said nothing as the governor swirled his wine. "I was sorry to learn of your son's injury. Major Pringle has approved your request to take him home to Trinity. I can tell you as well that we are forming a new regiment and I would like to see the young man return as one of its officers."

"It will be known as His Majesty's Newfoundland Regiment of Foot," Montague put in.

"What's more," said the governor, "I see no reason for you to return to St. John's before spring. As I say, the war in the North Atlantic is as good as ended for this year and you have done well, sir. You have earned your rest and your pay and prize money, as well as my thanks for your service."

Squibb acknowledged the gratitude with a nod.

"No doubt you have pieced together much of what has happened," the governor went on. "Let me tell you the rest. To begin with, in June it became evident to us that orders from my office were being passed to the enemy. Hence the loss of *Coureur* off Toad's Cove and nearly of *Independence*. We experimented with our system of delivery and eventually found the source. It was one of my clerks. He was passing information on the movement of our ships to two Yankee spies. They were then alerting the privateer with whom you became so familiar."

Something fluttered in Squibb's chest and he barely heard his own voice. "Salter was one of them. Who was the other?"

The governor was watching him. "A Yankee prisoner on parole. A ship's surgeon named Thaxter." Squibb stared at the fire. What he felt could not be called relief. He was unsure of what it was.

"Which brings us to Lieutenant Gardiner." Squibb looked up, surprised to hear the name.

"Gardiner was suspicious of Salter, after the *Egmont* affair. And in June he had seen Salter and Thaxter together. Without proof of what they were up to, he decided to take matters into his own hands."

"By goading Thaxter into a duel."

"Exactly. We had to move quickly on that one. It might have been avoided if we had shared our own suspicions with Gardiner, but we could not—in the interests of secrecy and out of fear that he would do something rash. Gardiner was spoken to quite strongly, of course, but he would not be deterred. Despite my considerable powers of persuasion."

"Gardiner sent Salter to me," Squibb said, "to be rid of him. But a month later he wanted him returned. Why was that?"

"Lieutenant Gardiner came to realize that by passing him on to you, he had put Salter in a position to do more mischief. He began to have second thoughts. By that time, I feared that Gardiner would upset the apple cart entirely."

"Which is why he was sent to Ferryland," Montague noted. Squibb took a moment to consider everything he'd been told.

"But all this time, Salter did nothing to arouse my suspicion. He certainly had other opportunities to betray *Independence*—in Toad's Cove and in Placentia Bay. Why did he wait?"

"As I said," the governor replied, "he was in a position to do great mischief but he was not given free rein to make those decisions. His handlers wished him to bide his time. Ensuring that *Mercury* and Henry Laurens were not captured was just the opportunity they were waiting for. The plan failed and later he was directed to sabotage your defence at the Virgin Rocks."

Governor Edwards drained his glass and Montague gave the barman a nod.

"Of course, I suspect that Thaxter had other accomplices as well." The governor paused to let his words sink in. "We do not know who they may have been, but I am taking the precaution of sending another shipload of prisoners to Halifax tomorrow, where they will join a cartel bound for Boston."

Squibb turned his eyes to the fire. He knew what he was about to hear. "Miss Adams, with whom I think you are acquainted, will be among them."

The flames from the burning logs danced before him but he did not see them. From the turmoil of his thoughts came the question that he could not escape. Had she cared for him at all, or had he simply been of use to her and Gridley Thaxter?

The governor looked thoughtfully at his empty glass. "Someone else became suspicious on learning of Miss Adams' dinners. I confess I missed it myself—American prisoners dining with naval officers and others who might provide important information. My wife made a point of befriending Miss Adams and learning as much as she could."

Squibb hardly knew what to say. "Mrs. Edwards!"

"Oh yes. A governor's wife is very like a business partner, you know." With a wistful smile he added, "Often the senior partner."

"But that is absurd," Squibb protested. "Reverend Langman and a few merchants? What could they possibly know?" As he spoke, his mind raced through the things he himself had told Harriett.

"Oh, we assume that some guests were invited to disguise the purpose. I say 'assume' because my wife could find no proof of Miss Adams' complicity in any of this." A full glass of wine was placed before the governor and he waited until the barman had withdrawn.

"As for Gridley Thaxter and my clerk, martial law has given me powers that the courts in England cannot overrule. They were tried and hanged three days ago."

"But why did you let it continue?" Squibb demanded. "You knew there was a spy and yet you placed my ship and crew in jeopardy more than once."

"I had confidence that if something were to happen, you would be competent enough to deal with it. And we needed time to determine who these spies were and how they operated."

"And on those occasions when you delayed my departure, it was to allow the message to reach the privateer?"

The governor smiled. "Exactly. The first was our attempt to lure Froggat into Placentia Bay. He learned, as we knew he would, that *Independence* would be there alone. He did not know that Captain Parker was to arrive soon after. The timing did not go quite as we intended and the privateer escaped, but you handled the matter very well. The second occasion was your rendezvous with the Halifax convoy and the transfer of our valuable prisoners."

"Only there was no convoy. And no prisoners to be transferred."

"Yes. But again, the enemy did not know that. Nor did he know that *Maidstone* would be following you once more. This time the plan worked rather better, don't you think?"

Squibb had no need to address the silent sentinel of The Rising Sun. With a glance she directed him to the private room and watched as he knocked and was admitted. The maid left quickly and he was alone with the woman whom, until a short time ago, he had hoped to marry. He'd been determined to come but, seeing her, he was at a loss as to why. Or what he thought he could possibly say.

Harriett Adams sat near the window, a picture of grief and mourning. Her eyes were swollen and her face was streaked with tears, though in his own eyes she was all the more beautiful for it. She would not look at him and he stayed where he was, turning his hat in his hands, as he tried to find the words to express what he felt.

In the end there were no words, because he could not define what he was feeling. Bitterness, betrayal, sorrow, anguish and more—they were all there, but in a simmering cauldron of emotion that would make no sense until it had cooled. He was acutely uncomfortable as well, in the knowledge that he'd felt this upheaval once before, on the death of his beloved wife. He had never expected to feel it again.

"Jonah," she said in a voice that was hoarse from weeping. He waited and said nothing. "There is one thing that you must know." There was a long pause as she sobbed quietly into her handkerchief.

"I had no wish to lead you on, but Gridley thought . . ." She began to cry again and turned her face away.

"He thought I might be useful." The words were not harshly spoken. He was not angry, he realized. He only wished to be somewhere else. She did not reply and he quietly left the room, knowing they would never meet again.

———————o———————

The first evening of autumn arrives with a clear, star-filled sky and a brilliant harvest moon. It lights *Amelia*'s way as she sails slowly north on the turn of a flood tide, her passengers and crew all on deck to marvel at the heavenly sight. Young Nancy Graham is among them, having received her parents' permission to travel with Ethan as his nurse. Before the next full moon, she is likely to be his betrothed as well.

Titus Greening sits near the fore chains, gazing at the sky with his head freshly bandaged. He has a month's leave to convalesce and is glad of the offer to do so in Trinity. Beside him sits Robert Hogarth, a musket ball newly removed from his back and a penny whistle held gingerly to his lips. He plays an old, gentle tune as the schooner sails through the silvery wash of the radiant moon.

Beyond them, out where the bowsprit joins the jib-boom, Eli Bailey and Henry Spurrell perch like seabirds roosting for the night. Young Henry holds an orange given to him by the skipper, the first he's ever held, and he slices it in half with his new sheath knife. The knife, on his friend's advice, is the only purchase from his pay and prize money. The rest will see him through this winter and possibly the next. Not that Henry is concerned in that regard, for Mr. Squibb wants him to stay on as his steward at the old house on Mackerel Point. He hands Eli one half of the remarkable orange, as happy as he's ever been in his short, eventful life.

Squibb stands at the wheel of his faithful *Amelia*, his thoughts turning to his house in Trinity. With Ethan and Nancy there, along with Greening and Henry, it will feel like a home again. His troubled summer of service is at an end and he is looking forward to spending the cool autumn days hunting and cutting firewood against the coming winter.

The schooner needs some work and Amy's grave must be tended. In a few months' time it will be Christmas, and after that he plans to spend the long winter evenings with old and neglected friends—his books.

He is trying to keep his spirits up, he knows, with thoughts of these simple pleasures. Some of his wounds are deep and unlikely to heal as quickly as the physical ones. It will take time, but he can think of no better place to let it happen than in Trinity, surrounded by family and shipmates.

From across the moon-bright deck he hears the laughter of two young people in love, whose lives stretch before them like a voyage yet to be taken. He wishes it will be a long, happy journey of smooth seas and fair winds, buoyed with patience, love, and understanding. There is sadness enough in his heart, and yet there is much to give him hope. And hope is the greatest healer of all.

Author's Note

Of the dozen or so Royal Navy ships that formed the Newfoundland squadron in 1780, four were particularly active. The frigates *Maidstone* and *Vestal*, working with the sloops *Fairy* and *Cygnet*, accounted for most of the captures in that year. Their commanders were bold and enterprising sailors, and all went on to achieve senior rank. William Parker died an admiral in 1802, after distinguishing himself in several major battles at sea. In 1797, during the Battle of Cape St. Vincent, he damaged the Spanish 112-gun *San Josef* so badly that Commodore Horatio Nelson was able to board and capture her. The boarding became part of the enduring legend of Nelson, much to Parker's disgust. He was never given proper credit for his role and felt the prize had been taken from under his nose.

Among the others in Newfoundland that summer, George Keppel went on to become a full admiral, while George Berkley, promoted to captain after helping take the *Mercury* packet, had the most interesting part of his career ahead of him. He participated in many of the great naval battles of the age and was in charge of supplying Wellington's army by sea during the Peninsular War. His daughter became the wife of Thomas Hardy, Nelson's flag captain at the Battle of Trafalgar. He also had the distinction of ordering HMS *Leopard* to board and search USS *Chesapeake*, thereby precipitating the War of 1812. He died an admiral in 1818.

John Gardiner's career does not appear to have recovered from the loss of HMS *Egmont*. Naval records carry no further mention of him. The French Admiral de Ternay delivered his force to New England, only to die on his ship off Rhode Island in December of 1780. Richard Edwards, twice governor of Newfoundland and husband to Carbonear-born Julia Pike, was promoted to vice-admiral in 1787 and admiral in 1794. Throughout his career he was known as a good-natured man, eccentric and amusing, with few of the finer social graces. He was also known by the nickname Toby, likely a reference to Sir Toby Belch, Shakespeare's boisterous character from *Twelfth Night*. Like Sir Toby, the admiral was a man of high spirits, a force for vitality, noise, and good cheer. He was also known for his astute leadership in time of war and his humanity toward American prisoners. One of the many naval men who governed Newfoundland from 1729 to 1824, he died in 1795.

The novel has a number of minor characters who were also present in Newfoundland at that time. These include the American surgeon and prisoner Gridley Thaxter, Commander Peter Baskerville, Reverend Edward Langman, Thomas Slade, and the various army officers of the local garrison. Henry Laurens and Winslow Warren were indeed prisoners at St. John's in 1780. Warren was aboard the captured brig *Pallas*, en route to France, while Laurens, bound for Holland, was aboard the *Mercury* packet when it was taken by *Vestal* and *Fairy*. His valuable papers were recovered by a sharp-eyed seaman after he threw them overboard. Both men were taken to England by Captain Keppel later that summer, where Laurens, the more valuable of the two, was imprisoned in the Tower of London.

All of the other ships named in the novel were serving on the Newfoundland station in 1780, including *Bonavista*, *Portland*, *Proteus*, *Surprise*, *Trepassey*, and *Coureur*. The last vessel was captured by the enemy in June of that year, though twenty of her crew were recovered shortly after. The armed American schooner *Independence* was in fact a prize of HMS *Maidstone* and Captain William Parker, taken on the Grand

Banks that summer with a cargo of Virginia tobacco. The author thought she would make a fine central character for the novel.

Commander Squibb's exploit in detaching several ships from an American convoy is based upon a celebrated event that occurred off Newfoundland in the year before the events of the novel. In thick fog, three American ships found themselves among a Jamaica convoy on July 18, 1779. Over the next three days they quietly took ten British prizes and sent them away with skeleton crews. Eight of the ships reached Boston, where they and their cargoes were valued at one million dollars.

An inn and tavern called The Ship was operating in St. John's in 1780. It was located above King's Beach (now Queen's Beach), in the area of the present-day Crow's Nest Officers' Club. Lord Nelson is known to have stayed there in 1782 when he arrived with his ship, HMS *Albemarle*. He was then plain Captain Nelson, twenty-three years old and escorting a convoy to Quebec. He thought St. John's "a disagreeable place." What St. John's thought of him is unrecorded. An inn named The Rising Sun also existed at that time and was still operating in 1833, when it housed the city's first Catholic school in a back room of the tavern. The school was founded by the newly arrived Irish Presentation Sisters.

The desire of Parrell and Tompkins to part ways with the Royal Navy was by no means unusual. Disenchantment with the seagoing life was extremely high during the war, when an estimated one in three sailors jumped ship. These were men recruited or impressed for the conflict, with little love for the hard naval life. Some 15,000 of them deserted on the North American station alone during the War of Independence. Sympathy for the rebel cause was a motivation for some, but most were simply seeking a better life in the new world. Desertion was not to be taken lightly, however. On September 7, 1780, a court martial at St. John's found nine men guilty of the crime. All but one belonged to the Corps of Newfoundland Volunteers. Three corporals were sentenced to be executed by firing squad, four privates to each receive 1,500 lashes, and two other deserters a thousand. The record shows that Corporal Jeremiah

Connolly's death sentence was commuted to a life sentence of banishment on the coast of Guinea.

These and other difficulties stemmed in part from the growth of the Irish population in Newfoundland. Manpower shortages resulted in many Irishmen serving as troops and sailors throughout the war, and not all of them were enamoured of British rule. The same would have been true of some of the Irish fishing servants who replaced the migratory workforce from southwest England. As well, suspension of the Protestant oath caused mayhem in London and much concern in Newfoundland, along with apprehension over the British court ruling on the governor's legal powers.

Jonah Squibb's words regarding the overlooked importance of the resident fishery in Newfoundland were prophetic. The war disrupted the migratory fishery so fully that the transatlantic movement of summer labour went into a sharp and permanent decline. By war's end, island residents were supplying seventy-five per cent of the salted cod sent to the Catholic nations of southern Europe, where it was in great demand for the many meatless holy days. Immigration of settlers from the British Isles continued into the early 1800s and consisted mainly of Irish labourers.

These notes would not be complete without a word about privateers. The name was applied to armed vessels owned and operated by private individuals and commissioned by a government to act against a hostile power. These commissions, or letters of marque, allowed captured privateer crews to claim prisoner of war status. Otherwise, they were guilty of piracy and sent to the gallows. Dozens of New England privateers operated in Newfoundland waters during the revolutionary war. The Royal Navy squadron captured six of them between May and September, 1780. Their vessels averaged 100 tons, with twelve to fourteen guns and crews of roughly fifty men. Many more were captured in the course of the war, but others were successful in disrupting local trade. Well-documented examples include *Minerva*'s raid on the

Labrador coast in 1778 and the exploits of *Centipede* at Twillingate in 1779. Lieutenant Gardiner made use of *Centipede*'s escapades to taunt Thomas Slade at Miss Adams' dinner party.

The sources for the novel are many and varied, from the invaluable records of the Colonial Office, held at The Rooms in St. John's, to the work of later Newfoundland historians, Olaf Janzen prominent among them. The author is also indebted to Aaron Thomas, a young British sailor whose *Newfoundland Journal* of 1794 provided the basis for two conversations between Squibb and Miss Adams.

A sincere thank you to Rebecca Rose, publisher of Breakwater Books, for taking on this project, and to editor Claire Wilkshire for her faith in it. Much credit and gratitude go to editor Sandy Newton for valuable suggestions and guidance in its final stages. Thanks as well to fellow novelist Glenn Deir, whose journalistic eye detected many an error early on, and a big, grateful hug to Brenda, my supportive wife and always my first reader.

—Derek Yetman
St. John's, 2022

Derek Yetman is a former journalist and editor, and the author of four previous books, including *Midshipman Squibb* and *The Beothuk Expedition*. His historical novels have an authenticity that comes from his many years as a sailing skipper and student of Newfoundland history. He has served as a naval reservist, officer of the Royal Newfoundland Regiment, secretary to the Crow's Nest Officers' Club, and communications manager for Canada's national ship and ocean technology research centre. His debut novel won first prize in the Atlantic Provinces Writing Competition, and later books have won praise for their depiction of life and events from the island's colourful past. He lives and works in St. John's and in Chance Cove, Trinity Bay.